Pirates!

Also by Celia Rees
in Large Print:

Witch Child

Pirates!

The true and remarkable
adventures of
Minerva Sharpe
and
Nancy Kington,
Female Pirates

Celia Rees

Thorndike Press • Waterville, Maine

Recommended for Young Adult Readers.

Published in 2004 by arrangement with Bloomsbury Publishing.

Thorndike Press® Large Print The Literacy Bridge.

The tree indicium is a trademark of Thorndike Press.

The text of this Large Print edition is unabridged.
Other aspects of the book may vary from the original edition.

Set in 16 pt. Plantin by Elena Picard.

Printed in the United States on permanent paper.

Library of Congress Cataloging-in-Publication Data

Rees, Celia.
    Pirates! : the true and remarkable adventures of Minerva
Sharpe and Nancy Kington, female pirates / Celia Rees.
        p. cm.
    Summary: In 1722, after arriving with her brother at the
family's Jamaican plantation where she is to be married off,
sixteen-year-old Nancy Kington escapes with her slave
friend, Minerva Sharpe, and together they become pirates
traveling the world in search of treasure.
    ISBN 0-7862-6685-6 (lg. print : hc : alk. paper)
    1. Large type books. [1. Pirates — Fiction. 2. Blacks —
Jamaica — Fiction. 3. Slavery — Fiction. 4. Jamaica —
History — 18th century — Fiction. 5. Adventure and
adventurers — Fiction. 6. Sea stories. 7. Large type books.]
I. Title.
PZ7.R25465Pi 2004
    [Fic]—dc22   2004049840

For Sarah

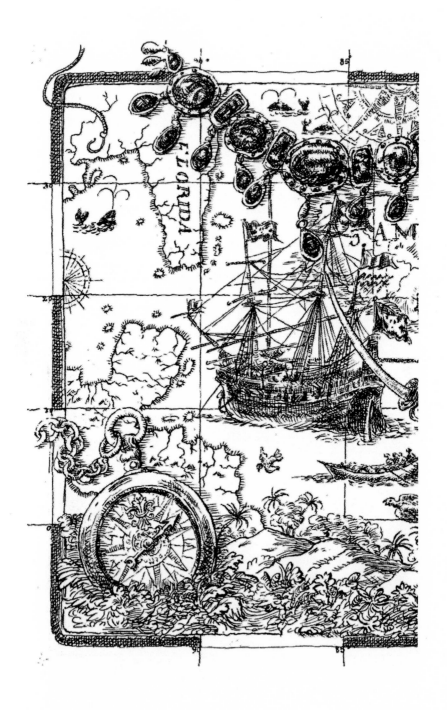

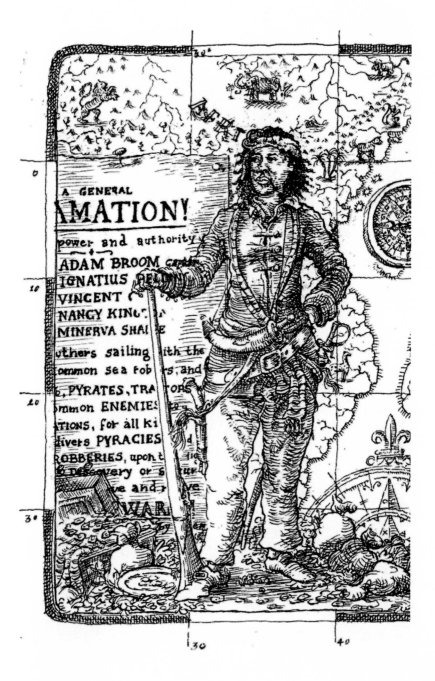

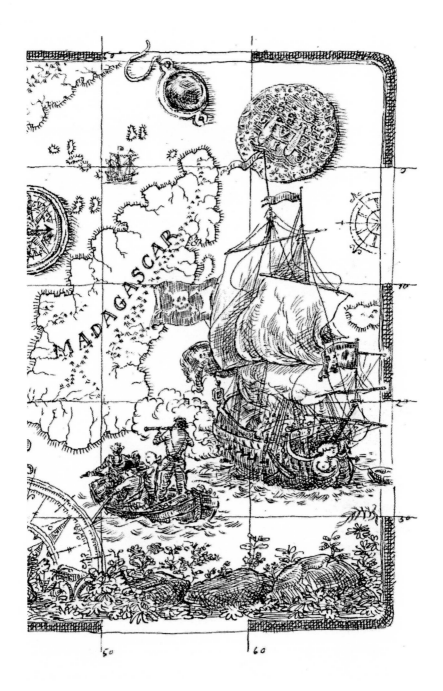

Author's Note

It is rare to be able to say, to the hour and day, exactly when a book began. This one started as an aside in an e-mail to my editor, Sarah Odedina, on an otherwise different matter. The initial remark was entirely frivolous, but her enthusiasm was as great as mine, and after three exchanges I'd agreed to write a book about a girl who becomes a pirate. It seemed that the idea had leapt, fully fledged, from this serendipitous exchange, but as I thought more about it, I realised that it had been there all the time, stored away from when I was about ten and spent my time drawing pirate ships and dreaming of lives more exciting than mine. There was a song, *Sweet Polly Oliver*, that we had learnt at school. Some of the lines stuck in my mind.

> *. . . a sudden strange fancy came into her head.*
> *Neither father or mother would make her false prove,*

She would list for a soldier and follow her love . . .

I remember thinking what a truly splendid idea, how remarkably daring and bold, and how brave and courageous of her to think of it, and how utterly romantic. I have loved ballads ever since then, and went to my record and CD collection to find the songs about sailors and their sweethearts, shipwrecks, strange magic ships, girls who dressed as boys and became sailors or soldiers to follow their hearts and destinies. Ballads gave me the spirit of the time (for my list see www.celiarees.co.uk), but I also went to contemporary writers. Above all, Daniel Defoe. I am most indebted to him and his *A General History of the Robberies and Murders of the Most Notorious Pyrates*, written under the pseudonym of Captain Johnson. This book told me almost all I needed to know, but I also read the work of modern historians who are rediscovering the lives of the sailors, slaves, rebels, radicals and the real Polly Olivers who made up the world I wished to recreate.

My reading can also be found at www.celiarees.co.uk, but reading is only part of it. I owe a debt of thanks to many people, in different measures. To my husband Terry, for his patient listening, his measured enthusiasm and careful reading. To my daughter, Catrin, who accompanied me to Bath, and on an exhaustive and exhausting walking tour of her adopted city of Bristol as, on a very hot day, we tried to find traces of the world Nancy had once inhabited. To Bristol art galleries and museums, for their wonderful collections of paintings and artefacts from the period, to Julia Griffiths-Jones, for drawing the necklace for me, and to David and Jenny Preston, for bringing back spices. I would also like to thank my agent, Rosemary Sandberg, and others for entering into the spirit of the book and letting me borrow what I would. This book is for all of them, and for everyone who ever dreamt of being a pirate.

I presume we need to make no Apology for giving the Name of History to the following Sheets, tho' they contain nothing but the Actions of a Parcel of Robbers. It is Bravery and Stratagem in War which makes Actions worthy of Record; in which Sense the Adventures here related will be thought to be deserving that Name.

Daniel Defoe, *A General History of the Robberies and Murders of the Most Notorious Pyrates* (Preface to the Fourth Edition)

Preface

1724

I write for many reasons.

I write, not least, to quiet my grief. I find that by reliving the adventures that I shared with Minerva, I can lessen the pain of our parting. Besides that, a long sea voyage can be tedious. I must find diversions that fit my station now that I have put up my pistols and cutlass and have exchanged my breeches for a dress.

What follows is my story. Mine and Minerva's. When I have finished writing down all that happened and how it came about, I plan to deliver my papers to Mr Daniel Defoe of London who, I understand, takes an interest in all those who have chosen to follow a piratical way of life.

If our story seems a little extravagant, to have something of the air of a novel, may I assure you that this is no fiction. Our adventures need no added invention, rather I find myself forced to leave out certain details in order not to shock. You will read of many things, both strange and terrible, and to many ways of thinking most unnatural; but I urge you, reader, to hold back your judgement of us until you have finished my account and know the full and exact circumstances of how we fell into that wicked way of life and found ourselves proclaimed notorious pirates.

The Merchant
of Bristol's Daughter

1

I was of a roving frame of mind, even as a child, and for years my fancy had been to set sail on one of my father's ships. One grey summer morning in 1722, my wish was granted, but not quite in the way I would have wanted.

I sailed out of the port of Bristol on board the *Sally-Anne* with sailors wearing black armbands and the colours flapping at half-mast. The day had dawned dull and cold. The wind was freshening, gusting rain into our faces. The sailors looked up, reading the scudding clouds, brows knitted with apprehension, but this was a squall, nothing more. The last dying breaths of the storm that had wrecked my father's life and mine alongside it.

My father was a sugar merchant and a trader in slaves. He owned plantations in Jamaica, and that's where I was bound, but I had not been told the why or wherefore of it. My father's dying wish, that was all my brothers would say. I was not yet sixteen years old, and a girl, so I was neither asked, nor consulted. They assumed I was stupid. But I am far from that. I knew enough not to trust either of them and time was to prove me right. They had sold me as surely as any African they trafficked from the coast of Guinea.

I might never see my home port again, but I did not cry as I left it. Neither did I look back as others did, hoping for a last glimpse of sweetheart or wife, looking up to the tall tower of St Mary Redcliffe, whispering a prayer: *Mother Mary, Star of the Sea, grant your blessing, watch over me.* My sweetheart was gone from the port, and in the church my father lay buried, his body corrupting and turning to clay. He had always been there to see his ships go out from the harbour. Perhaps he looked down as my ship left: a restless spirit, stricken by what he had done, helpless and raging in his ghostly impotence, knowing at last that the dead are powerless to influence the living.

If he was there, I had no sense of it. I just felt rain fall upon me, darkening my hair, running down my face in rivulets and dripping from my chin. The sky was crying for me. Misery wrapped itself around me like my sodden cloak.

We had left the harbour now and entered the snaking gorge. It reared high on either side, the tops of the cliffs lost in the descending cloud. Slowly the ship crept on, pulled by labouring oarsmen, inching its way between towering crags that seemed to narrow the Channel to a handspan and threatened to clash together and crush us like Jason and his Argonauts. The pilot yelled directions, calling the depths, guiding the ship as she crawled from the straits of the Avon and out towards Hungroad's mud flats and dismal marshes. There, a gibbet hung low over the water, freighted with the body of some poor convicted sailor, tarred and tied tight with chains, suspended in an iron cage to creak out a warning to every passing ship.

I should have taken more notice, but I'd seen gibbets before and did not give him more than a passing thought.

Once we had gained the open Channel, the towboats cast us off and turned for home. The few passengers had hurried out of the weather long ago, scurrying down below, leaving only the sailors on deck.

There is much to do when a ship puts to sea. The sailors busied themselves about their duties, working around me, keeping their eyes averted. I was not asked to move, or sent down below. They left me alone out of respect for my sorrow, the loss of my father. That's what I thought, but talk runs fast through portside inns and alehouses. Perhaps they knew more than I did.

The order rang out: 'Make sail!' and the sailors worked even harder. The sails filled and the ship heeled, tacking against the westerly wind to gain the deep sea roads. The water beneath us swirled red with mud swept down by the swollen Severn and the ship began to plunge as river and tide met together in choppy waves. I clung on tight, my hands white on the rail. As we drew away from the land, the rain intensified, blurring sea and sky together. All around the horizon disappeared into blowing greyness and I could see neither where I was going, nor from where I had come. The ship was beating against the tide and taking a buffeting from the wind. I was not used to a ship's motion and, as she dipped into a wave and rose again, I staggered and nearly fell, my feet slipping on the wet deck. I was gripped from behind and helped upright by my brother, Joseph.

'Come, Nancy,' he said. 'It's time to go below. You are getting in the way of the sailors. They have enough to do without the worry of you falling overboard!'

He escorted me below decks, making a show of smiling kindness and brotherly concern for the benefit of any who might have been watching. I understand now the reason for his concern. If I'd gone over-board, I would have taken his future with me.

Joseph left me in the hands of a steward, Abe Reynolds, who helped me out of my sodden cloak and fussed and clucked over the state of my clothes. He and my maid, Susan, shared a similar distrust of damp; it being, in their opinion, at the root of most illness. He brought me hot broth to drink, but at the sight and smell of it I suddenly felt abominably sick.

'I'm sure it's very nice, but . . .' I did not finish the sentence and barely reached the bucket in time.

I had to ask Abe to take the soup away.

'You don't want to get a chill, Miss,' he said, with exactly Susan's tone of concern and reproof.

It was too late for that. I was already shivering. He urged me out of my wet clothes and brought heated bricks to warm me. I lay in my bunk with the bricks tucked about my feet, shaking and puking by turns. I had never felt so ill. I thought I was going to die.

'That's what they all think, Miss,' he said with a grin. His front teeth had long ago been lost to scurvy. The eye teeth hung either side of the gap in his mouth like a pair of discoloured tusks. 'It'll get better given time. I'll look in later.'

I lay back in my bunk, thinking I could never be a sailor as long as I lived. Reynolds was right. In the end the sickness did subside, but it left me feeling weak and tired, fit for nothing but lying on my bunk.

They say that those who go to sea either look forward, or look back. What lay in front of me remained obscure, so I had no choice but to reflect on my life so far.

2

I was brought up in a household of men, my mother having died on the day that I was born. My father had loved her so much, so the story went, that he could not bear life in Bristol without her. I was handed straight over to a wet nurse, my brothers farmed out to relatives, and he had left on the next ship for Jamaica, not returning for more than a year. He came back with Robert, who took over the running of the household. Robert prepared our food, waited on table, showed guests into and out of the house. The only other servant was a boy, Nathan, who looked after the fires and did all the things that Robert didn't do. A woman came in for the washing, otherwise Robert and Nathan did everything. My father saw no reason to pay a houseful of women to sit about clacking and gossiping and eating his food, their backsides getting fatter by the day.

Robert looked after me well. He fed me, clothed me, made sure I was clean and tidy, especially for church on Sunday. He did not worship with us. We went to St Mary Redcliffe, while he went to the Baptist church in Broadmead. He went twice every Sunday. The congregation had welcomed him, despite his colour.

'God don't care what face you've got,' he declared. 'As long as the Glory of God shines in your heart.'

He was a gentle man, and a wise one. Since no one else seemed interested, he taught me to read at the kitchen table, where he had taught himself. We read what we could find: the Bible and prayer book, tracts and sermons that Robert brought back from his church, along with ballads and broadsides he collected in the street outside. As I became proficient, I prowled the house taking books from my brothers' rooms and my father's library. I chose anything that interested me, and read to Robert about the myths and legends of the Greeks and Romans, and from Exquemelin's *The Buccaneers of America* and *A New Voyage Round the World* by William Dampier. Adventure and discovery. That was the life for me. Would it not be splendid? Did Robert not agree? He shook his head at me, and his dark sad eyes took on an expression of pity and sorrow: such a life was not for me. I was a girl. Anyway, pirates were Godless men and all bound for Hell. I'd be better off reading *The Pilgrim's Progress.* I read on defiantly, holding my book so he could no longer see me. I had grown red and tears threatened to spill. I had not realised until then that being a girl would be such a grievous handicap. But Robert was just a servant, I thought to myself. What did he know?

By the time I was seven or eight years old, I had the run of the house. My brothers were away at school. Each one had his course in life planned from the cradle. Henry, the oldest, was to be a trader, like our father; Joseph was to be a planter; Little Ned, the youngest, was destined for a Regiment of Foot. There were no plans for me because, as Robert had pointed out, I was a girl. I seemed to be there as an afterthought, an addition, sometimes petted, more often bullied. Frequently ignored.

We lived in a street that ran down to the Welsh Backs, a stone's cast from the docks and the sugar house. Our house was old, tall but narrow, and jostled about by other houses. There was only a step between us and the cobbled street that rumbled with carts and echoed with shouts and cries from the early morning until late into the night. Our house was small compared to the grand houses that other sugar merchants were building. It was lined with panelling which made it dark, the stairs sagged and the ceilings were low, but my father saw no reason to move from it. He was not a man to welcome change, and he could see the masts of his ships from his bedroom window. He was near to his place of work and the inns and coffeehouses where he did business. Why would he want to live anywhere else?

He did not spend all of his time in Bristol. At least a part of every year he was in Jamaica, running our plantation. I knew that his trips were important; the plantation was the place the sugar came from and the sugar paid for everything, but as I grew older, I resented his long absences. When he came back, I would scold and berate him, even though he brought me presents. A monkey (which died) and a parrot that Ned taught to swear. A dead monkey and a foul-mouthed parrot did not make up for a father. When he was away I would wander into the room he called his library and curl up in his chair. The room was small and dark, like the others, and in his absence it grew dusty and smelt of ashes and stale tobacco smoke.

When he was at home and the lamps were lit and the fire burning, the library was my favourite place in the world. It was full of the most wonderful things that he had brought back from his travels, or that had been given to him by his captains. A tiny green crocodile on black wires hung from the ceiling, its stubby legs splayed out, little sharp white teeth bared in a long thin snout. A strange spiny puffed fish hung next to it, and shelves around the room held all sorts of other fascinating objects: carved effigies, curving lengths of elephants' tusks, plaques of tortoiseshell, a polished coconut set in a silver cup, a giant shell curled like a great pink fist. A battered globe occupied one corner of the cramped room, its surface worn and patterned with intersecting lines in red and black, showing the routes the ships took, outward and back, criss-crossing from Africa, to the Caribbean, and returning to Bristol. Sometimes my father would spin the globe and then stop it with both his hands, tracing the seaways with his fingers, telling off the names of the ships that sailed them, like a blind man reading a face. He was proud of his ships, and proud of his collection of curiosities. He would point to places, naming the lands where his treasures originated. To me, they became as familiar and ordinary as pewter or pottery might have been in some other person's house.

My father's family had been grocers but, being venturesome in his youth, and enterprising besides that, my father had broken away from that rather dull line of business and had shipped for the West Indies.

I loved to hear tales from that time in his life, and he loved to tell them. I would sit on his knee, with my head against his shoulder, taking comfort from the warmth of him and his heart beating next to mine, while he told me of his life when his associates were buccaneers and he had come to acquire Fountainhead.

Fountainhead was the name of our plantation. It had a sign that I thought looked a little like a weeping willow tree and it was stamped on everything. Even carved in the wood above the door to our house.

Besides the plantation, my father owned a sugar house, refining muscovado and molasses. Not only from his own plantation: he acted as factor and agent for other planters. If he was in Bristol, he was more often at his sugar house than he was at home.

Robert taught me to read, but I learned to letter and number in my father's office. My copy books were the invoices and accounts, ships' logs and bills of lading he used in his daily business. The room was small and warm with a round window, like a porthole, overlooking the docks. The air was filled with the sweet syrup smell of boiling sugar: it seeped everywhere, clinging to clothes and hair, the whole building steeped in it.

I would sit at his crowded desk, laboriously copying out lists of names and goods, balancing them against sums of money. I'd do this for mornings together, covering myself in ink and pages and pages in words and figures. Finally, he'd smile at me. Enough for today. He had business to conduct, captains and merchants waiting to see him.

I would run down to where the sugar was stored, begging twists of muscovado and a pocketful of chips from the sugar loaves, then I'd go to find William.

I had always known William. From my first memory we had been together. His mother, Mari, had been my wet nurse. I had lived with her until I was three or four, when I was plucked from her care like a puppy from a litter, and taken back into my own household. Perhaps my father no longer felt the loss of my mother so deeply now, for he made a great fuss of me and, as a young child, I only ever remembered kindness from him. He was an indulgent parent, some might say too indulgent, for he left me to do as I liked. I consequently ran wild, spending most of my time getting into mischief with the other children of the port.

I did not want for playmates. Docks and ships attract children like a shambles attracts flies. I led them on with my pockets full of glistening chunks of white sugar and dark crumbling muscovado done up in twisted paper. 'Spice', they called it. 'Got any spice, Nancy?' We made playthings out of whatever we found: swarming over barrels, playing king-of-the-castle, making seesaws with planks, rolling barrel hoops along with staves, swinging from nets, climbing ropes and rat lines.

William was our leader, and his word was law. I was mate to his captain, and together we led a marauding crew all over the town.

My mind was made up. Even then. I had it all worked out.

My father had no plans for me, other than that I would be married. That's where

I would prove myself helpful. He would not have to go to the bother of finding me a husband, because I would marry William. He would be a captain, like his father, and I would be his wife. Had we not already sworn a solemn oath to each other? Pricking our thumbs and bleeding them together? He would sail the seas, and I would go with him.

That much I had decided and, once my mind was made up, I seldom saw a reason to change it. If I willed it, then that is what would happen. It did not cross my mind that we would not always be together. A sailor's life would be my life, too.

We lived for each day, and each day was similar to the one before. We thought in the way of all children: life would go on much the same, with little change or difference, until one day we would arrive at the future that we saw.

3

I was ten, and William was twelve. It was springtime. I'd been hoping for a bright clear day, but when I awoke the sky was grey and heavy. Rain was spitting in my face as I went to our usual meeting place, a little courtyard behind Corn Street. I whistled our special whistle through my teeth as William had taught me. It was supposed to sound like a bo'sun's piping, but I had trouble getting it right. I expected to hear his answering shrill, but none came. William was not there. I tucked myself under the overhanging eaves, out of the rain, and waited for him. When the church clock struck one quarter hour and then another, I knew he would not be coming. I went in search of him at his mother's inn, The Seven Stars.

It was the middle of the morning, but the inn was busy enough, filled with sailors and women of the port. I peered through the blue drifts of tobacco smoke, trying to see if William were among the tables, collecting tankards and glasses. Sometimes he stayed behind to help when the inn was full, but I could see no sign of him, so I went to ask his mother.

'Upstairs,' Mari said, as she poured rum, running the bottle from one glass to another. When she looked up, her eyes were wary. I followed her glance. William's father, Jake Davies, was sitting in the corner with another man, a bottle on the table between them.

'I didn't know he was back.'

'Neither did we.' She sniffed, wiping her nose on the back of her hand. 'Arrived last night. Drunk ever since.'

William had inherited his mother's high colour, black hair and dark eyes, and smiling open face. She was not smiling that day. A fresh bruise showed under the edge of the kerchief she wore round her head; one eye was puffed and the left side of her face was swollen. When she saw me staring up at her, she gave a lopsided grin and winced.

'Been making his presence felt,' she said, gathering the glasses on to a tray. 'Now, shoo. This is no place for you. Your da would be angry if he knew you were here.'

I went up the narrow stairs behind the bar, worrying about William. His father liked to use his fists on his wife and his children. He usually started on Mari, then turned on William when he tried to protect her and the little ones. Everything they said, everything they did, seemed to enrage him. They lived their lives when he was not there; as soon as he returned they were silent and fearful, which only served to fuel his fury. They never saw a penny of his captain's share, and none of them would have shed a tear if the news had come back that his ship had gone down. But that never happened. He always came back without any mishap. Around the port he was thought of as lucky, although he was called Black Jake because of his moods, and few wanted to sail with him on account of his cruelty.

I found William in the room he shared with his smaller brothers, busy laying out his belongings on a square of canvas. He was wearing a sailor's clothes: a blue coat and wide trousers. The cloth was stiff and new. The clothes were too big and didn't look right on him. The sleeves of the jacket came over his hands and the wide trouser bottoms flapped round his narrow ankles. His neck stuck up from his collar, as thin and white as a stalk of celery. He looked as though he were masquerading, dressed up in clothes stolen from one of the sailors who lodged with his mother.

'I'm sorry, Nancy,' he said when I came into the room. 'I don't have time to play with you today. I have to get ready.'

'Ready?' I asked. 'Ready for what?' Even though I knew the answer.

He was not masquerading. He was leaving. Our ways were parting. I sensed, even then, that the next time we met things would not be the same. Things would never be the same between us again.

He was twelve years old. He sang with a boy's pure treble and the skin on his face had never felt the touch of a razor. His black hair fell on to his shoulders in soft silky curls and his big dark eyes and long lashes were the envy of many of the girls who came into his mother's inn. They used to tease him, saying he had skin as white as any milk and cheeks as red as roses — just like in the ballads. They did it to make him embarrassed. He blushed as easily as any girl.

His skin was flushing slightly, but he was a man now. I could see it plainly in the way he held himself, shoulders square, arms folded, chin pointed towards the ceiling. He looked at me in the same way my brothers did. Down his nose, as if I didn't

37

smell right to him. And perhaps I didn't. Being a girl.

'My father's found me a ship. The *Amelia*. Captain Thomas. I'm signed on as cabin boy. I have to leave right away. We anchor at Hungroad tonight to catch tomorrow's tide.'

The *Amelia*. I'd seen her name in my father's ledgers, but could not exactly recall the trade in which she was engaged.

'Where bound?' I asked him.

'Jamaica. Kingston.'

'Straight?'

He nodded. That was important. Any ship going by way of Africa was a slaver.

I should have wished him luck. Fair winds. A good voyage. Offered him something to remember me by. But I did not. I turned and ran down the stairs. The thought of saying goodbye to him made my eyes and nose sting with sudden tears. I did not want him to see me crying, and I wanted to get to my father as quickly as I could.

I went straight to his office, high up in the sugar house.

'He's of an age to go to sea,' he said with a shrug. 'It has nothing to do with me.'

'But it's your ship!'

'And it's his father's will. It doesn't do to

38

interfere between father and son. Which ship is it, my dear?'

'The *Amelia*.'

My father looked surprised at that. He stuck out his lower lip, pinching it gently between finger and thumb in the way he did when he was thinking.

'What's the matter? What's wrong with it?'

'The ship? Nothing. All my ships are sound. Anything less would be false economy.'

'The captain, then. Is he cruel?'

'No more'n usual. He's lately been in the Navy and runs a tight ship. He's no dancing master, that's for sure, but he's not a tyrant, neither.'

'So what is it, then?'

' 'Tis an odd choice for the boy's first voyage, that's all. But I dare say he'll survive.' He laughed. 'The sea is a hard school. If it's going to be his life, it's better he learns while he's young.'

There was a falseness in his laughter and, although he smiled down at me, smoothing my hair away from my cheek, I knew that he was lying. I ran out and down to the docks. I had to warn William. The *Amelia* was a slaver, sure.

I was too late. The water was ebbing

from the harbour. The *Amelia*'s berth was empty. She had already sailed, going out on the afternoon tide.

I wandered the quayside, disconsolate. Other children called out to me, but I ignored them. Sailors waved from other ships of my father's, but I did not see them. I could not imagine my life without William. He was to be found nowhere in the city and tonight his bed in The Seven Stars would be empty. He had been taken on to work a slaver. I should have saved him. I felt that it was all my fault.

Robert found me sitting on a bollard, staring down at the stinking mud of the harbour. The tide was now full out.

'Come, Miss Nancy. I've been looking for you everywhere.' He looked down at my dirty, tear-streaked face. 'You've got to come home and get ready. The master's expecting an important guest and he wants you looking your best.'

4

My father's guest was Mrs Wilkes. She will always be that to me. I never called her mother, or even Mrs Kington. She was always Mrs Wilkes. I never liked her. She had a face like folded dough, a pursed little mouth and eyes like tarnished threepenny pieces. She sat opposite my father at dinner that night and it was clear she was to become his second wife. After my mother, it had taken him a decade to decide to take another, and I wondered at his choice, but this was no affair of the heart. Mrs Wilkes was a wealthy woman, the widow of Benjamin Wilkes, my father's former partner. When he had dropped dead, right in the middle of Corn Street, some had expressed no surprise, saying he'd been worn to a nub by his wife's constant nagging, but even if my father heard such comments, he was not a man to allow gossip to fog his commercial sense. To combine their assets was the most profitable course of action. Love played no part in the marriage, as far as I could tell.

She began to make changes even before they were married. I fared better than the dogs, which were immediately banished to the stables, and better than Robert. If he had been younger, and more handsome, she might have dressed him in a powdered wig and fancy livery and had him walking behind her, carrying her packages. But Robert was tall and strongly built, brown-skinned, with big amber eyes and scarifications on his broad cheeks. Mrs Wilkes declared him too big and hulking, with eyes like a hound and not nearly dark enough; ladies liked African servants to be coal-black. She could see no use for him and was all for having him returned to the plantation, or sold, which was what people did when they had no further need for a black slave. Except Robert was not a slave. He was free. My father told her that, and said he had no intention of getting rid of him, but he agreed to have him moved from the house, so Robert was sent to the stables to look after the horses and dogs. Not that he seemed to mind. Horses and dogs being preferable to the general run of people. His place was taken by a cook, a housekeeper and a couple of maids and footmen. Staff that Mrs Wilkes had brought with her.

Once she had the household running to her satisfaction, she turned her attention to me.

She looked me over as if I were a filly at a horse fair.

'She strides about as if she were breeched, and the way she talks is enough to make a carter blush. It won't do, Ned!' She shook her head at my father. 'She cannot sew, she cannot sing, play an instrument, or do any useful thing. I don't know what you were thinking of, letting her run wild like that. Such freedom is not good for a child, a girl in particular. It gives them the wrong idea. If it goes on much longer, you'll have the devil of a job getting anyone to marry her.'

My father grew alarmed at that. What if I came in at a loss, like overvalued stock, a cargo about to spoil, gimcrack goods on a glutted market? He looked at me askance.

'Perhaps there's no helping her,' he said doubtfully, pinching his bottom lip. 'Perhaps it's gone too far . . .'

'No, no, no! There's always help!' Mrs Wilkes's eyes crinkled, the tarnished silver beginning to gleam. 'The size of her fortune will see to that. And she's not *bad*-looking. She's not got a squint, and her features are regular. Her mouth is a little too wide,' she pinched in my cheeks, making me gape like a fish, 'but her eyes could be fine, if they were to lose that sullenness. I've seen *far* worse prospects make *very* good matches. She'll never be pretty, I'll give you that, but she may have looks. Of a sort. But she wants refinement!' She held my chin between her squat forefinger and thumb, studying my face in the unblinking way she had, her small eyes as round as buttons. 'This mane of hair!' She pulled it away from my head. 'Like straw! And she's as tawny as a gypsy. As for her hands!' She looked down and shuddered. 'You leave her to me.' She took hold of my ear. 'I can make a silk purse from her.'

With that she called for her maid, Susan. A sharp-faced, dark-haired young woman came bustling into the room.

'Yes, Ma'am?'

'See what you can do with this,' said Mrs Wilkes, thrusting me forward.

'Yes, Ma'am.'

Susan bobbed a curtsey and took me away. I was not especially vain, but to be found so utterly wanting cut me to the core. I hid in my room and studied the mirror with my sullen green-eyed stare. Perhaps she was right. I could find no prettiness, either. My mouth was too full, and sulky besides, my nose too straight, jaw too wide, cheek bones too high. Perhaps if I tamed my mane and tied it back . . . So I tried that, but I looked more like a hand-some-faced boy than a dimple-cheeked girl.

'Who're you scowling at?' Susan came in followed by servants lugging a tub and water. 'Wind changes, you'll stick like that.' She looked at me, head on one side, her eyes bright and sharp like a bird sighting a worm. 'The name's Susan. Susan Smythe. I'm your maid.'

'I don't need a maid!'

'That's not what the Missis says.' She looked around my room. 'She says you need seeing after. We don't always see eye to eye, but this time I'd say she be right.'

'Not in *my* opinion,' I countered.

'Your opinion don't count for much round here now, do it?'

I turned away from her, watching in the mirror as she emptied out drawers and presses. She gathered it all into her arms.

'Fit for rags, the lot of it. As for you . . .' She looked me over, head on one side again, but her birdlike stare had softened. 'You're a challenge, and no mistake. I'll tell the Missis we're starting from new. I dare say your pa can bear the expense.'

45

5

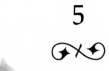

Susan dressed and groomed me until Mrs Wilkes could stand to look at me. I was inspected from every angle and made to walk up and down. Mrs Wilkes remained silent for a long time, then pronounced me 'not unsightly'. Susan's brows rose in two black bows and her eyes sparkled so that I was hard put not to laugh out loud.

I was still deemed too uncouth to join Mrs Wilkes's circle of ladies, but she no longer winced at my presence. She put me in the care of others who were employed to teach me the 'female arts', as she called them: a dancing master, a drawing master, a singing teacher, another for flute and harpsichord. I did not care to learn anything from any of them, apart from the dancing master. He also taught my brother Ned to fence. I persuaded him to teach me as well. When Ned was home from school we would fight in the grounds and up and down the servants' stairs. No mercy shown on either side.

Such acts of rebellion declined as Mrs Wilkes wore me down, breaking me like a horse to bridle and saddle. By the time I was fourteen, I could draw passably well, hold a tune, embroider a cushion cover, and dance a minuet. I was now allowed to wait on her visitors, handing round dainties as they sipped their glasses of Bristol Milk. I was even invited to stay and join in their conversation, discoursing on the weather, fashion, and what ribbons were best to trim bonnets.

We were living in a new house by this time. Mrs Wilkes had my father build one away from the centre of town. He had offered her Queen Anne's Square, but she had disdained to live there, declaring it common to live so close to the docks and that such low-lying ground would be prone to bad air and unhealthy miasmas. The new house was in Clifton, built from yellow stone brought from the quarries at Bath.

It was a fine house and, although my father grumbled at the expense and muttered that we'd rattle around it like peas in a drum, he was secretly pleased with the result. He would walk around, touching this, admiring that, commenting on the refinements that his wife had brought to the decorations and furnishings.

'A woman's touch,' he would declare, with an increasingly satisfied air. 'That's what was wanted.'

I would look up from my embroidery and know I was included in his judgement.

I'd had no word from William, and although he was often in my mind, I was no longer so free to go down to the port to visit his mother at The Seven Stars to find out how he did. The last I'd heard was that he'd signed on for another voyage. I had been looking forward to his returning and was puzzled by that, and more than a little disappointed. I had made my new life under Mrs Wilkes tolerable by thinking how I would describe it to him. I perfected commentaries on her friends and their doings and stored up stories to share with him, incidents carefully selected by me to demonstrate her vanity, greed and stupidity. I'd ever had a wicked tongue and had always been able to make him laugh, but in my mind we were still children together. I had not considered how time passing might have changed him, or me.

When I next saw him, we barely recognised each other.

He was sitting on the bench in the

stableyard, talking to Robert. His face and arms were tanned brown and he wore the clothes of a common sailor, neatly mended and patched, but bleached by the sun and stiff with tar and salt.

Robert made space and I sat on the bench next to them. William explained that he had been sent out by the footman.

'My father's wife, Mrs Wilkes, has ideas about how things should be,' I said, by way of apology.

'About you, too,' he laughed as he looked at me, and some of the old spark showed in his eyes as he surveyed my silk and brocade. 'She's made you into quite the lady.'

'Only on the outside.' I smiled.

He smiled back and I could see the boy he used to be. I knew that, beneath the surface, things had not really changed between us.

'What happened?' I asked. 'Why were you so long away?'

He shook his head and the laughter died in his eyes. 'I was duped by my own father.' He sighed. 'He told me that the *Amelia* was an ordinary trader, but she was a slaver. They began to build the platforms as soon as we were clear of the Channel. At first, I wondered what the hammering and sawing was,' he laughed, this time without any humour at all. 'I was that green. Green as the water in the bilges. When I asked someone, they didn't even answer. I went to the captain, to ask him, and got a beating for my trouble. I felt all kinds of fool. Most of the others were desperate for a berth, or else they had been crimped and spirited on board. I'd gone voluntary. Put there by my own father.'

'I found out that she was a slaver,' I said. 'I went to my father. But by the time I got down to the docks to warn you, it was too late. You had gone.'

'We were children.' He looked at me. 'What could we have done? I would still have sailed. I'd signed by then. And I had no way of knowing . . .'

He stopped what he was saying and stared at his hands, fine-boned, thin-fingered and supple. A boy's hands, but the backs were burnt deep brown and seamed with scars, the palms as callused and rough as a carter's glove.

'It's a dirty trade, Nancy,' he went on quietly. There was little of the boy I re-membered in his dark eyes now. 'Human beings treated worse, far worse than these horses here. Worse than cattle. Worse than any animal. And they ain't animals, no matter what folk say, they are people just like us. And it's not just the Africans who suffer, though it's worse for them, taken from everything they know, kept chained and shackled, packed in hundreds together as close as knives in a box.' He glanced over at Robert, who was currying the flank of my brother's bay until it shimmered like silver. 'It don't compare, I know that, but it's no bed of roses for us, either. We had a good surgeon, but we lost a third of the crew on the first trip, to fevers and fluxes, near half on the next.'

'If it was so bad, then why did you sign on for a second term?'

'It was either that, or find my own way back from Africa.' He sighed, as if the burden of memory were too much for him to carry. 'I'd have gone to be a pirate, if we'd met any, but even they were out to avoid us. They could smell us coming. A lot deserted, but I stuck at it. I completed my terms and I'm here for my wages.'

'Were you not paid?'

He shook his head. 'And I need my money. I intend to join the Navy.'

'Join the *Navy?*' I could hardly believe it.

Robert looked up in surprise. No one joined the Navy of their own free will. Men had to be pressed to it. Everyone in Bristol knew that.

'I know what they say, but it can't be worse than what I've known under Captain Thomas. No matter how little the pay, or how hard the conditions. It's a cleaner trade.'

He looked from me to the glossy horses, the gleaming carriage, and through the wide archway to the golden stone of the house. I followed his eyes, and with them his thought. My silks and satins, my brother's Arab stallion, each honey-coloured stone of our fine new house, all of our wealth depended on this trade that he had been describing. I knew what he was thinking, but I did not know how to reply. I turned my eyes away and saw in my mind the lists that I had copied from my father's ledgers, trying not to blot the ink, striving to keep my columns straight and my writing neat. I had transcribed without any thought for what I was seeing: brass manillas, iron bars, copper rods, cowry shells, pipes of beads, kegs of powder, guinea cloth. Trade goods balanced against men, women, boys, girls. Other columns with prices fetched. We were traders of human flesh. I knew none of the sailors liked to work a slaver. I had not thought why. Until now. I looked away from him, shocked by my own blind complacency, and flooded with shame.

'I'd not be joining as an ordinary hand,' he went on, looking down at himself. 'Not as I am now. I mean to be a midshipman, and have to present myself as a gentleman. I have to buy the necessary accoutrements and will need money besides for my premium, to buy myself a place. I have a little put by from trading on my own account and when I collect what's owed to me, then I should have enough.' He stood up. 'That's why I'm here.'

'Why has the captain not paid you already?'

'He's a villain and I do not trust him. He told me to come back tomorrow and that was two days ago. He's not on board ship, which means he's most likely drunk somewhere, or sleeping off his excesses.' He sighed. 'In any event, I cannot find him, though I've searched every inch of the port.'

'My father is in London with Henry. Joseph is in charge of the business when they are from home.'

Just then a horse clattered into the yard. Joseph swung himself down, throwing the bridle to Robert without even looking at him. Then he turned to me.

'What are you doing out here? Shouldn't you be embroidering something?' When he laughed, I could smell the spirits on his breath. 'All the money the old man's spending on making you a lady and you still prefer to spend your time with blacks and horses.' William stepped out from the shadow of the stable. Joseph's hand tightened on his whip. 'Who's this?'

'William Davies. Late of the *Amelia*.' William came towards him. 'At your service.'

Joseph ignored him and looked at me. 'Tars, as well, eh? Choice company.' He turned to William. 'Be off before I set the dogs on you.'

William stood his ground.

'You heard me!' Joseph glared at William, his lips compressed in a thin line. He was quick to anger, and brandy made him more so. He is fair-haired and fair-skinned, like me, although his eyes are paler than mine, blue rather than green. They were red rimmed from the drink he had taken, the whites all bloodshot. His flushed face darkened and veins stood out on his forehead at William's defiance.

'What are you waiting for? Get going, or I'll shoot you for trespassing.'

William stayed where he was. Even when

54

Joseph turned for the pistol holstered in his saddle, he did not move.

'I have business here.'

'Business? What business?' Joseph turned to Robert who was trying to lead horse and pistol away from his reach. 'Leave it!' he barked. 'Keep the horse where he is or I'll shoot you, too!'

'I want payment.' William stood his ground.

'Then go and see your captain. Why come to me?'

'I would if I could find him.'

Joseph squinted at him. 'What ship did you say? What captain?'

'Captain Thomas,' said William. 'The *Amelia*. We came in two days since.'

'Can't find him, you say?'

'No,' William shook his head.

'Didn't look very hard, did you? I've just left him in his cabin!' Joseph jeered. 'I have it all here.' He pulled the saddlebags from the horse and draped them over his shoulder. 'All his men are paid off. Except for a rascal who lost a whole parcel of slaves overboard. That wretch owes *him* money. Get your hands off me!' He shrugged Robert off and staggered off across the yard towards the house.

William turned from us, head held high

so we could not see his humiliation. As a boy in a man's world, he could expect to be cheated and mocked, and all he could do was endure it. Otherwise they would bait him to madness. He walked slowly towards the stables, came back shouldering his pack, and turned for the road.

'Where you going?' Robert called after him.

'Down to the ship to get my money.'

'No.' Robert followed, catching hold of his arm. 'You go on that ship and you won't be leaving it again. Cap'n says you owe *him* money. He'll keep you in the hold until it's time to sail. You'll wake up halfway across Biscay, if you wake at all.'

He was right. William was trapped and he knew it. He turned back, dropping his pack as if it were suddenly too heavy for him. His shoulders drooped as if he carried the world upon them.

'What am I to do?'

'You could sign to another ship,' Robert suggested.

'Without my money? Never!'

'You could join the Navy anyway.' Robert looked at him. 'It's a hard life, no doubting that, but as you say, it's a cleaner trade.'

'I do not want to join as a tar. It isn't the

56

harshness and hardship — I've endured that and more. I'd thought to join as a gentleman! Cut a decent figure!' He glanced at me. 'I have my reasons for that, and now they would cheat me of it. They've had near four years work out of me and I'll get nothing!' He held his hands up to show the cuts and calluses. 'For all this! Nothing! It was the only thing that kept me going . . . '

He looked as if he might weep.

'Wait! Wait there!' I left them in the yard and went into the house. I entered through a side door and paused to listen. Servants' voices carried faintly from the kitchen; a low murmur and cups clinking sounded from the drawing room. I stole across the clock-ticking silence of the hall, taking care not to let my shoes tap on the tiles of the floor. I stopped again at the foot of the stairs, then trod each step carefully, keeping to the centre so that the new Turkey carpet would deaden my footfall. I passed along the landing to my brother's room. The door stood ajar. I pushed it further and slipped inside.

Joseph was lying face down on the bed, his powdered wig askew, his boots muddying the counterpane, so deep asleep that a sharp tug on the ear failed to rouse him. I rolled him over and reached into his breast waistcoat pocket for the key to my father's bureau. I could have taken his gold chain, his watch, anything I wanted. I smiled to find him so stupid, reflecting that I was hardly the first to fleece him this way, and I would not be the last. Once I had the key secured, I backed towards the door. He didn't even stir.

The study door was open. I unlocked the bureau and counted out how much I thought was owed to William for the voyages he'd taken, then added some more for inconvenience caused. It came to a decent sum. I poured it into my own purse to take to William. On my way back, I threw the key in the shrubbery. Joseph would think he'd lost it in his drunkenness. He would get the blame for that, and for the money, once it was missed. The thought gave me great satisfaction. However much Joseph denied it, my father would assume that he had taken it to pay his gambling debts.

'This is what is owed to you.' I gave the purse to William. 'I'm paying you off on behalf of my father. Since my brother,' I smiled, 'is incommoded.'

William looked as if he would refuse, but Robert urged him.

'It's only what's due to you. Take it, son.'

William took the purse, heavy with gold,

weighing it in his hand.

'Very well!' He stuffed it inside his jerkin. 'I won't forget this, Nancy!'

'I'm sure you'll look very well in your Navy uniform. You must promise to come back so I can see it . . .'

'Of course I will! I mean to make you proud of me!' He held me by the shoulders and looked at me. He did not speak further, perhaps through shyness, perhaps because he did not have the words for what he was feeling. I, in turn, could find nothing to say. My mind emptied as I stared at him. All I could do was try to read his face, where one look followed hard on another, chasing each other like racing clouds.

He grinned down at me. We were once of a height, but now he was taller.

'I'll be back,' he said, touching my cheek. 'When I've received my commission. And then . . .'

'Then what?'

He grinned. '*Then* you'll see.'

He kissed me. His lips were cool, the kiss was light, but I could feel his lips on mine even after he stepped away. I put my hand up to my mouth, as if to confirm to myself what had just happened. It was not a clumsy salute of the kind exchanged by children, or a brother's cursory caress. It was my first proper kiss.

'You will wait for me, won't you?' he said. 'If I knew that, I'd brave anything . . .'

'Of course.' I caught his hand and held it fast. 'Of course I will. I promise.'

With that, he shouldered his pack and walked out of the yard and on to the short curving drive that led from the house. I followed him as far as the gate. He turned once to wave to me, then he went on, whistling a high thin plaintive melody. His step was light, carefree. A butterfly kept him company, stitching the air above his shoulder. I watched until the turn of the road took him out of sight.

There was no knowing when I would see him again, but I knew that I would wait for him. A lifetime if need be. I still hold to that promise. Even now.

My Dark-Eyed Sailor . . .

6

I did not see William for almost two years. In that time my life changed again. I no longer lacked for female company. I was surrounded at the day school I'd begun to attend and, with such a quantity of brothers on offer, we did not lack for young lady visitors accompanying their mothers to our home. The girls' giggling, twittering conversation revolved constantly round beaux and admirers. Their thoughts were all of marriage, but I never joined in their chatter and, no matter how much they teased, I would not tell them my secret and why I had no need to chase other young men. My love was a sailor and, when he came home, I would marry him. This was no idle fancy. It was what would happen.

When the wind came from the west carrying the tang of salt on its breath, I would sit with my window open, listening to the gulls crying about the rooftops and think where he was. In what port? Upon what ocean? At night, I would gaze up at a silver sixpence of a moon playing hide-and-seek with the clouds and imagine him on watch, wondering if he saw the same moon, the same stars, or if he sailed under a different sky. Then I would allow myself to dream. When we were married, I did not intend to stay lonely on the shore waiting for him. William would have his own ship and he would take me with him. We would sail the seas together, just as in my childhood dreams, but in those days I'd seen us as sister and brother. Now I would be his wife.

Susan was the only person who knew my secret. She was my close friend and confidante, and I could keep little from her, although I did not often speak to her about William. She said I was mad to love a sailor, for weren't they the worst of all in their falseness, and wouldn't she know, having had her own heart broke that many times that she'd stopped counting? Besides, we'd hardly seen each other since we were children. How did I know that he felt the same way? I was building up castles out of the clouds I studied so intently. I told myself that Susan did not understand. How could she? She was too quick to scoff and talk about calf love. What did she know of the kind of love I felt for William? I refused to listen to her. I did not want the fires of my passion doused by bucketfuls of her common sense.

'Even if he prove true. And even if he be the one for you,' she said in her matter-of-fact way. 'You won't be able to marry him. A poor sailor lad.'

'Why ever not?' I looked at her in amazement. 'If I love him and he loves me?'

'Love? Who marries for love?'

'Plenty, I'm sure.'

'Not in your class, they don't.'

I knew she was right. Of course. But I thought that such arrangements were for other people. Not for me.

'Well,' I said. 'I mean to marry my love and no other.' I stretched out on the bed, arms beneath my head, ready for dreaming.

'That's as maybe.' Susan busied herself about me. 'The Missis is making other plans.'

'If she is, she'll just have to unmake them.' I paused, not liking this conversation. I rose up on one elbow. 'What other plans?'

'To go to Bath.'

'Bath!' I sat up, alert now, cross-legged in my petticoat.

'We're all going for the season. Cook

told me. The whole household, barring your father. He's got important business. He's expecting a big convoy of ships, so can't be spared.'

Not that he would have gone anyway. He could not see what was wrong with Bristol's own spa at Hotwells and it was barely a mile from our house. People of fashion did not go to Bath just to take the waters, Mrs Wilkes declared. Father did not understand.

'Come over here, Miss.' Susan beckoned me to the dressing table. 'So I can do your hair.' She commenced brushing, as she did every night, first to get the tangles out, then to make it shine. 'The Missis has plans for you,' she winked at me in the mirror. 'Mark my words.'

'What kind of plans?'

'In the matrimony department.'

'But I'm too young!'

Susan laughed. 'Miss Contrary! What about yon sailor boy you've been mooning over. Not too young for him, are you?'

'But that's different! I do not mean to marry him *yet!*'

That was a dream belonging to sometime in the future. Not now. I was beginning to panic. The season was only weeks away . . .

'Never too young!' Susan winked again and I half wondered if she was teasing, but then she mentioned Elspeth Cooper who was already promised and younger than me. I'd seen the man who she was to marry. Twice her age with the marks of pox on him. I didn't want that to happen to me.

'I'll refuse to go.'

'Stand up to the Missis?' Susan guffawed at my chances. 'I'll see that when it happens!'

'It'll be a waste of time, let alone money! I'll tell Father! Who'd be interested in me?'

'Plenty. You're a handsome young woman, even if you ain't prepared to make the best of yourself. Don't know what you've got, that's your problem. I don't know how many would die for this colour.' She arranged my hair about my shoulders in a shimmering cloak of gold and copper, winding a strand round her finger to form a ringlet. 'Don't even need rags to curl it. There's been interest already.'

'In me?' I didn't know whether to be flattered, or alarmed. 'From whom?'

'Never you mind.' She commenced brushing again.

'I can't see how there could be. I don't go out in society. I mean, who's *seen* me?'

'You'd be surprised.' Susan gave me one of her knowing looks. 'I seen the way some of the gentlemen calling here look at you.'

'You mean friends of Father's? But they're all ancient!' I covered my face with my hands. I'd end up like Elspeth Cooper. I couldn't bear that.

' 'T'ain't just the beauty,' Susan went on, as if such a consideration were irrelevant. 'You'll bring a pretty penny when you marry. Someone'll get a rare prize in you, Miss Nancy, and that's a fact.'

Bath was a town wholly given over to pleasure. Mornings were spent at the bath and pump rooms, or else shopping for ribbons and trinkets, browsing in bookshops, or drinking in coffee houses. The afternoons were spent at Harrison's Assembly Rooms at the gaming tables, or drinking tea and perambulating about.

Susan was right. Young men did not go to Bath for the cure, that was for sure. They went there to hunt fortunes. My father was rich. That made me a fair prospect.

I found it all unutterably tedious.

The most important social event of every week was the ball held each Tuesday. Whatever the occasion, my brother Joseph went straight to the gaming tables. He would soon be returning to Jamaica to take over the plantation and he was behaving like a man under sentence. He was keen to enjoy every civilised pleasure, and what place was more civilised than Bath? His chief enjoyment was playing piquet or faro. He was very bad at both. My father's money flowed through his hands like sugar ground to sand.

Mrs Wilkes was not averse to a turn at the tables either, but her play was slow and deliberate, each card considered. Money stuck to her fingers like molasses. It was not what she was there for, however, and after a hand or two she would give up her place at the tables and accompany me into the ballroom. She had a deeper game to play.

The marriage game had its own rules and etiquette, winners and losers, like any other game of chance. The opening bid was an invitation to dance.

Mrs Wilkes had taken care to drop hints as to my wealth among her fellow card players, so I did not lack for partners. First one young man presented himself, then another. Mrs Wilkes watched, assessing each prospect, tallying them on a dance card of her own devising, rejecting those who were too old, too poor, too common, the fine lines about her mouth working like the drawstrings of a purse. If she thought one was right, off she went to secure an introduction to his mother. She would reel off to me their family history, going through their pedigree as if they were thoroughbred horses. Mr Amhurst, Barstow, Denton, Fitzherbert, Fitzgibbon; younger son, nephew, cousin; related, though distantly, to the Earl of somewhere or other. I could hardly tell them apart. Bowing figures in powdered wigs presented themselves in seemingly endless succession: sweating faces looking up at me, mouthing meaningless compliments; limp fingers in damp gloves leading me into the dance. All the time Mrs Wilkes watching everything, her fan fluttering faster than a dragonfly's wing.

I went through my paces, as expected, although all I wanted to do was to get out of there as soon as possible. The year was turning towards summer, the rooms wanted ventilation and were abominably crowded, filled with a continually milling press and throng of people. As the night wore on the exertions of the dancers added to the warmth given off by the candelabras and chandeliers. The musky stench of overheated heavily-perfumed bodies made the atmosphere close to intolerable. At the stroke of eleven, the ordeal was over. Beau Nash, the Master of Ceremonies, declared the ball to be at an end. I went home with my face aching from so much smiling; my feet and legs sore from standing and dancing all night in thin-soled pumps.

Mrs Wilkes scolded me for being too cold, too distant, too aloof. She was beginning to despair that I'd *ever* find a husband, when a likely prospect presented himself. Mr James Phillips Calthorpe, younger son of a baronet, well bred and well connected. He had hardly a penny in his own right, and altogether no prospects, but he had the tastes that went with his station, liked the gaming tables quite as much as my brother, played with similar skill and enjoyed the same degree of success. I was under no illusion. His ardour was fuelled entirely by his own greed and the size of my fortune.

Mrs Wilkes was beside herself. Calthorpe was considered handsome by some, although I thought his blue eyes altogether too pale, his colouring too vivid, and there was a weakness about his mouth and chin that I did not find attractive. I was envied for his attentions, but I cared for him not at all, finding him shallow and vain with a vastly inflated opinion of himself. I did my best to ignore him and to act cold towards him, but he took my indifference as haughtiness and this served to stoke rather than dampen his interest, which rendered his attentions even more tiresome.

I was steeling myself for another evening of more of them when a young naval officer presented himself.

'May I request the pleasure?' He bowed before me.

I was waiting for Calthorpe, saving my energies for him. I did not want to dance before I had to, and began to refuse him, but when he straightened up and grinned at me, I saw that it was William.

Suddenly, everything was different. I tore up my card for the evening and determined to dance with him all night. The room now glowed with a golden light thrown out by the glittering chandeliers. The rows of dancers facing each other looked handsome, beautiful. The normal lines of callow youths and ageing rakes, overpainted women, elderly spinsters and awkward plain-faced girls seemed to have stayed at home. Everyone moved with grace and agility. No one turned the wrong way, barging into me, or treading on my toes. The windows were open. The scent of lilac came in on the air.

Calthorpe arrived too late. He was with his friend Bruton and, when it was clear that I would not leave my new partner for him, Bruton said something that did not improve Calthorpe's temper. He turned on his heel and marched out, fury and humiliation painting his cheeks, but what did I care? I was being partnered by quite the handsomest man in Bath.

My head filled with so many questions to ask William. What was he doing here? How long had he been in Bath? How long was he going to stay? But there was little chance to talk. I had to content myself with looking. I had not seen him for two years and he had changed. He was a man now. His uniform made him look very dashing, buttons and buckles shining, white stockings and white gloves immaculate. Maturity had carved away the boyish roundness from his cheeks and chin, but his dark eyes were as expressive as ever and his mouth still quirked up at the corners showing that he had not lost his humour or sweetness of nature. I'm sure that I had changed as much as he, but I knew in an instant that all was the same between us. I did not need words. His eyes and the touch of his hand told me enough.

Looks and smiles can convey a great deal in the intricate motions of the dance. My heart beat faster as each step brought him closer and closer, then stopped altogether when his face, his lips, were only inches away. I ached with the waiting as the dance took him away from me, and seethed with jealousy to see him join hands with another. Then he was coming back to me and the delicious rising excitement began all over again. I knew then what dancing was all about.

I thought that there would be time to talk in the interval, but as the last dance ended he told me that he had to go.

'But why?' My eyes filled as if I had received a sudden blow. To have such happiness offered and then snatched away was cruel.

'I have stayed longer than I intended. I only came to deliver a message. My captain's wife is here. I had a letter for her. Now I must get back to my ship.'

I looked at him. There was no opportunity even to say farewell. Our words were lost in the din of those around us. We were being pushed apart by a crowd of people, all struggling to gain the refreshment rooms at the same time.

'Meet me!' I whispered in his ear. 'Meet me outside!'

William went to collect his cloak and sword, and I went back for my wrap. I tripped down the stairs and out of the doors. I stood looking about, ignoring the link boys' curious looks, fanning myself as if I needed air, although it was scarcely cooler outside than inside the building. Then I heard his whistle.

He was at the archway that marked the beginning of Harrison's Walks that ran down by the Avon.

'Will you walk with me, Miss Nancy?' He offered me his arm. 'How long have you been in Bath?'

'Three weeks or so,' I replied.

'And do you enjoy yourself? With all the entertainments, music, dancing, and so on?'

'What do I want with dancing? I despise dancing.'

He laughed. 'Come, Nancy. That's not true! You seemed to enjoy it well enough just now.' He was teasing, his mouth curved up in a broad smile, but his eyes held a deeper seriousness, a sadness even. He knew as well as I did why young ladies were taken to Bath.

'That's because I was dancing with you.'

'What about all the other young men that you have met? Do you not like to dance with them?'

I shook my head. 'I like to meet young men rather less than I like to dance.'

He smiled again. 'I thought the two things went together.' He was silent for a while, running his hand over the nodding heads of the roses that lined the walk, releasing their scent. 'Perhaps you already have a young man, and do not want to meet another.'

'Perhaps I have,' I said.

He blinked as if at some sudden sharp pain, then he looked away. He walked in silence, eyes cast down in resignation, and he sighed as if he'd heard what he most dreaded and most expected, all in the same breath.

We went on for a few paces, then he turned to me.

'In that case . . .' He looked about, at a loss for what to do, what to say.

'No.' I gripped his arm tighter. 'That's not what I meant. I meant . . .'

I stopped. I'd suddenly run out of words as well. Perhaps I had no words for it.

'I have no young man. Other than . . .'

'Other than?'

76

He was looking at me now, his dark eyes bright and intense.

I took a deep breath. 'Other than you.'

'Do not trifle with me, Nancy.'

'I'm not trifling with you. Why would I trifle? I do not trifle.'

'Truly?' He looked down at me, his face still serious.

'Truly. Of course. I am not the trifling sort.'

He began to smile again and his smile spread wide, reaching his eyes.

'I have thought of you every night, and every day since I went away.' He paused, as though to collect his thoughts. 'If it had not been for you, I would never have obtained a place with Captain Robinson on the frigate, *Colchester*, and he's been like a father to me. You were my saviour, Nancy, but you are more, much more.' He stopped again, as if these words were hard for him. 'You had always been there, from our earliest years, like a sister. Always a friend: strong, and brave, and loyal. When we were playmates, do you remember?' I nodded. 'But when I came back, you were different. You were dressed like a lady, in silks and satins. You seemed to have gone so far above me, a common sailor, and you a rich man's daughter. I thought that I could never . . .' He shook his head. 'You were the finest, cleanest, prettiest thing I'd seen in an age. I was so glad to see you, but it seemed so hopeless . . .' He sighed. 'I vowed that I would not come back until I had made my way in life. Until I was in a position . . .'

'In a position to do what?'

'To ask your father for your hand. I have my commission now, Nancy.' He pointed to the gold at his collar. 'I have money from prizes and my wages. My prospects are good. I should make captain —'

'I do not care a fig for that.' I put my fingers to his mouth to hush him. 'I am not my father, you can save the speeches for him.' I drew him closer. 'You could come home barefoot in a sailor's rig and I would still want to marry you.'

'In that case . . .' He bent his head to kiss me. His arms went about me and he held me close, his mouth warm on mine. I felt suddenly breathless, almost as though I were swooning, as though my very bones were melting. I wanted the kiss to last for ever, but eventually he broke the embrace.

'We will be sweethearts, you and I. Promised to each other,' he murmured. 'Take this as a token.'

He drew a ring from off his finger. It was

a man's ring, heavy gold, and so big that it would only fit on my thumb.

'Then you must have this.'

I reached for the ring I wore on the middle finger of my left hand. It had belonged to my mother. I had been given her jewellery on my last birthday.

It reached the knuckle of William's little finger.

'I'll wear it around my neck.' He took the ring and kissed it, slipping it into his uniform pocket. 'Now I must go.' He looked up at the sky. 'I have to ride back to Bristol and there is going to be a storm.'

In the distance, thunder growled as if to confirm his prediction. Rain was beginning to spot as he kissed me in parting. I had to hurry back to the Assembly Rooms to avoid a soaking. I ran up the stairs, humming a merry dance tune. The second half of the evening had already begun, but I wouldn't be dancing. If we had come to Bath to find me a husband, then as far as I was concerned the search was done. William had to return to his ship, but I didn't care. I was sure of him and he'd be speaking to my father just as soon as his duties allowed.

I came to the last turn of the stairs and met two men lounging there. James

Calthorpe and his friend Edward Bruton. I smiled a greeting by way of apology for slighting him earlier and was about to explain about William, but Calthorpe ignored me and carried on his conversation with Bruton, turning his back as they began to descend the stairs. It was, perhaps, little more than I deserved, and I was not disposed to think the worst of him for it, but then he made a comment and I could not but overhear it.

'What did you say?'

They looked at each other and smirked. They were both in varying degrees drunk, although Calthorpe was the less steady of the two.

'A merchant's daughter is bad enough,' Calthorpe repeated, enunciating his words louder and more clearly. 'But a sailor's whore, I could never endure —' He looked at his friend and they both fell to laughing. I could not bear the insult, to William, or to me.

'At least he's not a rake like you two. He risks his life for King and country. Who do you think you are, to slight the jacket blue?'

That set them laughing louder, so much so that I could not endure it. Temper and pride flared together as I looked down at

Calthorpe's braying face a step or so below me. I reached back my arm and punched him square on the nose. It was not a girl's slap, or a wild swing, but a short, sharp jab from the shoulder just as Ned had taught me. It was a well-placed blow. Brother Ned would have applauded. I heard the bone crack. Blood spurted and splattered, adding a poppy-petal pattern to the pale embroidered silk of his waistcoat.

Calthorpe reeled back, holding his face. If Bruton had not caught him, he would have gone toppling down the stairs. Blood seeped between his fingers as he snorted and swore, his words thick and indistinct. I turned on my heel and left them.

A storm *was* coming. William had been right. It came full force in the night. The wind screamed about the houses and rain hit the windows like scattering shot. Mrs Wilkes had to raise her voice to have her orders heard above the commotion, but the growing tempest did not seem to trouble her, beyond a fear for the slates and chimney pots.

Those who live by the sea always keep an eye on the weather. Susan declared that she would not sleep a wink.

'I don't like the sound of it,' she said

81

when she came to help me undress. 'If it be like this here, what's it going to be like in Bristol? Or out in the Channel?'

The windows were shaking in their sashes as she looked out into the rain-streaked blackness. The wind that screamed about the houses of Bath would be blowing twice as strong out at sea. Any ship caught far from shore would stand little chance. The captain would have to make safe harbour or be at the mercy of the storm.

'There'll be wrecks tonight.' She rubbed at the gooseflesh on her arms. 'You see if there's not.'

Susan and I knelt together that night to pray for all those who might be in peril on the sea and for any whose ships were driven on to the shore. I added a silent prayer for William, giving thanks that he wasn't at sea, and asking God to keep him safe.

By morning, the storm had hardly abated. Instead, it continued, growing and building, turning itself into one of the worst storms in living memory. It went on all that day and into the next. Up at King Road, the safe anchorage at the mouth of the Avon, ships were thrown up on the shore. That had happened only once before. By the end of the third day, the damage was grievous. Word slowly filtered into Bristol of the number of vessels wrecked and lives lost. Whole fleets had gone down, although we knew nothing of that in Bath. Trees blocked the roads and the rivers were swollen to bursting. It took a further two days for the first coach to reach us from home.

It brought Robert with a letter from my father. Mrs Wilkes read it quickly. She did not share the contents with us, but whatever news it contained made her white about the mouth.

'What's that all about?' Susan asked Robert as she fed him in the kitchen.

Robert shook his big head, his long face graver than I had ever seen it.

'The Master says to come home.'

7

My father sat in his study, encased in gloom.
His clothes were wrinkled, as though he had
slept in them, and his wig was dishevelled
and set at a slant. He looked shrunken as if
he'd lost flesh. His waistcoat no longer
strained at the buttons; his florid face was
dull as putty and sunken under a three-day
silvering of stubble. His eyes were lustreless,
rheumy and red from lack of sleep. He
looked far older than when I had last seen
him, as if he had aged twenty years in as
many days.

He had been expecting a convoy of ships
from Jamaica. Only one had arrived safe in
port.

'Don't fuss, Madam!' he roared at Mrs
Wilkes. He waved her away as if warding
off a buzzing insect. 'I can't bear it!'

'Father —' Joseph began, but got no further.

'You be quiet, Sir!' My father half rose
from his chair. 'If we are ruined, it is

largely your doing. What you have done is near criminal. Where are the funds I forwarded to you in order to secure the cargoes?'

My brother had no answer. He didn't even bluster, just hung his head as if he were ten again and been caught pilfering by some shopkeeper.

'You borrowed on expectation of profit, and now the whole lot is lost. All at the bottom of the sea.' My father rose, leaning on his desk to face his son. 'How am I to pay the creditors? How am I to pay the planters whose sugar we were shipping, the merchants who have bought it? Perhaps you could tell me? I have to stand surety. How can I do that without ships and money? You are guilty of fraud, Sir, or as near as dammit! I could turn you over to the justices, and will do if you are not very careful.' Joseph opened his mouth to say something, but thought better of it. Father's fury left him gaping like a fish. 'I'll speak to you later. Now get out of my sight!'

I thought he meant me, too, so I went to follow my brother out of the room.

'Not you, Missy.' He called me back. 'I want to speak to you.'

I stood waiting, but it was as if I were

85

not there. He sat down and remained lost in thought, staring out of the window at the city spread below.

'Father?' I stepped forward to remind him of my presence.

'Is a husband found for you?'

I shook my head.

'Prospects? In your mother's last letter, she had hopes of someone . . .'

I saw James Calthorpe's bloody nose and shook my head.

'Good. Good.' He rubbed his hands as though warming them. 'These younger sons — they've not got a pot to piss in. Never mind that they're aristocratic. No point in throwing good money after bad. So you're not committed?'

'Well, not exactly . . .'

'What do you mean?' He looked at me sharply. 'Speak plain.'

I took a deep breath, determined to tell him and get it over. Hope surged within me. If I played my cards correctly, I might marry William directly. It would be one less expense for him. It was a way of getting me off his hands.

I did not play my hand well.

'I'm promised.'

'Oh?' His eyes narrowed. 'Who to?'

'William. He was in Bath. We met and . . .'

'William? What William?'

'William Davies. You know him.'

He rubbed the stubble on his chin. 'Father used to captain the *Andrew and John*? Mother keeps The Seven Stars?'

'Yes. That's him. He's . . .'

'A sailor. You'll not marry a tar.'

'He's not a tar. He's a naval officer.'

'Naval officer!' My father gave a short bark of a laugh. 'He's still a tar. They all are.'

'But we're promised . . .'

'Not now you're not. You can't marry without my permission and I'm not giving it.' He read the expression on my face. 'Think me harsh, do you? Think me cruel? Go and ask the widows and orphans of Bristol, let them tell you what's cruel. I've lost everything. Everything!' His voice was trembling. 'What ships I have left will have to be sold to repay the debt. Do you understand?' He stood up and came towards me. 'You would do your part, wouldn't you? If I asked you to. For me? For the family?' He touched my cheeks, his fingers tracing over my skin with an old man's tremor.

'Of course, Papa!' I had no idea what he was talking about, no idea what I was promising, but his distress and sudden infirmity frightened me. What else could I say?

'Good girl! My good girl. My Nancy! Always honest and true! Your brother Joseph has turned out a sot and a waster, but I knew I could depend on you. You are my daughter and you will do your duty.' He leaned on to the side of the desk, edging his way back to his chair, going hand over hand, like a man on a tilting deck. 'I have one chance left,' he said as he dropped into his seat. 'One chance, and one chance only.'

He muttered the words with his chin sunk into his chest, so they sounded slightly slurred. Then he looked up at me, his mood changed, his old self snapped back again.

'There will be no more talk of marrying sailors. I'm expecting a guest at dinner. Make sure you've lost that sulky expression by then, Miss. It's enough to sour milk. I want you at your most charming. I want you looking your best. Tell Susan. Now send Joseph to me. We must see what we can salvage from this mess.'

The destruction at sea had been general; my father was not the only one to suffer. His, however, was the greatest loss. A whole convoy had gone down, its crews drowned, its cargoes hauled away by wreckers or dissolving in the waters of the Channel. The only ships my father had left were those that had been in port, or far off abroad and not expected home for a long while.

'It's all over Bristol. Only one ship saved out of the whole lot coming in,' Susan told me when she came back from town. 'Crewed by foreigners, all dark-skinned fellows, with gold in their ears and coal-black ringlets. Not a jack of them speaks a word of English. Came through the storm with hardly a sail torn or a spar broken. Must have been captained by the Devil himself, that's what they are saying in the port.'

The harbourside gossips were nearer to the truth than they could have ever guessed.

The mysterious captain of the sole surviving ship was to be our dinner guest, but the dinner was never given. The roast beef my father loved so much charred on the spit; the plum pudding he'd ordered to be made boiled away on the stove until it was as solid as a cannonball. My hair was half brushed, spread about my shoulders, when we heard a scream from downstairs and the sound of pounding feet, then further cries and shouting from all around the house.

I was not yet dressed, so Susan ran out to see what could have happened to cause such a commotion. She came back slowly, her thin face pale and pinched.

'What is it, Susan?' I turned from the mirror. 'Whatever is the matter?'

'It's your father, Miss,' she said quietly, her eyes filling with tears. 'He's been took badly. They're bringing him upstairs now.'

I ran from my room, still in my corset. Robert and the footman were carrying my father between them. His head lay slumped against Robert's chest, one hand hung down, knocking against the banisters. I ran to help, taking his arm by the sleeve. It was limp and heavy as I lifted it on to his chest. His face was grey and his jaw hung slack. The cheek towards me was puckered, lifted as if by a giant hook. His eye was half open, the white suffused with blood.

'Is he —' I looked up at Robert, who shook his head, frowning as if to say, 'Not yet.'

'The doctor's been called for.'

They took him to his room and Robert laid him down as gently as if he were a sleeping child. He stood for a moment, looking down at him. He sent the footman away and asked for warm water and clean linen. I left him tending to his master, tears in his eyes.

' 'Tis apoplexy, the Missis says,' Susan told me. 'Her last husband was took with it. She knows the signs.'

The doctor came and shook his head. There was nothing he could do. Most people thought Mrs Wilkes might go to pieces, but after the first shock she kept her head. She sent for Henry to come from London, and Ned from his regiment.

It took my father three days to die, so they both arrived in time to say their good-byes. We were called to his bedside when it seemed he couldn't last much longer. Henry and Joseph were already there, standing each side of him. I stood at the end of the bed, Ned next to me, listening to each shallow whistling breath, counting the seconds between them, wondering if there would be another. Just as it seemed that he could last no longer, his hand gripped Henry's sleeve and he pulled his son to him. Joseph and Henry bent down, their ears close to his mouth. His words were slurred, his voice a hoarse bird caw. I could not hear what he said, but they both nodded.

'We promise, Father,' they said together.

His hand went slack and he turned his head away from them. He never spoke again.

Outside the house, straw was strewn in the drive to deaden the sound of hooves and wheels. Inside, the mirrors were turned, shutters closed and curtains drawn. My father lay in his coffin in the dining room, surrounded by tall clear-burning beeswax candles, Robert standing over him in quiet vigil. Men came to see my brothers, to pay their respects and offer condolences. They spoke in murmurs and stepped softly, but many were owed money and they were anxious to know what would happen to their investment. Business wouldn't wait, even for the funeral. Henry offered them Bristol Milk and cake along with placating words and reassurances that all was well. They drank their sherry, brushed the crumbs from their waistcoats and agreed to give Henry a little more time to order his father's affairs.

'That's all I need,' he said. 'Just a little while.'

After they had gone, he'd retire to the library to spend hours bent over the books, looking at agreements. He would come out hollow-eyed, and drawn. We were ruined; no two ways about it. Only a miracle could save us. The creditors would wait until after the funeral, but after that they would take it all.

I do not know to whom he prayed, but our saviour was the foreign sea captain who had come through the storm unscathed. Bartholome, the Brazilian, came to our house the day before the funeral. His very presence set everyone talking and whispering in corners. The man was a mystery. Nothing was known about him. It was as if he had sprung up among us like a devil from a trap door, brandishing a pitch fork. No one even knew his full name. Legend gathered around him, swirling about him like a great black cloak. His age, the country of his birth, his early history, were all unknown. Even his looks were deceptive. He must have been as old as my father, but he looked much younger. He wore no wig and the thick black hair falling to his shoulders had no grey in it. There was no surplus flesh upon him and his face was curiously ageless. His prominent features seemed carved from some hard wood. His thin moustache and beard were clipped close as though they had been painted on to his dark skin.

He had been a buccaneer and had acquired fabulous wealth during his years as a freebooter, that was all Bristol knew. To us, he was a planter with a colourful past. He had used his booty to buy land and his Jamaican holding was next to ours. My father had been in business with him for many years, providing slaves and acting as factor for his sugar. He'd been a guest at our house before, and now he'd come to offer his condolences and something more. He spent hours locked away with my brothers and when he left, he took our troubles with him.

I met them in the hall just as the Brazilian was leaving.

'Miss Nancy.' He bowed to me. 'I'm so charmed to see you again, even at this sad time.' He took my hand. His long fingers were heavy with rings, square-cut rubies and emeralds. He stood looking down at me with eyes so black as to show no pupil. They held a gleam of red, almost purple, like overripe cherries, or deadly nightshade berries. 'I am truly sorry for your loss,' he murmured as he lifted my hand to his mouth. 'Whatever assistance I can give . . .'

His lips were warm and moist inside the close-clipped soft silkiness of his beard and moustache. It was like being caressed by a panther. I had to steel myself not to snatch my hand away.

'Thank you, Sir. You are most kind.'

'The last time we met you were but a child . . .' He smiled, his red lips parting to show a gap between his front teeth. A gap shows lust, so Susan said.

'Yes, I remember.'

I'd been thirteen, maybe fourteen. Hardly a child.

'Now you are quite the young lady.' His eyes left my face.

'As you see.' I looked down at myself.

When he smiled, the skin around his eyes wrinkled, betraying his age. He continued to stare at me expectantly, but I could think of nothing more to say. Then he seemed to recollect himself.

'Yes, Sirs.' He turned to my brothers and shook hands with them. 'We do well. Very well.'

I assumed he was referring to whatever had been agreed, and that it would be enough to save the business. My brothers shook his hand warmly and saw him out. I suspected nothing, although they would have been laughing if my father had not still been in the house. They were talking loudly about getting cargoes in and of buying ships again. I felt glad, I remember, relieved. I might even have felt grateful to the Brazilian for helping us out, for showing such generosity.

When I think of it now, my innocence makes me shudder.

The next day, my father was to be buried at St Mary Redcliffe, the church that he had attended since he was a boy. He'd never missed a Sunday when he was in Bristol; now he'd be there for ever more.

The church was dim and gloomy. Black clouds outside threatened more rain and brought darkness to the early afternoon. The candles were lit, their flames guttering as more mourners entered. The only splash of brightness was Ned's red jacket; then, as I turned round, my eyes caught a glitter and spark. Bartholome had come in behind us. Halfway to the altar, he dropped to one knee in genuflection. The diamond cross he wore on his chest swung out, catching the candlelight and shining like a constellation of stars in the gloomy aisle. People shook their heads in disbelief and disgust. No one had done such a thing here for more than a hundred years. Nostrils flared at this whiff of popery and the God-fearing folk of Bristol turned away in disapproval. Bartholome seemed unconcerned and, when he saw me staring, he smiled, his gap-tooth grin white against his black beard. Susan dug me in the back, as if I needed reminding not to gawk about at my father's funeral.

The service was over quickly. We were soon all filing out into the driving rain. Only my father remained behind, soon to lie under the flagstones where all men walked.

My brothers had commissioned an alabaster plaque to be carved, with no cost spared. The design was to be of things to do with the sea and the plantation: ships, sugar cane, kneeling slaves. There was to be a weeping fountainhead at the top, the mark of my father's business, and a skull in the corner, like on the other memorials: a reminder that death comes to us all.

The will was read in my father's study. I was not yet sixteen, and not invited to attend. Henry and Joseph were appointed my joint guardians. Henry was to take over the business in Bristol, with Joseph going to Jamaica. They quarrelled about that as they had quarrelled about everything else since they were boys. Henry prevailed just as he always did. Besides, it was father's will. Even Joseph would not defy his dying wish, although it left him angry and resentful, muttering that Henry had always been Father's favourite and had the best of everything. I almost felt sorry for him, but when I offered my sympathy, he told me to save it for myself.

'You're coming with me. Didn't you know?'

I had no idea. The shock I showed at the news quite cheered him.

'Why? Why should I go?'

He put his hands together in mock prayer. 'Father's will.'

I was living in a house of secrets. Everyone knew more than I did. Even Susan.

I went in search of her, and found her in my bedroom sorting through my summer clothes.

'I'm sorry for it, Miss Nancy, I truly am. It'll not be the same with you gone.'

'You knew, didn't you?'

Susan nodded.

'Why did you not tell me?'

'I was told not to.' She busied herself folding and refolding one of my dresses.

'But why?'

'In case . . . in case you ran away —'

'Ran away!' I sat down on the bed, mystified. 'Where would I go?'

'I'm sure I couldn't say . . .' Susan looked at her hands. She was hiding something else. I could tell by her face.

'Well?'

'The Missis thought you might panic and bolt off.'

'Who with? Where to?'

'With William. 'Twasn't me, Miss.' She hurried on. 'Honest. I never said a word, but she's got eyes in her head. She seen you with him at Bath.'

'I've not even heard from him.'

Pride made it hard for me to admit this, for I had expected word from him and that hope had been the only bright spot in all this grey misery, but every day my hope had faded. Now its stock was almost nothing.

'I dare say it's for the best,' Susan said, with a false jollity. 'You'll probably meet some young planter out there with pots of money.'

'I don't want any young planter.' I stared at her. 'You know something else, don't you? What is it, Susan? Tell me!'

She looked at me, obviously in two minds.

'He called.'

'When?'

'Just before the Master was took bad.'

'Why was I not told?'

'Been forgotten in all the confusion.' She

hesitated, unsure whether to go on. 'There was a note, though,' she said, finally. 'From him.'

I felt my expectation unfurling from the place where I had folded it away.

'When? What did it say?'

'T'other day. What it said, I couldn't say. Missis got hold of it and threw it in the back of the fire. Said that what you didn't know wouldn't hurt you. Notes from him would only put ideas in your head and encourage you to do summat stupid.'

'But you could still have told me!'

'She said if you found out, she'd know who'd told you, and she'd dismiss me.' Susan began to cry, dabbed at her eyes with her apron.

I reached for my writing things. 'Perhaps it's not too late. I could send a note to William.'

'There'd be no point.' Susan sniffed and shook her head. 'Navy left for Portsmouth this morning. Cook told me. Her Noah is serving on one of the ships. I am sorry, Miss, truly! But there's nothing you can do!'

She was right. I could do nothing to prevent what was happening to me, so I helped to sort my summer clothes, taking them out of their presses ready to be packed into trunks. As I worked, I tried to put William out of my mind, but how could I? Where was he? What would he think of me? To send word, and yet to receive no reply? I certainly would have run away with him, if I had known, if the chance had been offered to me. My life seemed blighted. Bleak as a winter's day.

I didn't blame Susan. She had been a true friend, and I didn't want to think ill of her. I even gave her some trifles of jewellery: a pearl brooch that she'd always fancied, along with a coral necklace and matching earrings.

Perhaps Mrs Wilkes sensed a change in me, or perhaps she felt sorry now for what she had done, for that night she treated me differently. She poured chocolate from her special silver pot and talked about my new life in Jamaica and what would be expected of me. It was as if I had crossed some kind of line, some invisible divide between girl and womanhood.

'It's a shock for a young girl . . .' She paused, pleating her skirt with her fingers. 'Especially at first. Not at all what one expects. Takes some getting used to . . .'

'I'm sure,' I said, thinking that she was still talking about life on a plantation.

'I'm the nearest thing you have to a

mother, so it rests on me . . .' She paused again.

I looked at her expectantly. She was rarely at a loss for something to say.

'But he's hardly ever at home, so I hear,' she finished. 'So he shouldn't bother you over much.'

She hurried off to organise Susan and to supervise the last of the packing. I followed after her and the conversation went out of my mind. In the morning, I would be departing. I had other things to think about. Anyway, I thought that she was talking about Joseph. And since when had he bothered me?

It draws a bitter laugh, even now, to think that I was ever so naive.

8

I don't know how many days I kept to my cabin, confined by seasickness and general wretchedness. The steward, Abe Reynolds, came and went, bringing me food I couldn't even look at without wanting to heave.

'You got to eat, Miss,' he said, tugging at one of his long earlobes and looking aggrieved as I rejected yet another little delicacy meant to tempt me. 'Perhaps you're in need of some air. Ship's steady now. Wind's set fair. How about a turn on the deck? Other passengers find it quite a reviver.'

I told him I had no desire for company of any sort.

'Prefer your own, do you?' he asked, taking my tray of untouched food.

'I do,' I said firmly.

It was not strictly true, and the time I was spending in solitary reflection was only adding to my misery, but there was no one I wanted to see, no one I could count as a friend to me, and I did not like the thought of being among strangers.

When another knock came at the door, I thought it was Abe again and I told him to go away, but the knocking persisted. A voice I did not recognise demanded entry. I went to answer, stepping down on to a deck that no longer shifted and tilted. It was as steady as a drawing-room floor, but I still staggered as I opened the door and nearly fell into the arms of the man standing before me.

He helped me back into the cabin and sat me down in a chair. He was crew of some sort, but clearly a gentleman, with shoes and stockings on his feet, and although in shirt sleeves, he wore a waistcoat.

I guessed his hair to be sandy under his powdered wig, for his face was pale and speckled with freckles. His eyebrows were bleached almost white and grew tangled and thick, jutting like loops of unravelling rope. His eyes were a faded blue, as if the sun had taken the colour from them, too. He had the worried, tired air of a man who takes the troubles of others on to himself. He looked as if the sight of me had increased his burden still more.

'What do you want?' I asked.

'To see you.' He rolled his sleeves higher. 'I'm Graham, Niall Graham. Ship's surgeon. I've come to see how you are.'

'Very well, thank you.'

'That's not what I hear.'

'Why should you care? I'm not your patient.'

'You have no choice.' He gave a wan smile. 'Everyone on board is my patient, be they passenger or crew.' He came closer. 'Now let me see you. I can't have Miss Kington falling sick. Your family owns this ship. How would that look on my record?'

'I am not sick.'

'That's for me to judge. Reynolds tells me you will take no sustenance.' He held down my lids and looked into my eyes. 'Bodily affliction is not the only illness we have to fear. It is possible to fall into melancholy.' Somehow he knew. His blue eyes might be faded, but they were shrewd and astute. 'I am a doctor. The nearest thing we have to a priest on board. Talk eases the soul, or so they say.' He held his arm towards me. 'Perhaps you would do me the honour of taking a turn or two about the deck. The fresh air will do you good, Abe is right about that, and I always find talk comes easier when accompanied by exercise.'

I went with him up the companionway and stepped into a light which hurt my eyes. I wanted to turn and go back to the dark and gloom below decks, to hide myself away again, but Graham gently urged me forward. My sight cleared to see white sails against blue sky. I felt the sun burning through my dress, and turned to feel a warm wind on my face. It would be hard for me to admit, but I was glad to have exchanged the stuffy confines of my cabin for the open deck. I had closed myself off for too long, beset by melancholy, as Graham had rightly judged. From that moment on, I began to feel better. He was a clever doctor.

Graham offered me his arm, and I took it. I felt the urge to confide even though I did not know this man. As we paced the deck I found myself telling him everything. It was nearing midday and the sun grew hot. Graham led me to the shelter of the quarterdeck and there we stayed, using a couple of upturned buckets for seats, until I had finished my tale.

Graham listened with great seriousness, and did not offer false cheerfulness. He agreed that, indeed, my position was grave.

'But you should not give up hope. You are young. There's always hope for the young. And this young man of yours, William, he'll not give up on you. He's a stout fellow.'

'You speak as though you know him.'

'Indeed, I do. We served together.'

'On the slave ship, the *Amelia*?'

'The very one!'

'Why did you not say earlier?'

He laughed. 'You scarcely gave me the chance. He was a good lad and did his duty in difficult circumstances, believe me. I'm glad he's joined the Navy. He will make an excellent officer. I'm pleased to hear that he is doing well in the service.'

The thought of William brought all my sorrows back again.

'He doesn't know where I am! Or what has happened!' I had not yet cried, but now tears pricked my eyes. 'I had no time to explain to him. He will think I've forgotten him, or deserted him for another . . .'

'Now, now, my dear.' Graham patted my hand. 'We'll get a message to him; acquaint him with what has occurred.'

'How?'

'Write him a letter. On my return to England, I promise to deliver it myself.'

Just then, our conversation was interrupted by another officer.

'There you are, Graham.' He swung in under the jutting timbers of the quarter-deck. 'Is this your idea of how to entertain a young lady? Have her sitting on an up-turned bucket like a swab? For shame! You should have taken her to the grand cabin for a glass of punch or a dish of tea.'

He looked down at me, his brown eyes shining. He was about thirty, younger than Graham, and handsome in a florid kind of way. His broad face split into a grin and I found myself smiling back at him. 'My name is Adam Broom. I'm first mate here and navigator. You must be Miss Kington. How d'you do?' He held out his hand and shook mine like a man's. 'Glad to see you feeling better.' He kept hold of my hand and pulled me to my feet. 'He is a grisly fellow.' He nodded towards Graham. 'He's no use with ladies. Always talking about ill-nesses and other gruesome subjects. I hope his company has not distressed you too much.'

I had not laughed for a long time, but Broom's teasing made me smile.

'I'm not distressed because of that!'

'Miss Kington wants me to get a mes-sage to her young man,' Graham supplied.

'Oh,' Broom turned to me with his quick bright eyes. 'What young man is that?'

'Young William,' Graham replied.

'William? Which William? Every other tar is a William.'

'Ship's boy on the *Amelia*. *You* remember.'

'Oh. *That* William.'

'He's Navy now.'

'*Is* he?'

'Could we get a message to him, d'you think?'

'I'm sure we could. Between us we know someone on every ship in the fleet.'

I knew they exaggerated, but the promise cheered me, as did their company. It was part of Graham's treatment, as I realised much later. The idea of writing to William gave me hope, and that's what I needed, even though I thought at the time that my message was as likely to reach him as if I had cast it over the side in a bottle.

'Don't it feel good to be in the sun again?' Broom turned closed lids up to the great bright disc above us, and bid me do the same. 'Feel the wind warming the skin.' I opened my eyes to find him smiling at me. 'That's the Trades, Miss Kington, set fair to take us straight to the Islands. Damned if my soul doesn't lift as soon as we are beyond the line. I long for southern climes, not like Graham here who pines for a landsman's life and longs to hang his doctor's shingle in some fetid, fog-bound northern town. This is your first trip, I take it?'

'Indeed, Sir, it is,' I replied.

'I envy you then, Miss Kington. Indeed, I do. To view the Islands for the first time, with fresh eyes. To see their mountains and forests rising up from the sea, like emeralds heaped on a silver salver.' He described a distant land with his hands, his eyes fixed on the southern horizon. 'And when you get there! Such riches! Such beauty! Little birds, smaller than this,' he made a walnut shape, curling his fingers into a fist, 'more brilliant than any jewel, flitting about flowers brighter than any silk that you will ever see. Fruit for the picking, sweet as anything you could name; the very air about you, scented with spices. The Islands are paradise on earth, it seems to me. You could search the world over, and not find their equal anywhere on it.'

'Why do you not live there?' I asked, 'if you find it so agreeable. Keep an inn perhaps, or be a planter, or trader.'

'Oh, no, Miss Kington,' he shook his head vigorously, as if shocked by the very idea. 'That could not be. I have an affliction beyond the help of physick; even my good friend Graham has no cure for it. No sooner am I ashore, than I wish to be away again. My home is the ship. My country is the sea.'

He grinned, his teeth white and even against skin tanned from many days sailing. He did not wear a wig; his long dark hair was tied back with a red velvet ribbon. He did not dress like the other ship's officers. His shoes had silver buckles, lace frothed at his throat. He wore silk beneath his plain sea coat, and his breeches were woven with ribbons.

I should have guessed his destiny. He was half pirate already.

He looked up as canvas cracked above us. 'The wind is freshening, turning east nor'east. You bring us luck, Miss Kington, damn me, if you don't! With this behind us, we'll be there in no time.' He winked at me. 'If I didn't know better, I'd say you whistled for it.' He bowed. 'Now I regret I must leave you in the company of this ugly fellow,' he nodded towards Graham. 'There is work to do!'

He went off, barking orders that sent sailors scampering up the ropes and the helmsman spinning the wheel.

'Don't mind Broom.' Graham smiled, watching his friend with affection. 'He is an excellent fellow, despite his teasing ways. The men would go to hell and back for him. There's no better sailor either side of the Atlantic, you have my word upon that. Now you must excuse me. I hope you will join us later in the great cabin. I'll make sure that Cook prepares something palatable for dinner, and I'm certain that Broom will want you to sample his punch.'

They left me to wander the deck and I had reason to thank both of them, for their words began to heal me of my melancholy. I leaned at the bow, watching the prow cut through the waves, folding lacy white foam on to the shining deep blue water, and I saw the beauty there. A hint of Broom's sentiment touched me like the breath of the wind on my cheek. The heat of the sun seemed to melt the coldness that had grown around my heart and my drooping spirits lifted with the steady warm wind blowing over me.

That evening I joined the company in the grand cabin. The other passengers were merchants, or planters like my brother. They seemed jolly enough fellows and the captain and his officers were charming and gallant, declaring themselves glad to have me there, for a female presence among them would stop their growing rough and grim. After supper, we were entertained by a pair of fiddlers and a boy on the penny whistle. Sailors danced for us, as nimble-footed and agile as any who played the theatres at home. Only my brother seemed unamused. He sat apart, drinking brandy, his face set and sullen, muttering that the other passengers were low, common, rooking fellows who cheated at cards, and cursing the crew equally as surly dogs who refused to do his bidding.

I spent most days on deck after that, often in the company of First Mate Broom. He told me to look sharp about, for we were approaching the latitudes where pirates lurked in the sea lanes, waiting for fat merchant ships such as ourselves.

'What would happen if they found us?' I asked, more curious than fearful.

'If a black hoist were to be sighted, we would strike our flag. They would board us and take whatever they wanted.'

'We would not fight back?' I was a little surprised at that.

'And risk being put to the slaughter? Not likely!'

'What would happen? Once we were boarded?'

'Most of the crew would join them, given

half the chance. Not the captain, of course.' He said nothing about himself or Graham. 'The captain is a fair man, so he would probably be spared, put in an open boat, the passengers along with him.' He laughed, although I did not think pirates any laughing matter. 'Your brother might not fare so well. He treats the men like servants and no sailor likes that. Captain's the only one allowed to order them about. That's until they go on the account, then the captain is not much different from the men.'

'On the account?'

'That's what we call pirating. They ain't *all* bad fellows. They call themselves gentlemen of fortune, and some are exactly that.'

'I am the only woman on board. What about me?'

He patted the hilt of his sword. 'I would skewer any man who came near you until they were heaped up in piles.'

'Give me a blade,' I said, joining in his banter, 'and I'll do that for myself.'

'You can use a sword?'

'Tolerably. I learned to fence with my brother.'

'I see.' He rubbed his smooth-shaved chin. 'I'm glad that we are on the same side, then. What a surprising young lady you are, Miss Kington.'

A watch was kept at all times, but although we saw ships on the horizon, none approached us. No black hoist bore down upon us. We had fair winds and good weather. We began to pass small islands surrounded by crescent-shaped reefs. They were uninhabited, but we stopped to take on water if they offered it, and whatever else they could provide by way of fresh produce.

I felt none of Broom's predicted excitement when we sighted the northern coast of Hispaniola. Neither did I share in the celebrations of the other passengers. Great bowls of punch were prepared and endless toasts drunk, chiefly to friendship, as is often the way on voyages, vows of undying affection made between men who will likely never set eyes on each other again. I thought them fools and kept separate. Instead of joy and hope, I felt a great weight descending. Journey's end was nearing. The next island would be Jamaica.

It was unto the West Indies
our gallant ship did steer . . .

9

The town of Port Royal lay at the end of a narrow spit that arced from the land like an arm flung as a defence from the sun. The bay that lay on the inside of it was deep, the water clear as crystal. The anchor ran straight down, scattering shoals of bright fish, sending them feinting and glittering like shards of falling mirror, until the flukes came to rest, catching on the fat lumps of coral that studded the white sand fathoms below.

The scene on shore was as busy as the Welsh Backs in Bristol. Ships stood at the docks. Wharves and warehouses lined the quays, but the men and women toiling to load and unload the cargoes were slaves. Sweat glistened on black skin. The female slaves laboured alongside the men, heaving sacks and rolling barrels, or moving with slow and stately grace, one hand held high to balance the great burdens which they carried on their brightly turbaned heads.

Behind them, the town spread away from the waterfront, mounting the hill in a tumbled pattern of wooden huts and red-roofed, white-painted houses crowded one upon another.

There was a carriage waiting for us.

'Thomas, this is my sister, Miss Nancy,' my brother said as he handed me into the seat behind the driver. 'You are to take her to Fountainhead directly. I have business here in town.'

He left us with a slap to the nearside horse's flank. The animal was nervous and skittered sideways, knocking against its pair.

'You all right, Miss Nancy? Horses didn't jar you?'

'I'm perfectly fine, thank you, Thomas.'

He nodded, satisfied that no harm had come to me, and called a boy to hold the horses as he got down to load the luggage. Thomas was a tall man and powerfully built. He lifted with ease trunks that it had taken two men to carry off the boat. He said little, just swung himself back into his seat, and we were away.

We were traversing the narrow spit that led to the mainland. The ground dropped away sharply on either side of the road, shelving down to strips of white sand. On one side, the pale green Caribbean curled in long low lines of surf; on the other, the waters of the lagoon lay blue and still. The horses pulling our carriage were high-stepping and skittish. Suddenly, one shied, swerving from something that lay in our path, causing the other to rear. The carriage lurched and we veered perilously close to the crumbling edge of the road. I clung to my seat, fearing that we might end up in the ditch, while Thomas fought to right us and to control the panicked animals. I peered over the edge of the carriage, wondering what had caused us to come so close to mishap. At first, I thought that a twisted pile of wood had fallen from a passing cart. Then I saw that the sticks were moving, jerking in a strange random way. There must have been some dreadful accident. I started up in horror, marvelling at the cruelty of anyone who could just drive on and leave a living creature broken in the road.

The creature lying there was so coated in sand and dust, the shape so contorted that I could not see exactly what it might be. Too large for a dog, but too small for a donkey. I shouted to Thomas that we must stop. He showed no signs of hearing, so I tugged his sleeve. When he still did not respond, I tapped him sharply on the back. He winced and turned round, pulling the horses to a halt.

'What is it, Miss?'

'It's still alive,' I indicated the heap by the side of the road. 'We must stop and help.'

He shook his head.

'No, Miss.'

He raised his whip while I stared back. What I'd taken at first for a thing inanimate, and then for an injured animal, was a human being. What I'd seen as hanks of twine, or a halter, or collar, were scraps and rags of clothing. This was a woman. Half skeleton already. Her skin dull, greyish under a powdering of fine white sand.

I was fumbling to open the door of the carriage, wondering if she were still alive, if we might help her, but Thomas reached back and pulled it closed.

'She's old. She'll die soon,' he said with a shrug, indicating that any efforts we might make on her behalf would be wasted. 'Refuse slaves, they're good for nothing.'

He pointed with his whip to where others lay tumbled in the ditch, then past the narrow fringe of grass and scrub to the margins of the lagoon. Dark shapes littered the beach like flotsam cast up by the sea. I could detect no movement. They lay like driftwood logs drying in the sun. He shrugged again and shook his head, his dark eyes bleak and empty. What was the point of saving one, when there were so many?

He turned away from me and whipped up the horses. This was my first sight of the cruelty that lay at the heart of this place that Broom called paradise, eating away at it, day by day, with a voracious appetite that would never be sated, like some hideous worm. The effect on me was profound. I stared back at the woman until she was just a tiny mound, a speck of black on the bone-white ground. I stared until my eyes ached and the heat shimmering up from the sun-baked track took her away.

10

Thomas drove the horses at a good pace along mile after mile of dusty red road. To the right was forest, with moss and vines draping it, and beyond that lay the sea. To the left the land was cultivated.

'All this here? Belongs to your father,' Thomas remarked, waving his whip in a great arc that took in a vast plain that sloped up from the road to the distant mist-shrouded mountains.

The land had been divided into fields of chequer-board exactness. The cane was being cut and rough stubble stretched away, just as it might in England at harvest time, except the stalks were knee high and thicker than a man's arm. The effect was strange, as if these were the acres of some farming giant. The uncut cane stood much taller than a man, dwarfing the figures swarming among the stalks. They worked like an army of ants, diligently and me-thodically, cutting, binding, pitching bundles into the waiting wagons.

The cultivated land was not fenced or walled along the road. The entrance to the estate was marked by a pair of impressive stone pillars standing alone. An overarching curve of wrought-iron letters announced that we were entering *Fountainhead*. The letters were surmounted by twin gushing springs frozen in silvery metal. Before, I had always seen the sign as a weeping willow. It was only as I went underneath that I could see what it was really meant to be. There were no weeping willows in this country. The long straight drive was bordered either side by tall palm trees, their leaves flopping down, the fronds spread wide in leathery fingers, like cormorants' wings drying in the sun. Thomas whipped the horses into a smart high-stepping trot and we drove on towards the house.

It stood alone on a small promontory, shaded by tall pine trees, set apart from the other buildings. White smoke and steam billowed from the direction of the mill and boiling house, obscuring a collection of roughly-thatched hovels. Behind the plantation, the land ascended in giant steps to form the foothills of a high mountain range of individual peaks and serrated ridges, the tops of which were lost in torn cloud and trailing mist.

The house was not grand in the style of some plantation houses, and was considered old-fashioned, being made of white painted wood with only two storeys, but it was artfully constructed and carefully situated to catch every breath of wind. I could sense my father's preferences in the design of it; he was not a man to put fashion before comfort. At home, in England, he had hated a draught and had liked the old house because it was packed in with others, easy to keep warm. He had complained about the new house, saying that it was like living in a barn. Here, he would have wanted to keep cool. The windows were large, with bright painted shutters folded back and thin muslin curtains billowing with the constant breeze blowing through the rooms. A wide veranda threw shade on all sides, so no part was directly in sunlight. My eyes pricked at the thought of him. I could almost see him sitting out there as the heat of the day faded, comfortable in an old sagging armchair, sipping a rum punch and smoking his pipe.

Wide double doors stood open at the top of a flight of stone steps. A man stood in front of them, obviously waiting for me.

Mr Duke, the overseer, was a small man of stoutish build. He stood splay-legged with his chest puffed out and his head thrust forward, belligerent as a bantam cock. He was pale, as if he always kept his face shaded from the fierce sun, and smooth-skinned with a little mouth, his upper lip protruding over his teeth in a parrot pout. He held a whip under his right arm. A black plaited thing, rolled in a snakelike coil with a handle as thick as my wrist. As he waited, he allowed its iron tip to fall from his grip before flipping it back into his palm.

Thomas helped me out of the carriage and, as I mounted the steps, Duke came forward to meet me. He removed his sweat-banded broad-brimmed tricorn hat to reveal a cap of shiny brown hair, greased by some rancid oil, straggling down to his shoulders. His dark eyes were flecked with grey and oddly opaque, like gun flints. He was near-sighted, I was to learn, and growing more so by the day.

'Miss Kington!' He held out his hand to me before I had reached the top of the steps. His palm was soft and moist. His shirt was marked with sweat, fresh patches ringing the yellowed armpits, soaking the stiffened fabric. 'Welcome to Fountainhead! I hope your journey here was not too arduous, but you must be fatigued. You will need to rest and refresh yourself.'

He took my elbow, propelling me towards the house. Two women had appeared, standing either side of the doorway, as still as caryatids. One was old, the other young, and both were dressed in shapeless shifts of some faded blue stuff. They looked like mother and daughter. The girl was lighter skinned, but the resemblance between them was strong. They were tall, long-limbed and, in the way they stood, in their carriage, they exactly mirrored each other.

'Phillis, Minerva.' Duke addressed the older, then the younger. 'This is your new mistress.' He let more of the whip down, cracking it back on itself with a flick of the wrist. They curtsied to me and sprang forwards. 'Look after her well, or it will be your skin.'

'Yes, Master,' the women said together. The whip cracked softly, a mere caress of leather on leather. They did not look at either of us, but focused on spots on the ground.

'Get those trunks into the house!' Duke roared down the steps to Thomas, who was unloading them from the back of the carriage. 'And look sharp about it, you lazy, good-for-nothing black bastard! Excuse me, Miss.' He turned back to me with exaggerated politeness, touching the brim of his greasy tricorn hat. 'I have duties to attend to, but after that, it will be my pleasure to show you around.'

With that, he stepped past me. His clothes might have been sweat-stained and reeking, but in boots he rivalled Beau Nash of Bath. They were as polished as mirrors and his high heels rang on the stone as he tripped down the steps.

I was left in the charge of the two women, who ushered me into the house. The rooms inside were large and airy, one opening out on to another. Many of the furnishings I recognised as being from our old house in Bristol. To discover familiar objects in such a foreign place was jarring to the senses. A bright green lizard skittered down the white-painted wall and across a portrait of my father. A white marble table that had stood in our hall now held a bowl heaped with oranges, mangoes and guava. It was like walking into a dream.

The older woman, Phillis, showed me upstairs to a cool, wide room under the eaves of the house. The floor was polished wood. A bed stood in the corner, draped in thin white muslin. There was a china bowl of warm water for me to wash with and a tablet of lilac soap. The sharp sweet scent reminded me of home. Phillis stood by with a soft towel to pat me dry. I said that I would like to rest and she stepped forwards to disrobe me, but I told her that I could do that for myself.

She went away and I stripped down to my petticoat, climbing into the muslin drapes as into a tent. I must have slept, for when I awoke the light was softer, the room cooler, and filled with a chirping, chirring sound. Not loud, but persistent and utterly unfamiliar. I thought it was that which had woken me, but I opened my eyes to find the girl, Minerva, looking down at me through the shifting muslin.

She had brought a tray of fruit and fresh-baked bread, and a draught of cold spring water. She laid it down on the table next to the bed without looking at me, or saying a word. When I thanked her, she glanced up, startled. I smiled, but her face stayed impassive as she drew the netting back. While I ate, she went to lay fresh clothes out for me, then stood by the wall, with her head down and her hands clasped behind her back. She sprang back to life as

I rose from the bed, and came forwards to help me dress.

'What's that noise I can hear?' I asked her.

She looked at me, surprised at the question.

'Cicadas,' she answered. 'Insects. They rub their wings together.' She demonstrated with one thin brown hand on the back of the other.

'They sound like nutmegs on a grater,' I said, and was rewarded with the faintest trace of a smile.

'Mr Duke,' she said, her voice low and musical. 'He's waiting downstairs. When you're ready, Miss.'

The overseer was pacing the veranda with the thick whip clasped tightly behind his back. He wore a long brown coat now, much stained with use.

Outside, a new racket had joined the other. This one much louder. I asked him what it was.

'Frogs,' Duke said. 'Start up about now. Get worse after sundown. Make the devil of a din. Now you're rested, I'll show you about.' He pointed with his curled whip to the windmill set on a small hill. 'Over there is the grinding house.'

Carts pulled by teams of long-eared

131

mules stood waiting to be unloaded, the cane stacked as high as stooks on a hay wain. A gang of men threw the bundles down and others formed a chain, passing the cane, one to another, until it reached the jaws of the grinders: huge metal rollers which crushed the thick stems like so much grass, squeezing the juice into a wedge-shaped trough which ran down to the boiling room built on lower ground.

'You there! Look lively!' Duke's whip leaped like a live thing, wrapping itself round the back of a slave who had let a bundle drop and scatter. The man showed no reaction, just carried on, even though the iron tip ripped through his shirt. 'Can't waste a minute. Cane has to be crushed as soon as possible after cutting, or the sugar won't crystallise.' He coiled the whip back. 'Helps to keep their wits about 'em. Such wits as they've got.' He laughed at his own joke. 'Need 'em near them things.' He nodded to the great vertical grinders which dwarfed the men sweating to feed them. 'Them rollers'll have your arm off in no time. Which is why we keep that there.' He pointed to a sharp-bladed machete hanging by the machine. 'Just in case.' He laughed again. 'Even these idle bastards learn to pay attention when they work in here.'

Feeding the grinders went on twenty-four hours a day, seven days a week, all through the harvesting season. It was back-breaking work, carried on at a cruel pace set by the slave boss and the prowling Duke.

He took me down the hill to the boiling house.

'The juice has to be boiled within twenty minutes or it ferments and turns into molasses and will never crystallise. It comes down this channel, a little lime wash is added to help it granulate. Then it is emptied into the copper vats.'

The copper vats were vast, heated by huge blazing furnaces fed with faggots of wood and trash — sugar-cane waste from the crushers. We did not go in, but even outside the heat was searing. Men and women moved like ghosts through clouds of smoking vapour, wielding long-handled copper ladles, skimming scum from the bubbling liquid. These skimmings drained into yet another basin. At each stage, waste molasses was carefully collected to be made into rum.

The boiling went on night and day through the harvest, the furnaces never dying down. Accidents were frequent; the results horrific. Molten sugar sticks to flesh and burns to the bone.

The crystallising sugar drained into vats, Duke explained, and was then packed into hogshead barrels, stamped with the Fountainhead sign, and sent to Bristol.

He stood back, looking at me, as if expecting my admiration, or my approval. I stared at him, shaken to the very seat of my being by what I had seen. All this was here because of us. The Kington family. It shamed me deeply that I'd never before really thought about where the sugar came from. I'd really had no idea how hard the work was, how relentless, or how dangerous.

Duke then took me to see the slave quarters, rows of two-roomed wattle-and-daub thatch cabins. A few children played, naked in the red dust. It was coming towards evening. Gangs of men and women were returning from the fields, while others were leaving to go to the grinding and boiling houses. They all looked equally weary and none of them looked at us. Only the children stared with solemn round eyes, before bolting into their houses as if running from malevolent spirits.

Behind the huts the land was divided up into little plots.

'We let 'em grow some stuff of their own:

Indian corn, yam, beans and such, a little tobacco. Saves on fodder and gives 'em something to barter or sell at market for the kind of bright-coloured cloth and gew-gaws they like.'

'You hold a market here?'

He nodded. '*They* do. Over there. That's the marketplace.'

He indicated a space of red beaten earth shaded by a great forest tree. Immense branches spread out, shading the whole area, as a great oak or chestnut might shelter a village green at home. Judging by its girth, the tree must have been very old. This was no shady chestnut, or English oak. Chains and manacles had been driven into the trunk about two feet above a man's height from the ground. Over that point the bark was smooth, but from there to the ground, the tree was torn and scarred, mutilated and marked with a complex criss-cross pattern as if someone had taken a knife to it. Great patches had been flayed away. In other places sap oozed, congealing in great crusted resinous clumps, dripping down like gouts of blood. All the bark had been ripped and torn, apart from one central column which branched either side to make the shape of a man in cruciform shadow.

'Doesn't do to be sentimental,' Duke said, as if he divined what I was thinking. 'God ordained blacks to be for our use and benefit, or else why make 'em in the first place?' He looked at me with his clouded eyes. 'Some says they're like children. Well, they ain't. Thinking that way brings danger to all of us. They ain't like us, that's for certain. I've studied 'em for many years now, Miss Kington.' He leaned forward earnestly. 'In my opinion, they are like animals, wild and vicious, but possessed of a cunning that makes 'em far more treacherous than any beast you could mention. You can't tame 'em, and you can't trust 'em. All they respect is this,' the whip reared and cracked in the air. 'Don't do to be too trusting, or get too familiar. Keep that in mind.'

He walked me back to the steps of the house and then excused himself. A new batch of slaves had been delivered the week before and needed seasoning in.

'Get 'em used to the work. Used to the discipline. First of all we brand 'em with this.' He took an implement from his pocket. The end was about as big as a shilling and bore initials surmounted by a fountain, like a seal. It was delicately wrought, more like a brooch than a branding iron. 'We had to have a new one made to reflect the change of ownership.' He turned the face for me to see. *N* and *K* reversed. 'Silver, see? Silver makes a sharper scar. Got to rub a little oil on first.' He moved thumb against forefinger. 'To stop the skin sticking to the metal.'

My attention was fixed by the object he held between his fingers. I found it most shocking and hideous in the way it combined prettiness with an utter vileness of purpose. I looked at the initials. I'd assumed the *N* was for Ned, my father. But that would be *E* . . .

The sudden realisation made me light-headed. I felt as though I might faint.

'Change of ownership?' I parroted his words like an idiot. 'Do you mean me?'

'Who else?' He looked at me, owl-eyed, peering close at my expression to see if I were mocking him. 'All this is yours. I've been showing you your own property.'

'I — I didn't know.' I tried to stop my voice from shaking. 'I assure you that I did not know.'

'I have it in a letter by your father's own hand. It's in his will. You are a very rich young lady.' He looked up uneasily. Phillis and Minerva were standing at the top of the steps. 'The old witch, and the young 'un.' He leaned towards me, taking my arm. Another turn about the yard took us out of earshot. 'You keep a close watch on those two. I'd have sold 'em both years ago, not kept 'em together, but your father would not allow it. Now,' he tipped his greasy tricorn hat, 'if you'll excuse me.'

'Should I expect you for dinner?' I did not know if I should invite him to dine with me. I had no idea what the etiquette should be, or even if there was any.

He was clearly surprised by the invitation.

'Very kind, I'm sure,' he said after a moment. 'But I have my own arrangements. Thank you, Miss Kington.'

That evening, I stood on the balcony outside my window, watching the sun go down: a great shimmering ball of red falling through bars of black cloud into the distant sea. The dark came more quickly than I had expected. Suddenly it was night. The air was hot, heavy with the perfume of flowers and full of the beat of wings and the sounds made by small unseen creatures. Birds or monkeys, I could not tell which, cried from the forest. The sound was almost human, jarring and sudden and utterly foreign. First one call, then another.

Each made me start, and gooseflesh crept up my bare arms despite the heat. Below me, a myriad of tiny lights glimmered in spangling pinpoints, littering the earth as though the stars had fallen, so I could no longer tell the sky from the ground.

All this was mine, I told myself, and everything that went with it. These people. I owned them. Their flesh would be burnt with my initials. I went back inside, rubbing my arms as the full chill of it came upon me. How could I ever get used to the strangeness of that? And why had my brothers not told me? They were seeking some way to cheat me out of it, I knew them well enough to see that. I could have told them not to waste their energies, that such deviousness was unnecessary. If they'd asked me, I would have told them. They could have the plantation and welcome. I wanted no part of it.

Light wavered on the walls around me. Minerva had come in on silent feet bearing candles. She came over to the window.

'What are those?' I pointed to the little lights on the ground.

'Fireflies,' she replied. 'You can collect them. Make a lantern. Close the shutters now, Miss.' She reached up to unlatch them. 'Moths and insects will fly in.'

She had brought a tray laden with food and a beautiful stem of papery purple flowers in a little earthen pot.

'Phillis hopes you like your dinner.'

'Am I to dine up here? I thought Mr Duke might dine with me, but I understand he makes other arrangements.'

'Mr Duke don't live here. He has a small house next door. He has his own woman prepare his food for him.'

'I do not like to dine alone.' I looked at her. 'Perhaps you would join me? You and Phillis?'

At home, I would have dined with Cook and Susan if no one else was in the house.

'Oh, no, Miss.' Her eyes grew wide and the shake of her head was emphatic. 'That would not be allowed. Will there be anything else?'

She stood looking straight ahead, her hands clasped behind her back. I had thought her older than me, now I could see that she was probably younger. She was a handsome-looking girl, with fine eyes, the colour somewhere between hazel and amber. A mix of races showed in her face, the best of both physiognomies combined in the shade of her eyes, her slanting cheekbones, her long straight nose, generous mouth and strong chin. The candlelight played across the planes of her face, bringing out rich tones in the bronze of her skin: ochre, umber and burnt sienna.

'No, nothing else,' I said. 'You may go.'

She withdrew quickly, with her head down. My scrutiny had brought the colour up into her cheeks and made her uncomfortable. I felt sorry, even shamed by it. She had no way to protest, or show how she felt. I was the mistress. Anything I chose to do, she would have to endure it.

11

So it went on. My first week seemed to stretch to eternity. I had no idea how to spend my time. Phillis and Minerva came and went on silent feet, heads bowed, never meeting my eyes. It was as though they weren't really there, as if I were being served by sprites. My attempted friendliness came to nothing; if anything it made them even more wary. They saw us all as immensely dangerous, like monstrous children who were as likely to kill or discard, with the utmost hardness of heart, anything that ceased to please them, or that threatened to make them angry. They took care to meet every wish, every need. Every desire was anticipated and gratified, sometimes even before I had thought of it myself. It was as though they knew all about me instantly: what I liked, what I disliked, what I enjoyed, what would displease me; while I would never know a thing about them, even if we were to live a lifetime together in the same house.

I came to be lonely, pining for companionship. My loneliness drove me to find ways to break down their reserve.

I spent the days sleeping, reading, or just drifting round the house. My brother had not come back, so I had no company at all. I thought I would die of boredom. I needed to get outside. If I owned the land, I should at least view it. The best way to do that was on horseback. Duke had offered to show me, but I did not think I could stand a day in his company. I asked Minerva to come with me instead.

Duke didn't object. 'I dare say she can ride a mule,' he said, when I told him my plan. 'Most of the blacks can do that.'

I ordered horses to be brought round. My brother kept a tolerable stable and I would have us ride the best animals.

Minerva rode like a man, her long brown legs showing to the knees on either side of the saddle. I envied the control this gave her and determined to do the same when we were out of sight of the house. She sat a horse well, with strength, natural grace and balance. We were able to set up a good pace along the straight tracks that ran between the square stands of sugar. We came to where the last stands were being cut at a far corner pocket of the property.

Minerva dismounted, took a machete from one of the men and lopped off a growing stem. She chopped off a section and, with a few sweeps of the razor-sharp blade, she cut away the tough outer skin to expose the pithy inner core.

'Here.' She handed the peeled cane to me. 'It tastes good. Refreshes the mouth after riding.'

I sucked at the oozing liquid. It was much less sweet than I had thought it might be, and did serve to quench the thirst. I nodded. It was good.

She smiled and cut a length for herself, then we rode on, turning from the endless fields of sugar up towards the mountains. The trees on the lower slopes would shade us from the sun's fierce heat and it would be cooler once we reached higher ground. We left the plantation far below us. It was soon out of sight as we gained one ridge, then another. As we rode further into the wilderness, the distance between us seemed to narrow. Talk became easier, and there was even laughter as we followed a wide, shallow, fast-running river, riding sometimes in, sometimes out of the water, the cold spray arcing up and splashing our legs.

We rode on, the stream becoming ever

shallower, until we came to a glade, a semi-circular clearing in the forest dominated by a sheer rock-face. Water gushed in a torrent from a fissure halfway up the towering cliff and fell in a white rush down to a limpid pool, wide and deep, clear right to the bottom. Bright green ferns extended feathery fronds, making shadows on the surface. Tiny silver fish darted and turned, catching the sun like silver coins.

Minerva pointed to the cascading water. 'That is the fountain. The plantation is named after it.' Her voice dropped to a whisper. 'It is obeah. A place of spirit.'

A diamond fountain falling into a crystal pool set in an emerald forest. It was a truly magical place.

We were not the only people to think so. Minerva showed me a smooth black boulder with primitive carvings upon it in the shape of a man and a woman, god and goddess.

'They were made by the people here before us.'

Across the water floated a garland of flowers made from the orchids that I'd seen growing in the forest. Minerva did not tell me who might have left it there.

She stepped into the water, cupping her hands to drink and splashing shining drops over her face and head. Then she stepped out of her shift and stood naked, as if she were about to step into a bathtub. She waded into the water, going deeper and deeper. I watched her in envy and wonder. *I* had never done such a thing in my life. At home it would have been unthinkable.

But I was not at home, was I? There was nobody there to see me. I slid off my horse and followed her lead.

I stepped in almost to my waist. The water was so cold it made me gasp for breath. Minerva waded back, smiling, splashing the water towards me. She shook her head and her wet hair fell in dark glistening coils about her naked shoulders.

Suddenly, I could not look at her. I saw her face change to dismay, as I turned away. Perhaps she thought that she'd embarrassed me, that I'd been overcome by sudden modesty, that she had presumed too far. But it had nothing to do with modesty, hers or mine. There was a mark on her shoulder, about the size of a shilling piece. The Fountainhead sign. I had seen it stencilled on the sacks of sugar coming into the warehouse in Bristol, burnt into barrels and packing cases, printed on documents, stamped on to leather-bound ledgers, carved above our door, but to see it branded on to the skin of another human being? I remembered what Duke had said about why they used silver and felt sick.

Her hand went to her shoulder.

'It does not hurt.'

I shook my head, unable to explain what I was thinking, took a step back and faltered, taken by sudden dizziness and dazzled by the light shining off the water. A sharp stone cut into my instep and I slipped, missing my footing altogether, plunging headlong. I must have stumbled into a place where the water was deeper, for I went down. I struggled for the surface, puffing and blowing, only to find that I was still out of my depth. I felt for the bottom, or a ledge, but my feet encountered nothing. For a second time I sank down, and I began to panic. I was choking, my breath coming out in great bubbles. I could not take any air in and my lungs were emptying. I feared that I might drown. Then long brown arms were round me, pulling me up to the surface. Minerva hooked me under the arm and turned for the side of the pool, towing me behind her. I staggered from the water and she helped me to a flat sun-warmed rock, where I sat with my head between my knees, coughing and spitting and trying to recover.

Minerva was shocked that I could not swim.

'Is there no sea where you live? No river?'

There was both sea and river, I explained, but no one learns to swim. Not even the sailors.

'Sailors think that there is no point,' I said. 'They believe that you cannot cheat the sea.'

Minerva grimaced and shuddered, as if she found such reasoning hateful. Then she smoothed her features and smiled at me, as if she had forgotten herself momentarily in showing her feelings to such a degree.

'We are not in the sea. I can teach you. It is easy.'

I did not find it easy, but the lesson was very pleasant. We were girls together and of an age, and that is how we behaved, laughing and playing in the water. As we lay on the smooth rocks, letting the sun dry our skin, she asked me about the ring that I wore on the gold chain about my neck. I found myself telling her all about William, things that I had never told anyone, not even Susan. We were not mistress and slave from that day on. We were more like friends. Like sisters.

The pool had done its magic.

148

12

We went back as the shadows began to lengthen. We composed ourselves as we neared the plantation, but the length of time that we had been absent had not escaped Duke.

'Where have you been?' Duke greeted me, eyeing me closely. My hair was still wet and my dress was damp. He was very observant for a near-sighted man. 'Thought the maroons had got you. I was about to send out a search party.'

'Maroons?'

'Live in the mountains. Escaped slaves and runaway servants, all sorts of rogues and runagate scum.' He let down his whip, lashing it across the ground, making a cracking sound. 'Should be hunted down with dogs and hung, every man and woman. There's a nest of 'em, not too far from here, led by a black demon called Hero, but they're devilish hard to find. I told Master Joseph, he should bring back bloodhounds. That Brazilian's got 'em. I told him, we could do with some here. Train 'em up from pups to hunt down blacks. He was all for it. Thought it'd be marvellous sport.' He gave me a look of enquiry. 'Perhaps he had some with him?'

I shook my head.

'Pity.'

Duke flicked the tip of his whip towards a nearby bush and a large creamy blossom exploded in a shower of scent and petals.

'When will my brother be here? Has he sent word? Do you know?'

He would not be back for another week, Duke said. Delayed by business. I did not want Joseph to hurry back, fearing that his presence might curtail the freedom that I was just beginning to enjoy, although I thought he might bring news from home, maybe letters. Perhaps there might be one from William. My heart leaped at the thought of it. I spent a great deal of the time on my rides with Minerva wondering what his letter might say, wondering how I would reply to it. We visited the magical pool again and my swimming lessons continued. We rode by clear rivers and up into the high country. The air was cooler here and scented by pine trees. The forests were brilliant with birds, the air heavy with the smell of flowers. I began to see why Broom loved the islands so much.

My brother's further week extended to a fortnight. He arrived in the back of the wagonette, stinking of rum. Thomas heaved him on to his shoulder and carried him into the house like a sack of sugar. I did not see him again until late the next day when he appeared, pale and clean shaven, for dinner.

'Are there any letters for me?' I asked when he came in.

'No.' He looked at me sharply, as if my question startled him. 'Why should there be?'

'No reason,' I replied, as we sat down at opposite ends of the long table.

He hardly spoke to me after that, and ate little of the food that Phillis had prepared: chicken and rice, sweet potato and beans, complaining loudly that she had added too much spice. Instead he drank, pouring pale golden rum from the decanter he kept at his elbow. When I had finished, he left me, carrying decanter and glass on to the veranda. There he sat in a rocking chair, staring out, profiled against the glow from the boiling house and the billowing ghost-white clouds of smoke and steam. I followed him out on to the veranda. All around the frogs and cicadas played their overtures, and fireflies glowed, tiny specks of gold in the velvet blackness.

'I think it's beautiful here,' I said.

'You do?' He seemed genuinely surprised. 'I loathe it.' He laughed and poured himself another glass. All the rum he'd drunk had failed to blunt the edge of his misery and self-pity. 'You always did like the opposite.' He motioned to the chair by his side. 'Why don't you join me? Thomas! This decanter's near empty, and bring another glass!'

'Oh, no,' I began to protest, but he ignored me.

'Yes! Thomas!' he roared, half getting to his feet. 'Where is he? He's getting above himself. I'll have him flogged. Thom—'

Thomas appeared, silent as a shadow, bearing a tray with a glass for me and a full decanter. He put the tray down and poured the rum. I took a sip of the golden liquid. It tasted of spice and caramel. It was fiery on the tongue, and warming to the throat and stomach. Not at all unpleasant.

'To my darling sister!' Joseph threw back his measure and poured another. 'Come on! Drink up!'

'Why did you not tell me that Father left

this plantation to me?'

He paused, the glass halfway to his lips. 'How did you know that?'

'Duke told me.'

'He had no right! He should keep his nose out of business that does not concern him.' Joseph banged his glass down, causing the rum to spill. 'There's another needs taking down a peg or two.'

'He thought I knew already. He was surprised that I did not. Don't you think I have a right to know such a thing? What were you thinking of?'

'Why should you? You are a child. Henry and I are your guardians. You cannot inherit before you are twenty-one. Even then . . .'

'Even then . . . ?'

'Depends on your husband, don't it?'

'Husband?' Despite the warmth of the rum, I felt a coldness spreading inside me. 'What husband?'

'Now that *would* be telling.' Joseph gave an exaggerated wink and took another drink. Then he laughed. 'We have plans. Men's business.' He wagged a finger at me. 'Don't you worry your pretty little head.'

He sank back into his chair, eyes closed. I sat for a while, sipping my rum, watching as moths fluttered out of the darkness, white and yellow, on wings as delicate as tissue paper. Some bumped against the shaded lamp; others fed on the pools of spilt rum. They flew off as I put down my glass and rose to go.

Joseph chuckled, laughter gargling from him, as if he dreamt something amusing. ' 'S good,' he said. ' 'S good you like it. Going to be here long, long time.'

The words came out all in one mutter, slurred by the rum that he'd been drinking all night. I could not tell if he was sleeping, or waking, or somewhere between the two states. He jerked as a dog might when it is dreaming. The glass dangling from his fingers dropped and smashed on the floor.

Day by day, whatever constraints I might have felt in my former life dropped away. I drank rum and rode like a boy. I swam naked in pool, river, sea and fountain and felt no shame. I ate strange food: land crab and lobster, crawfish and mullet, young pig and goat dry-roasted on an open pit in a way called barbicue, all seasoned with peppers and spiced in the manner my brother found so distasteful.

Every morning, I went riding. Sometimes Minerva came with me, sometimes she did not. By noon, I had returned home and I stayed in my room in the hottest part of the day, or out on the veranda at the side of the house, staying there until the sun dipped towards the sea. My brother was either in Port Royal, or asleep in his room, and Duke was out in the fields, or in his hovel, so Minerva and Phillis often came to join me on those long afternoons.

Phillis would bring out the vegetables she was preparing, and we'd sit together, shelling beans and peas, peeling potatoes, stripping corn, and she would tell me about what had happened to her, and how her life was here.

The story began with her being taken from her home in Africa. When she spoke of it, she would stir, flexing and shifting in her seat, as though the memory brought on pains, like rheumatism in the rainy season. Minerva would watch, her eyes on her mother, attending to every word, although she had heard it all many times before.

'It an old, old tale, nothing new about it. Happen to thousands every year. I was a young girl, younger than you two now . . .'

Phillis had been taken when she was twelve years old, from Abomey, the capital city of Dahomey. Her family had been high-born nobles. She herself was destined to become a woman warrior. One of an

155

elite guard whose job it was to protect the king. She had been chosen because her father was one of the king's most trusted commanders, but life at court was uncertain, full of intrigue. One day, her father was accused of plotting against the king. He was arrested and his whole family was sold into slavery, tied at the neck in coffles and forced to march a hundred miles or more through swamp and forest to the port of Whydah. They were bought by different traders and put on ships owned by different nations, destined for different places. She never saw any of her family again.

'All that time, I never cried. Never dropped a tear. Not then. Not since. I am a Dahomey warrior woman. We show no fear.'

Minerva looked at her with pride. As I got to know her better, I came to realise how much she had learned from her mother about courage and fearlessness. I had cause to remember and be grateful that she came from a line of warriors.

Phillis was bought by a Portuguese trader. She spoke a little of the language, having been taught by her father. This made her passage easier, as she could act as interpreter. The ship was destined for

Brazil, but was blown off course and landed at St Kitts. The captain sold his slaves there, eager to take a profit rather than risk losing more slaves in further storms and mishaps. She was sold to a man named Sharpe, who brought her to Jamaica with another parcel of slaves where she was bought by my father.

Phillis told her tale over many days. Her narrative led her to the plantation and ended with Minerva, although she said nothing of the circumstances of her daughter's birth, or who her father might be.

I thought to add my own part, by telling her about Robert. Phillis had said that she and Robert had been part of the parcel of slaves brought from St Kitts and that he had been her man until my father had decided to take him to Bristol. I assumed that Robert was Minerva's father and was anxious for them both to know that he did well. I told them that Robert had been granted his freedom, and had been given money in my father's will and that, last I heard, he was thinking of starting a tobacco shop. I told them of the times we had spent together, of his care of me from when I was a young child. Phillis's worn face softened as I spoke, and split into a rare smile.

'Robert is a good man, and kind. He always loved children. He had a way with them. Your father too was a good man, a good master. We were all sorry to hear of his passing. He taught me English. Not just speaking, but writing and reading, and I taught Minerva. Now she can learn from you.' Minerva looked up at her name and smiled. 'She can read your books, learn to speak well. Not like a slave. Your father named me and her, too. He was good to me. To both of us.' She stopped speaking for a moment. When she went on it was in a low voice, as if the words were hard to say. 'We looked for him in the springtime, every year. His ships come, but he was not there. More's the pity. It was a shame to leave Fountainhead in the hands of a man who don't give a damn.'

She did not say if she meant my brother or Duke. One thing she did not have to tell me about was the cruelty with which the overseer ran the plantation. It sickened me so much that I felt I had to speak to him about it. I had ordered him to stop his savage treatment and the whippings for no reason, but he barely listened to my protests. Even when I threatened to go to my brother, he carried on just the same.

'That man is like a cockroach,' Phillis

commented. 'Stamp on him and he'll just come out somewhere else.'

The description was apt. He even looked like a cockroach, especially from the back. His shiny cap of greased brown hair emerged from his long rusty coat which was split like a wing case and stuck out over his polished-booted legs. Her description made me laugh out loud.

Phillis did not laugh with me.

'He hates me, always has done.' She sighed as if he were an affliction that could not be avoided, like biting flies or scorpions. 'He's suspicious of everyone. He only eats food cooked by his woman, even then he makes her taste it. He worries about poison. I say, why worry? He's already poison to the root. You smelt him?' She waved a hand under her nose. 'He can kill a snake with just one breath.' This time she laughed with me, but then her face grew guarded. 'That man makes a bad enemy. You be wary.'

'What of? This is *my* plantation,' I replied, haughty in the knowledge of ownership. 'He can't hurt *me!*'

Phillis excused herself, saying she had to start dinner. Minerva went with her. I sat on the veranda, secure in my superior position. It did not occur to me to think that my behaviour might be putting others in danger; I assumed that Phillis's warning was for myself.

I decided to speak to my brother about Duke, despite what Phillis had said, and to suggest that we get rid of him. I chose noon, when he was breakfasting, before he'd had time to start drinking.

'Ah,' he said. 'Yes. I've been meaning to talk to you about this.'

My hopes rose. I thought that, for once, we agreed on something. I should have known that was not the case.

'It's, ah, it's about . . .' he cleared his throat, '. . . it's about your attitude to the blacks.'

'Oh.' That was not what I had expected. 'What about it?'

'Well, it's too familiar. A sight too familiar.' He chopped the top off a boiled egg. 'It won't do, Nancy. It's bad for them. They take advantage.'

'Who says? Duke?'

'Not just him.' He spoke through a mouthful of egg. 'I do. You haven't been out here long enough, or you'd see the difficulty. Take Phillis and Minerva, you are too close to them. They ain't our kind.' He dabbed his lips with his napkin. 'You can't trust 'em, Nancy. You miss female company, I understand that. You used to have Mrs Kington and her friends in Bristol, and so on.'

'You understand nothing.'

'I understand more than you think. I ain't a complete brute. One thing I do know, you can't make friends of them. It just don't work.'

'Why not?'

'Because they are *slaves.*' He pronounced the last word with slow deliberation, as if speaking to an imbecile.

'They are human beings. Flesh and blood. Just like us.' I looked at him. 'What if I were to say I don't believe one people should enslave another?'

He look genuinely shocked. 'I'd say you were a foolish girl and tell you not to speak like that. Then I'd remind you what puts bread on your table and clothes on your back. Besides, it's *natural* for one people to enslave another. We're just taking advantage, putting it to profit, you might say. The Africans sell the slaves to *us,* for God's sake. All we do is collect 'em from the forts. You don't understand, Nancy. It's how things are and ever will be.' He paused. 'Duke's a hard man, I'll own that, but we need him. You might not like his methods, but they are necessary. Plantations cannot be run without discipline.' He wagged a finger at me. 'So don't you go thinking about interfering. You cannot change things. You will only make difficulties for everybody, including your favourites.' He thought for a minute. 'For them, especially. You're giving them ideas above their station, for one thing, and that ain't fair to them. Don't be stubborn about this, Nancy. You might think you're helping them, but all you are likely to do is cause them unhappiness.'

He went to his study, shouting for Thomas to bring rum. It was clear that Duke had already been to him, complaining about my behaviour. I did not know that he had also been advising him to get rid of Phillis and Minerva, urging him to sell them separately. Phillis as a field hand, Minerva to a woman he knew who kept a brothel in Kingston.

If I'd known that, I might have changed my behaviour, but I was young and headstrong. I never liked being told what to do, my natural inclination being to do precisely the opposite, and my brother's reprimand made me smart. I took absolutely no notice and carried on exactly as before, putting myself before everyone around me. I had no idea then how evil men could be.

If I'd had any inkling as to how things would turn out, then I would have acted differently. But such could be said at every twist and turn of this story.

Duke continued to watch me, but I still thought there was nothing he could do. I tried to make light of him, but he was an oppressive and malevolent presence. My brother was weak, but he was not inhumane. He did not condone overly harsh treatment of the slaves, but he was easily swayed, and the beatings increased. The great tree in the marketplace was put to use more frequently. Duke administered punishments himself, that great black whip of his tearing huge gouts from the backs of the unfortunates he singled out. He punished even trivial misdemeanours in the same way, with no difference or moderation.

When I went to my brother, he told me again not to interfere.

'Duke has plans for your favourites,' he said, by way of warning. 'Ones that you will not like. If you want to save them, keep your distance and turn a blind eye.'

Phillis and Minerva became subdued in my presence. They fulfilled their duties, but withdrew their companionship. I did not understand how great the threat was to them and was hurt and puzzled when they failed to meet my gaze, or looked at me with vacant expressions.

Things might have gone on in much the same way, my life settling into patterns that I was powerless to alter, but then one day came that changed everything. I remember it particularly, because it was my sixteenth birthday, but I remember it for other reasons besides that. A rider came up to the house. He was mounted on a bay horse and dressed all in black. He was fine-boned and handsome, his skin was the deepest shade of ebony, and his crisp curled hair was cropped close to his head. He reached into a saddle bag marked with the letter *B* in an elaborate swirl of serifs and brought out a note. It was sealed with the initial of his master: Bartholome, the Brazilian.

13

The note was for my brother and contained a dinner invitation. Joseph replied immediately. He came out on to the veranda, pale and unshaven, but sober enough. He handed the man a note, folded and sealed, the writing on it shaky but legible. He did not tell me the contents, but called for Thomas to shave him and told Phillis and Minerva to lay out my finest clothes and make me look like a lady, or he'd sell them to the swamps of Surinam.

'And how could that be worse than here?' Phillis muttered to herself, but she did as she was told and when they had finished I hardly recognised the girl in the mirror.

My brother waited for me on the veranda. He wore a dove-grey coat with gold frogging over a cream silk waistcoat delicately embroidered with butterflies and flowers. Lace spilled from his cuffs and shirt front. His breeches were of soft chamois, his boots shone like mirrors. I hadn't seen him dressed like that since Bath. He was freshly barbered. He smiled when he saw me, and gave me a look of relief and admiring approval, as if for once I was doing right by him. He took one swift shot of rum, for the tremor in his hands, he said, then conducted me to the open carriage.

Thomas was dressed in livery and wore a pistol at his side. My brother had a pistol, also. And a sword. Out of the little kingdom of one's own plantation, the island was a dangerous place. Runaways, black and white, lurked in the forests and there were maroons camped up in the hills. The road we were to travel took us by the coast and pirates sometimes roamed up from the shoreline. It was best to be prepared.

The evening was coming on as we left the plantation. Parrots and cockatoos darted through the forest trees, splashes of brilliant colour, blue, red and yellow against the green, adding their harsh calls to the shrilling din of the cicadas. The sea lay rippling like a cloth of gold, lit by the setting sun. A skein of pelicans beat its way on broad wings, the birds flying low to the water, as if their heavy beaks weighed them down.

'They feed their young on their own blood,' Joseph remarked. 'Or so it is said.'

I made no reply, only thought of how free they seemed, leaving the land far behind them and flying off west into the sunset.

The entrance to Bartholome's plantation was flanked by two huge trees. A single letter *B* swung between them, made with the same curling serifs as on the slave's saddlebag.

Thomas turned in at the sign. Before us lay a long drive made up of small white stones, shining chips of marble which turned the road to silver in the twilight gloom.

A sudden fluttering movement in one of the great trees that lined the drive caused our horses to shy. The wheels skidded on the chippings, and the carriage lurched, threatening to spill. Joseph cursed, roaring at Thomas, calling him an incompetent fool. Thomas looked back at us, his face grey in the half light, his eyes huge and wide. He looked as if he had seen a ghost.

There was something suspended from one of the great branches of the tree before us, something large and heavy, swinging ever so slightly. Shapes moved above it. Huge black birds fought with each other, trying to keep their balance on a surface too small for them. Our approach had disturbed them and they had flown up with a heavy flap of wings into the spreading tree branches. Thomas fought to quieten the frightened horses, bringing us up right in front of the creaking gibbet. The birds settled back down, their ragged plumage hanging about them like filthy gowns as they vied for purchase on the iron cage that hung from the tree.

I had seen gibbeted men before. Bleached bones dropping through the bars at the top of Gallows Acre Lane. A body, roped and tarred, slung low over the marsh out at Hungroad. This was different. The man inside the cage was still alive. The birds had pecked out his eyes. Their cruel beaks had slashed his face and shoulders to the bone. Blood dripped like tears down his ruined cheeks, dropping into black pools on the dusty ground. I covered my nose, for the stench was terrible, as though the body were already corrupting, but a convulsive movement from the man jerked the iron cage on its chain, sending out a frenzied black cloud of furiously buzzing flies. His hand twitched. His lips drew back, as if he would speak.

We were only stopped there for seconds

as the horses regained their footing, but in my memory it seems a much longer time. I saw everything, every detail. I can never cleanse my mind of it. If I close my eyes, I can see him still. We all stared, transfixed and unbelieving, unable quite to take in what we were seeing, until my brother roared to Thomas, 'Drive on!'

'Who would do that?' I turned to my brother. I could see he, too, was shaken, although he was trying not to show it. 'Why?'

'He must have done something bad. Hit an overseer, something like that. Dare say the rogue deserved it,' he added, trying to regain his composure, but his lips were white and his hand was shaking as he took out the silver flask he kept about him and took a swig. He offered the flask to me, but I declined. 'Don't say anything. Don't say a word.' He leaned forward, keeping his voice low so that Thomas would not hear him. 'That's how life is out here. I told you. There's nothing you can do about it. So it's time you left your sensitivities at home and grew up.'

I did not reply. I had no words, there were no words to express the shock I was feeling. I stared from the back of the carriage until a sweep of the drive took us away from that dismal sight.

Bartholome, the Brazilian, waited for us on his veranda. He wore a suit of black velvet, just like the last time I had seen him, but he was adorned with far greater opulence than before. A rainbow of rings studded the knuckles gripping the rail. His silk neckcloth was secured with a sapphire; his jacket hung open to show a shirt of cream satin buttoned by pearls the size of peas. He came down the steps to greet us, taking my hand in his. His gap teeth gleamed inside his black beard, and his night-shade eyes smiled down into mine.

'Miss Nancy.' He touched my fingers to his lips. 'I am honoured to welcome you to my home.' He held on to my hand and led me up into his mansion, the stones and metal of his rings feeling cold and hard against my skin.

It was a great house with marble floors and stone-built walls that made ours seem like a flimsy cabin. Half of Europe had been ransacked to furnish it; the rest of the world plundered to provide suitable decoration. Jewelled icons and masks made of gold looked down from the walls. A face made up of plaques of turquoise grinned with what looked like human teeth and stared with glinting eyes formed from some kind of shiny black stone. Antique marble statuary stood on plinths next to pagan idols and golden animals encrusted with jewels. A cross bright with huge square-cut emeralds stood at least a foot tall and made an altar of a table set with gold patens, ruby-embossed chalices, pierce-work boxes carved from ivory and jade. Chinese silks and Indian carpets hung next to Italian oil paintings. I had never seen anything like it. I was walking into a robber's cave, a glittering magpie's nest filled with booty acquired from every continent.

'I cannot resist beauty.' He waved his hand to indicate the priceless furnishings. 'I am a collector, as you see. I will go to considerable trouble to get what I want. No price is too much, and no place is too far for me. I have objects from India, China, even Japan. When I have something, I like to keep it here, where I can see it and enjoy it. Come.'

He offered me his arm and conducted me to the dining room, shuttered and panelled in dark wood, illuminated by crystal chandeliers suspended from the carved ceiling. The long table was set with the finest ware. Silver and crystal glittered. Milky-blue porcelain gleamed with duck-egg translucency in the steady light given by golden branches of fine beeswax candles. Servants stood round the walls, still as statues.

He escorted me to my place, pulling out the chair for me to be seated.

'This is my dear sister, Isabella.'

A lady seated at the end of the table inclined her head to me. She was wearing a towering black mantilla with the veils drawn back. I thought that perhaps she had been widowed, but later discovered that she had never married. It was the custom among these people for ladies to go veiled in mantillas, as we might wear a bonnet. I looked for a family resemblance, and could see none, although brother and sister shared the same oddly ageless quality. She was pale complexioned and very thin. One side of her mouth lifted up slightly, catching her in a permanent sneer. Her dark hair was pulled back under the mantilla, stretching the skin taut, making her gaunt face almost cadaverous. Her black silk dress was of heavy brocade and tight fitting with a high bodice and long sleeves, a style more suited to a European court than a tropical plantation, yet she seemed to feel no discomfort. She watched me, still as a spider, her hands loosely clasped, her long, thin arms gleaming green in the candlelight.

She spoke no English, her brother interpreting for her. Although she said very little, her dark eyes followed the conversation, flicking from person to person, and I began to suspect that she understood a great deal.

The table was set for an elaborate meal. Course followed course: choice foods of that bountiful country, perfectly prepared and elaborately presented. My brother ate heartily and drank copiously, complimenting his host on the quality of the wines he kept, exclaiming that he'd tasted nothing like them since Bristol. The Brazilian smiled at the praise, for they all came from his estates in Portugal. He declared Joseph to be a connoisseur, inviting him to try more, until my brother was quite drunk.

I, in contrast, ate very little, and drank only water. The Brazilian's sister was equally abstemious, so perhaps they thought it appropriate behaviour. I did not want to explain my lack of appetite. I had eaten almost nothing since breakfast, and would normally have been ravenous, but the very sight and smell of the food made my throat close and my stomach clench like a fist inside me. How could they eat, drink, and enjoy such luxury, conversing about every kind of frivolity, when all the while outside a man was dying in the cruellest way that it was possible to imagine? I could not get him out of my mind. I looked at faces smiling, laughing, mouths chewing, gullets swallowing, and all I could see was a man hanging at their very gate, being eaten alive inside his gibbet.

At last, the table was cleared and set with candied fruit and nuts and various sweetmeats along with decanters of Madeira and port and bottles of French brandy.

Bartholome insisted I had at least a taste of ruby-red port, and when all our glasses were filled, he called for a toast.

'I understand it is your birthday, Miss Nancy. We must drink to that.'

I wondered how he knew, as they all raised their glasses to salute me. Joseph must have told him, I decided, but I could not think why.

'To friendship between our families,' the Brazilian went on. 'And to ties that will shortly bind us even closer.' I thought that was the toast and was about to drink, when he lifted his glass even higher. 'To Miss Nancy!'

I stared in confusion as they turned their glasses and drank to me. The Brazilian drank deep, the red wine seeping into his beard and staining his lips. He smiled, his eyes like those of the mask behind him: little black mirrors, flecked with tiny points of candlelight.

'I have spoken to your brothers about this matter so close to my heart, and indeed to your father just before his sad and untimely death. He assured me it was his dearest wish, and that I had his blessing, although he desired me to wait until the occasion of your sixteenth birthday. I, of course, have respected his request of me, but now that day has come.' He paused to clear his throat and his voice rose, becoming more sonorous and formal. 'Miss Nancy, I have every hope that you will make me the happiest of men . . .'

He was proposing to me. For a second, I just stared at him, unable to think of a word to say. Then I looked to my brother, but he would not, or could not, meet my gaze.

The Brazilian faltered. 'You do know of this?' he said to me.

I opened my mouth, but no words came out. I heard my father's voice again, as if he were there in the room with me: *You*

175

would do your part, wouldn't you? For me? For the family? And my answer. *Of course, Papa.*

He turned to Joseph. His black-eyed stare as dark and cold as the waters of a bottomless well. The chill of his look seemed to sober my brother.

'Not in so many words, maybe,' Joseph began, twirling the stem of his port glass. 'But Nancy understands how important such an alliance would be to the family and all who depend on us.' He glanced at me, his pale eyes as hard as marble. 'Susan, for example, and Robert; the captains of our ships, their families, the men that serve upon them. Henry has many friends at the Admiralty. A good word, or bad, can make all the difference to a man's career. Many trade on our good name and need our patronage.'

I was caught in a trap laid by pitiless men: my brothers, my father, this Brazilian. All in it together. Their ruthlessness made me gasp. My mind raced as my brother spoke, trying to take in the depths of their duplicity, trying to find a path through the field full of hidden pitfalls and sudden dangers that I now found in front of me.

'This comes as a very great surprise,' I

said at last. 'I do not know what to say, Sir. You have utterly overwhelmed me.' Which was very near to the truth. As I struggled to come to terms with the very idea, his sister spoke from the end of the table. I looked up, startled to hear her speak. Her voice was gruff, pitched low, with an almost masculine timbre.

Her brother translated for her. 'She says you are very young.' He seemed to accept that girlish modesty explained my confusion, although even in a foreign tongue, the words coming from her twisted mouth had sounded more like a warning, or a judgement.

'You pay me a very great compliment, Sir,' I went on, 'and you must forgive me, but your proposal comes as a shock. I did not know that you would honour me in this way. I have had no warning, as you can see. I must beg you for time to think.'

'I understand . . .' he said, but it was clear that he did not. The look he gave my brother was full of questioning reproach, but Joseph did not meet his eyes. He studied his glass as if the answer to that, and to much else besides, were to be found at the bottom of it.

The Brazilian's sister laughed, her mouth jerking up on one side, her eyes glittered hard as she spoke again.

'What does she say?' I asked.

'She says, "What is there to know? Men decide. Woman obey." But *I* understand that it is perhaps not your English way. So, of course, I will give you time to make your decision. Meanwhile, I have a gift for you.'

He reached inside his coat and brought out a long flat case of sage-green calfskin and laid it on the white cloth. Then he undid the gold catch and flipped open the lid. He sat back as my brother and I leaned closer. Joseph took in a breath; his eyes lost their glaze and became greedy with wonder. I knew little of stones then, but even to my untutored eye these were magnificent. A string of perfectly matched rubies, set in finely wrought gold, graduating in size, even the smallest as big as my fingernail. They were arranged in a crescent around a pair of earrings shaped like bulging tears. The stones gleamed in the candlelight like drops of heart's blood.

'I put my faith in stones,' he smiled at me across the table. 'They do not fade, they do not rot, and they do not lose their value. They are light to carry and easy to keep close.' He patted his pocket. 'They will never let you down.'

I have remembered his words. I live by

them now. His advice has proved valuable in ways that he never intended.

'These are rare stones.' He held one of the earrings up to the light. 'Especially fine.'

'Perfect!' My brother put out his hand, but the Brazilian turned the jewel to me.

'No. Not perfect. The very best rubies have a flaw in them. There! See? It is almost as if another world lies within . . .'

The stone dangled from his fingers, eclipsing the candle flame. At the centre lay a tiny fleck that made the heart glow a darker red, filling it with a deep burning fire.

He laid the earring back in the case, handling it with careful reverence and respect. These were jewels of royal provenance. They must have been destined for some Spanish queen, or a Moghul's favourite concubine when they were snatched by this thief of the sea. Even now, I have rarely seen their equal. My brother's eyes gleamed. Their worth would have bought half a fleet of ships.

'That's generous,' he breathed. 'Very generous indeed.' He reached to take the case, but the Brazilian held his hand.

'They are not for you,' he said, his voice quiet, almost amused. 'They are a gift to your sister.' He swept the earrings up and handed them to me. 'Try them.'

I fixed them in my ears with shaking fingers while he took the necklace from its case and rose from his place. He came behind my chair, and placed the necklace around my neck, fastening it there with practised deftness. His fingers rested warm and pliant on my skin, while the stones and gold circled my neck close in a cold hard collar.

'There. Let us see how they become you.'

He bid me rise and led me to look in the mirror over the mantelpiece. He stood behind me, his long dark fingers resting on my shoulders. The necklace badged my throat like a bloody handspan. He stared at our twin reflections and frowned.

'You have a beautiful neck and shoulders.' His hands glided over my skin, stopping just below the angle of my jaw, moving back down again, coming to rest at the base of my throat. 'But rubies look best against milk-white skin, as though they rest on white satin. I fear our island sun is too strong for you, my dear.' He looked down at me with distaste. The skin on my shoulders, neck and face had changed from white to golden brown. 'But like all stones,

180

they respond to the warmth of the blood, rubies more than most. See how the colour deepens?' He brought his eyes down to the level of mine. 'They would look so very much better if your skin were to fade to its former paleness. Like alabaster . . .' His fingers travelled my bare shoulders in long feathery strokes, as if caressing a memory. In the mirror, his eyes took on a dreamy intensity, as if by some alchemy he could make a previous version of me. 'My sister never goes out in the day, unless heavily veiled. If you are to regain your complexion, I suggest that you follow her example.'

His sister looked at me, half sneering, half smiling, and a new note of fear crept into my heart. If I were to marry him, I would be a prisoner in this house, never allowed out, with only his sister for company. I found it hard to repress a shudder. In the mirror, the earrings shimmered like drops of blood. I put my hands up to remove them, lest their trembling betray my fear.

'You shiver.' The Brazilian looked down at me in surprise. 'Not cold, surely?'

'No, Sir. Rather the opposite. I think I may have a fever. In fact, I feel more than a little unwell.'

14

So the gruesome evening was brought to a
close. My brother was too drunk to return
with us, but I insisted that I be taken home
by Thomas. I waited for the carriage to be
brought, my head reeling with all that had
happened. The nausea that I had felt all
night threatened to overwhelm me, and I
was beginning to fear that I really was ill, but
I could not bear to spend another minute in
that house and pleaded that I would recover
better back at Fountainhead with my own
slaves to attend me. The Brazilian showed
every concern, and was reluctant to let me
go, but at length he relented. He offered to
have me escorted, but I said that Thomas
and I would manage well enough. Thomas
was armed and I took my brother's pistol.

I made my farewells brief, hardly able to
speak, thinking all the time that I might
vomit, but as soon as I was in the carriage,
the motion made me feel better. I ceased
from shivering and uncurled my fists. I'd

been holding my hands tightly clenched and they hurt as though my nails had bitten into the palms. A huge moon had risen, casting a white light over everything. When I looked down, I thought that I had indeed cut myself. I was still holding the ruby earrings. They lay in the palms of my hands like pools of blood.

I tucked them into the purse I wore from my sash and we drove on through bars of shade cast by the trees across the shining drive. Where the shadows were darkest, I bade Thomas stop. The great birds were still there by the gibbet, tenebrous shapes within the blackness. When I took out my pistol, I thought just to fire into the air, to scare these scavengers away from the living carrion upon which they were feasting. Then I changed my target. I took aim between the iron strips that made up the top of the cage, and prayed that I would not hit metal. The gun went off with a roar. The birds rose like the Furies in a flurry of powerful wings, causing the cage to swing and the horses to plunge forward. Thomas whipped them up, in panic at what I had done, so I had no time to see if my ball had found its mark. All I could do was pray that it was so, and that I had put an end to that poor soul's torment.

I was not afraid to be out at night, but I reloaded the gun as we drove along, so I would be ready for any danger that we might encounter. Jamaica was a lawless place, but so were the Downs at home — to drive along any lonely road was to risk an encounter with a highwayman.

We met no traffic and all was quiet when we reached the plantation. The house was in darkness as I went up the steps. I wondered that no lamp was burning and called for Phillis or Minerva to come and attend me, but was greeted by silence. I sparked a flint and lit a candle for myself and went in search of them. One or the other usually stayed in the house at night to see to our needs, and I'd expected to see both on our return as we had not planned to stay at the Brazilian's plantation. I had no sense of foreboding. I just thought it unusual. Neglectful in a way that was not like them. Perhaps I had in mind some gentle scolding as I made my way to the kitchen.

Phillis was there, sitting at the table, perfectly still against the moonlight, like a statue carved from ironwood.

She roused herself and turned to the glow from the candle in my hand. Her face changed as she saw me, her eyes show ing white in the darkness. She looked at me as if I were a ghost.

'What's the matter with your neck?'

My hand went to Bartholome's rubies. I was still wearing them.

'A gift from the Brazilian.' I paused. 'He wants to marry me.'

'So Duke say.' Her voice dropped to a murmur. 'I thought I saw your death upon you. I thought you come back in spirit. Looks like someone cut your throat.'

She went to rise, to come to me, but her arm trembled on the table edge and she slumped back down as if the effort were too much for her. She had always seemed so strong, tireless and indomitable. I was alarmed to see this sudden weakness and immediately put the candlestick down and went to see what ailed her. She held the neck of her gown clutched in one hand. Now I could see that it was torn, split front and back, hanging in pieces, like two flags striped and stained with fresh blood.

She tried to turn away from me in a slow wincing movement, as if she were ashamed for me to see her condition.

'Who did this to you?' I asked. As if I could not guess.

'Duke beat me.'

'Why?'

'Because he likes to. Because that is what

he likes to do.' She put her hand to her head, brushing her fingers over her eyes in a gesture of weary despair. 'Don't bother yourself with this, Miss Nancy. It's nothing to do with you.'

I'd be the one to decide what was, and was not, to do with me. I felt anger growing inside me, fuelled by all the things I'd seen since I came to this beautiful blighted country. I felt it bloom into fury as I brought the candle round to see what he had done. The scars on her back were not new. Fresh stripes glistened in long streaking criss-cross patterns across a back where the flesh was ruched into sharp ridged peaks, so rucked and buckled that it no longer resembled flesh at all, but looked as though she was encased in a garland of thorns.

'Where is he?'

'In his house.' Phillis looked up at me. She had endured everything, never been known to cry, but now the tears spilled from her eyes. 'He took Minerva. I tried to stop him . . .'

'That's why he beat you?'

'Yes. But ain't nothing you can do, Miss Nancy. Best not to interfere. Don't need to make trouble for yourself. You be married soon . . .' Her voice faltered. Her gaze flickered away as if she could no longer look at me.

I left her staring at the steady flame of the candle. I still wore the pistol, stuck in my sash, and I almost smiled as I felt the carved wooden grip snug in my hand. Nothing I could do. How many people had told me that? Well, now we would see . . .

Duke's woman sat squatting by the hearth, stirring a pot, her thin, worn body folded up on itself. She turned when she heard me come in, her face in the fire light as creased as a satchel. She appeared old, but she could have been young, broken past caring by a life not worth living. She took one look at me, at the pistol gripped in my hand, and bolted for the door.

My fury had grown cold now, congealing into an absolute sense of purpose as I stole up the stairs, quiet and careful as a hunting cat. Although I could have been a regiment of foot and I doubt that Duke would have heard me. He had his mind on other matters. Light spilled from the cracks between the boards of the door as I paused to listen and spy there. He was kneeling over her, his back to me. He held her trapped, laughing as she tried to get away from him. She was backed up towards the head of the bed, her breath coming short and shallow, her long limbs bent awkwardly, pinned by his hulking body, like a deer caught in the grip of a bear. I pushed at the door. It swung back silently and I stepped into the room.

She saw me before he did, her eyes growing wide, and she gasped to see me there. He gave a whistling grunt, thinking her eyes flared in fresh terror of him. He was toying with her, enjoying the power he had over her, allowing her fear to feed his lust. I grabbed him by the greasy tail of hair that trailed on to his thick white shoulders, yanking his head back as I jammed the barrel of the pistol into the base of his skull.

'Get off her.'

His head strained to the side; the lust dulling in his small deep-set eyes.

'Don't turn round,' I whispered. 'Just do as I say.'

The mechanism of the gun was near his ear. His head jerked, registering the click as I pulled the hammer back.

He tried to speak. A dry croaking coming from his mouth.

'Don't speak.'

I could see Minerva, under his shoulder, her face as rigid as a mask. Once released from his weight, she moved fast. He used her movement to try to squirm away from me. His arm shot out, reaching for that murderous whip that hung in loose coils from the head of the bed. In a second it would be in his hand. I did it without even thinking. I pulled the trigger.

15

I had never seen so much blood, and I tried not to see what was cast across the wall above the bed. Acrid smoke drifted thick in the air, and the sound of the shot in the small room still rang in my ears as I looked at Minerva, unable to believe what I had just done.

'I didn't mean . . .' I started to say, as we stared at each other over the ruin of Duke's body. 'I never could do such a thing . . .'

But I did mean it. And I'd just done it. Killed a man. I expected to see the horror I felt at myself reflected in Minerva's eyes. Instead, I saw the fear and shock that had been there dissolve into something verging on admiration.

'You don't need to apologise, or feel guilty,' she said, gathering up what remained of her dress. 'You saved my life this day, for I surely would have killed myself if he'd had his way with me. So you're not to feel bad. You hear me?'

I nodded and swallowed. I understood. She was absolving me from this terrible thing. For that I will always be grateful to her. We did not speak again, just stared at each other, knowing that nothing would ever be the same after what had just happened in that close and stinking room. The onward flow of our lives had been diverted, as though by rocks falling into a stream. We would have to find a different direction, but there was no telling yet what it would be, or where it would take us from here.

Then Thomas was there, with Phillis. Thomas looked at the mess and his face went grey.

'Go now,' he whispered in my ear as he prised the gun out of my hand. 'We will take care of this.' He held me by the shoulders; his strong fingers biting into my flesh as he looked into my face. His brow was fissured and hatched with deep lines of worry and fear, whether for me, or for the trouble I'd brought down on all of them, I could not tell.

Phillis came to us, wrapping Minerva in a shawl, taking me by the arm, shepherding us both from that bloody chamber.

'What will they do with him?' Minerva asked.

'Feed him to the crocodiles,' Phillis replied. 'They will feed on anything. Even trash like that. As long as it's flesh, they will eat up every last bit. They ain't fussy. It'll look like he just disappeared.'

There were plenty of crocodiles in the swamp that lay between the plantation and the sea. I'd seen them when I was out riding. Huge blunt-nosed beasts basking on the mud, their plated bodies glistening in the sun, jaws gaping, showing rows of great teeth set in wide and crooked grins.

'What about his woman?' I feared she might tell my brother what had happened.

'She hates him more than anyone. She came to fetch Thomas soon as she saw you come in. She's helping him right now. Ain't her I'm worried 'bout. We got to think what's best to do now 'bout this trouble.'

We were sitting at the kitchen table at the plantation house. Phillis rose to put wood on the fire. After midnight, the air sometimes had a chill in it and I could not stop from shivering. Minerva fetched my shawl, anticipating my need, as was her training; although her days as my slave were at an end. Of the two of us, her ordeal had been the greater, but she seemed to recover more quickly. In some ways, she is the stronger. I took my lead from her.

'We could make it look as though he's robbed us and run off to Port Royal,' I suggested, rallying somewhat. We could not sit and do nothing. We had to make some plan before my brother came back. 'Thomas has given me Duke's keys. I can open the safe in my brother's office, remove the money kept there, rifle the papers —'

Minerva nodded, as though she thought it a good idea, but Phillis cut me off.

'Duke and what happened to him ain't our problem. He sleeps with the crocodiles now.' She shook her head, dismissing him. 'I see bigger trouble coming that makes this small.' Phillis sometimes spoke like a kind of oracle. 'Like a trifle of wind before a hurricane.'

Phillis had a reputation among the slaves for knowing about medicines and herbs and other things besides. It was knowledge that she had brought with her. Magic from Africa that the slaves called obeah. They had no other faith, so they kept to their own belief. I knew that she had the power of augury. Minerva had told me how she could see things in clouds, in smoke, in flames and fire, in the lace of leaves against the sky. Such things are highly secret, kept hidden from white eyes. For me to pry would be dangerous, so Minerva said, so I never asked to know more.

Just before I had left Phillis to go after Duke, she had taken her attention from me to stare into the red-gold flame of the candle. Perhaps she'd seen a vision in its flickering heart.

'What did you see, Mamma?' Minerva asked now.

'I see Bartholome. The Brazilian. That black-hearted man.' She looked at me sharply. 'Take that thing off your neck!' She almost spat the words out. I put my hand to my throat. I still wore the rubies. I unclasped them and put them down on the table. 'You should cast them away. They are obeah. They carry death in them: the time, the place, the way it will happen. I have seen. If you stay here, you will marry him. And one day — he will kill you sure . . .'

'But what can I do? I cannot avoid this marriage. My brother is set on it. My whole family depends on it. I can see no way to escape.'

'That is where you are wrong. Listen to me, and listen carefully.'

Phillis's plan was as drastic as it was bold and, as we worked to put it into effect that night, my spirit grew lighter, lighter than it had been for many days, months even. Minerva seemed to feel it, too. She smiled at me and it was as if we were back in those first fine days when we rode out together, before it all began to be spoiled.

I did everything Phillis said, disobeying her in only one respect. I would not get rid of the rubies. I wish now that I had cast them away, as she had told me to, let them sink deep into the swamp along with Duke. There was something devilish about them, and it came from the man who had given them to me. Phillis was right in that, as she was about so much else.

I had seen it myself. When I had looked down and thought that I saw blood pooling in my hands, it was an omen. Of that, I am certain. Although I did not see it at the time. I did not make the connection. I considered the rubies far too valuable to cast away. They might come in useful one day.

Put your faith in stones . . .

I remembered the Brazilian's words, heard them whisper in my head. Jewellery was light to carry and keep close, easy to hide from Phillis. I tucked the rubies into the body belt that I wore inside my clothes.

I put on man's array, for ease of travelling, and we left before dawn. Thomas leading, with Minerva and I following on horseback, and Phillis on a pack mule be-hind. My saddlebag bulged with gold from the safe. I had taxed my brother a quantity of coin, thinking it fair exchange for the in-heritance I was forfeiting. Then I had found a letter with my name upon it, which made me furious, so I helped myself to everything that was left. My brother could believe that Duke and I had robbed him and run away together for all I cared; he would never guess at the truth. I was off to join the maroons.

A Parcel of Rogues

16

By dawn, we had left Fountainhead far behind. We had been climbing all the time and were now high above the plain in the foothills of the mountains. The whole plantation was spread out, the vast fields shrunk to handkerchief size, the buildings like a child's toy farm. Thomas urged us on into a stand of gnarled and twisted pines, glad to have gained some cover as the light grew behind the eastern slopes.

We made our way into the mountains, climbing all the while, going backwards on ourselves as we followed the crooked path higher. In places, whole sections of hillside had fallen away, leaving a gash of red earth and loose rock which slid dangerously as soon as a hoof was set upon it. We gained the ridge top, hoping to find clear country at last. Instead we found a series of mist-filled ravines, with cloudy vapour escaping in ragged wisps, like steam from a lidded cauldron. We rode with our heads pressed to our horses' necks, into dense dripping trees swathed with moss and hanging vines and spiky-leafed dangling plants that seemed to feed only on air. We had to dismount and scramble down steep valley sides, leading the horses in a skittering slide to a swift-flowing stream, then the way was up to gain the next ridge, and the next.

There were many such to cross and by midday I was quite exhausted and glad when Thomas called for a halt. We had come to a broad river. Here, we watered the horses and drank ourselves, bathing our scratches and insect bites. Phillis found leaves and told us to rub them on ourselves to repel the biting flies that hung in clouds at the bottom of the ravines, ready to blacken our skin and suck our blood.

Phillis and Minerva went to pick fruit that grew in the forest all around, and Thomas went to scout the way ahead. I took out my letter. It was written on paper creased and then flattened, as if someone had balled it up and tossed it away, only to think better of it. It showed signs of being written at different times, in different inks, with different quills, as if the writer had been at a loss for what to say, or in two minds about whether to say anything at all.

My Dearest Nancy,

I have sat down many times to write this letter. I have gone over in my mind what I will say, but every time I pick up a quill, the words just flee away. I feel that I no longer know you, Nancy. I received the letter you wrote from the Sally-Anne *and you seemed as true as ever. I thought then that the wide ocean was but a shallow pond between us, and now I learn that you are to be married to a planter! I hardly know what to say.*

By some cruel turn of fate, we are bound for Kingston, but I understand from your brother, Henry, that you will be a wife long before our ships come in to port. I had my hopes of you. I have been given promotion to First Lieutenant on the third rater, Eagle, *under Captain Dunstan, and I went to call on your brother on the strength of it, for my pay has increased, and above that I have the prospect of prize money, &c. I went to declare my intentions, but he told me that you were already spoken for. So my hopes are dashed. You have slipped away from me as a ship steals from harbour on the morning tide. I hold no hard feelings, Nancy. For who could fail to love you? And if this planter fellow has stolen your heart in return, as your brother says he has, then all that remains is for me to wish you happiness.*

But I want you to know that my love will never change. It will always remain the same. If I cannot have you, then I will have no other. My life is the Navy and I will do my duty. When we reach Kingston, our commission is to hunt down the pirates who infest the waters of the Caribbean. It will be torture for me to be so near and never to see you, so I hope our cruise keeps us far from shore. You may look for me where the fighting is thickest. If the service demands the highest sacrifice, then I will give it. For what else is left for me to do?

I am, and will always remain, your truest friend. If you are ever in need of one, you may count on me.

Your loving and ever faithful,

William

I read through a misting blur of tears. How could my brothers have been so perfidious? William probably knew of my 'marriage' before I did. I felt as though he was lost to me for ever. I would never forgive them, for they had ruined his life along with mine.

I sat by the side of the river pondering my position. To think he might be here, on the same island as me, was an added torture. If only I had known before. I had escaped the Brazilian, but it had brought me no closer to William. Further away, if anything. I was moving outside the law. How would he ever find me now? Even if he did, would he still want me? Dressed in men's clothes, with blood on my hands? I would have to tell him everything. I could never bear to lie to him. Thinking of the cruel turns that my life had taken made me cry even harder, bitterness and anger dissolving the ink and threatening the paper. Before the letter disintegrated altogether, I folded it small and tucked it into my body belt.

We rested through the heat of the day, then waded on up the river. The valley was deep, the tops of the ridges lost in a dense overhanging mass of trees that grew right down to the water's edge. Birds called to each other, their cries echoing from side to side, loud notes of alarm, strange and sudden, that made us startle and jump. We had met no one, nor seen any evidence of habitation at any time since we had left the plantation, but now I had an uneasy feeling, as though we were being watched.

Thomas looked up every now and then, peering around as if he felt it, or as if he feared that he might have lost the way and be leading us into danger. We turned another bend in the winding river and a cliff rose up, sheer in front of us. All around, the forest was silent. Even the birds had ceased calling. I searched about, but could see no way up through the crowded vegetation. I feared that Thomas had led us into a trap.

He waded towards the cliff without looking back. Vines and hanging plants grew in every crevice on the rock-face, tumbling down it like a green waterfall. Thomas parted this living curtain and showed us the place where the river gushed out as if from a great open mouth. The cavity was wide and high enough for the horses to walk through. Not that they were very willing to enter. Thomas had to come back to help with them, stroking their noses and talking in gentle whispers. The mule was the most reluctant: he had to be driven; but eventually all of the animals were persuaded into the dark, dripping interior.

The cave opened out, the sides spreading wide, the ceiling rising high as a church. Light filtered through unseen apertures, the slender fluted shafts falling from above. The animals stood with their heads down, ears laid back to show their unhappiness, while we stood looking about us in wonder and awe, for everywhere the solid rock was sculpted into fantastic forms, swirling and writhing like frozen waterfalls. Folded sheets hung from the ceiling, as thin and delicate as tobacco leaves in a drying shed. Globules of water collected on every surface and dropped, as regular as the tick of clocks, measuring the time of our passage along the course of the underground river towards the point where the end of the tunnel showed as a lens of emerald light.

The sun filtering through the leaves of the overhanging trees coloured the water, making it seem as if we waded through liquid jade. We were at the bottom of a deep bowl cut into the hills and lined by thickly growing forest. All around us the air rang and buzzed with bird cries and animal sounds.

'I sense we are surrounded,' I whispered to Minerva. 'Yet I see no one.'

'Use your eyes!' she replied.

Each thing was cunningly disguised, designed to blend with the surroundings and so appear to be something natural. Canoes at the bank looked like drifting logs. The huts tucked between the trees were thatched with leaves and hidden by drooping canopies. The fields were tilled in little clearings, impossible to see from any distance.

From above, no one would form any idea that people lived here. That was how they managed to survive. Even the weapons brought to bear on us were used by those who hunt silently. We were entering the village of the maroons.

A spear thudded into the bank opposite; an arrow whistled past, so close I felt the draft from its flight. They were meant as warnings only. We would have been skewered if they had meant to find their mark. Thomas waded to the shore and laid his cutlass there. We did the same, laying our weapons next to his. The men stepped out now, bows drawn and spears pointed towards us. The maroons were a motley mix of Africans, long-haired Indians, dark-faced mulattos, Spaniards and paler-skinned men who looked to be British in origin. None wore any shoes and their clothes hung in tatters, but they were a fiercesome-looking crew.

Their commander stepped forward. A large man, bare-legged and bare-chested, with a mass of fiery red hair growing straight out from his head. His face was broad and sunburnt above a great tangle of beard.

'Who are ye?' he demanded. 'And what do you want here?'

'We have come to see Hero,' Thomas spoke up. 'Ask his help.'

'Oh, aye.' This seemed to amuse him. He crossed his brawny arms. 'Well, he's away. And why should he help the likes of ye?'

'I'm Thomas. Hero's son. I come to ask protection. I travel with Phillis, his good friend, and her daughter, Minerva. And . . .'

'And?' The big man came nearer. 'Who are ye?'

'I am Nancy Kington. Late of Fountain-head Plantation.'

'Well, I'm Tam McGregor, late of no-where in particular. While Hero's away, I'm in charge here.' He scratched his beard. 'Kington of Fountainhead?' His blue eyes narrowed. 'Don't yer daddy own the place?'

I nodded, wondering what he would make of it.

'Well, we can always sell ye.' He laughed. 'Sell the owner's daughter, eh?' He looked round at the others. 'What d'you think of that, boys?'

17

The men went into a huddle to discuss our sudden arrival, but decided to do nothing until Hero returned. We were kept in open view in the clearing in the centre of the village and told that we must wait.

Whatever doubts might have been harboured about us were dispelled as soon as Hero arrived. He was an imposing man, over six foot tall and well built, with coal-black skin. His wide cheeks were scarified with tribal markings and he wore a bright red parrot feather stuck in the band that bound his thick curling hair. He had a broad smile and uptilted eyes that flashed with fire. He was dressed only in a tattered pair of canvas trousers secured with a broad leather belt, but he bore himself like a king. As soon as he saw Thomas he gave a shout, and when he saw Phillis, he let out a rich laugh of delight and welcome.

'Welcome, sister!' He took both her hands in his. 'What took you so long?'

He was captain here, and deferred to as such, but all decisions were made in common. He could not go against the council.

The men disappeared to discuss our fate and we were left alone in the clearing. All was quiet for a little while, then the children came out, too curious to be contained, only to be scolded and shooed back again by the women who came sidling from their huts for a better view of us.

Two of them recognised Phillis and greeted her in the language of their own land, their old land, speaking words I did not understand. Phillis spoke urgently, making frequent nods towards Minerva and me. The women's faces became serious, their tongues clucking with sympathy. They went to their neighbours and they all stood in a little huddle, then they hurried off to tell others. They came back carrying gourds of fresh water and calabashes full of a kind of porridge made with meat and vegetables, corn and beans. They invited us to sit and eat. Phillis asked if they would join us, then she winked at me.

'Don't matter what the men think. It's already been decided.'

Phillis smiled as she looked around the village. Her eyes lost their hollow haunted look, the tension and strain disappearing from her face. The houses were simple structures, thatched with palm leaves, but each with its own little yard and garden, surrounded by fruit trees: breadfruit, banana, oranges, lemons, pineapple, mango and papaya.

'It feels like I've come home,' she said.

The men followed the women's acceptance of us and we were allowed to stay.

The whole village worked to build us a hut. The women helped us to make it homelike, while the men cleared a patch of forest for our garden. Minerva and I helped Phillis with the tilling and planting with yam, sweet potato, corn and manioc. Until our first harvest, the other villagers promised a share of their produce in return for work on their plots. Not that we were a burden. There was food in abundance. Fruit and vegetables grew in great profusion. Pigs rooted, chickens scuttled and clucked through the common spaces of the villages, goats wandered, shooed from the gardens by the children.

The life here suited Phillis. Her skin lost its grey, dusty pallor, and her body gained weight, its angular thinness disappearing as the ever-present fear and gnawing bitterness that had made up her life for so many years began to retreat. She could laugh now, and smile. She showed every symptom of being contented, and was soon spending more time in Hero's hut than in ours.

Thomas soon found a mate, a tall, quiet young woman, originally from Senegal, and went to live with her. He seemed settled and contented, like Phillis.

Minerva and I slept side by side in the hut. I lay awake, listening to her breathing. I did not want anything to happen to threaten this newly discovered happiness, but I feared that it could not last. As time went on, I felt dangers crowding nearer, and found it hard to rest for worrying and thinking. I often did not sleep until the early hours of the morning, just as the cocks began crowing, heralding the first light of dawn.

We had been at the maroon's camp for several weeks and this feeling of dread had been growing. One night, I woke in a sweat and lay staring at the woven roof above my head, not daring to close my eyes again. I'd had the most terrible dream.

The dream was to haunt me for many months, but that first time, I remembered almost nothing but the whispered warning that roused me:

He's coming after you . . .

The voice was not loud, but it sounded so real that I started awake, heart thumping, expecting to find someone leaning over me, breathing into my ear.

'What is the matter?' Minerva's voice came to me out of the darkness. I must have cried out and woken her.

'I had a dream.' The terror was still upon me. Telling her calmed me, made my breath come less ragged. 'They are coming after me. I know it. My brother and the Brazilian. They are hunting for me even now. My very presence brings danger to you all. I cannot bear that. I must go away.'

Minerva was silent for a long time. Like her mother, she put a great deal of faith in dreams.

'Perhaps it will not come to that,' she said at last. 'Perhaps they will not find us.'

'They have dogs. Duke told me. And spies they can bribe.'

'Even so, the camp is well hidden,' she answered from the darkness. 'They have not found it before.'

'They did not have such a strong reason to look for it,' I replied. 'The maroons were merely an irritant, not worth the trouble of finding. Their camp did not harbour one such as me. An English heiress, promised

212

in marriage. They will not let me go easily, not when money and land are involved.' I knew them well enough to know that.

'Even if they come, the camp is well defended,' Minerva countered. 'The people can escape into the caves.'

'But why should they have to? If they came, they would destroy everything. The huts and gardens that the people have worked so hard to build and cultivate. I could not stand to see it all laid to waste.' I rose on my elbow, trying to see her face. 'It grieves my heart to leave you and Phillis, but I fear I have to go.'

'When?' asked Minerva.

'I don't know, but it must be soon. Each day I'm here brings danger nearer.'

Sleep was denied to both of us. Minerva got up as the first thin grey light filtered into the hut, and started a fire. The early morning could be cold before the sun rose to warm the high mountain valleys. I drew my blanket round my shoulders and joined her, glad of the warm tea she had brewed.

'If you go,' she did not look at me as we sipped the bitter liquid, 'I go with you.'

'You can't!' I was genuinely shocked. 'What about Phillis? You are free here, and safe, or will be once I'm gone. Your place is here, with your people, not with me!'

Part of me leaped for joy at the thought of Minerva coming with me, for I was full of fear, having no idea where I would go, and equally deep in misery at the idea of being parted from those whom I'd grown to love. But I quickly condemned my own selfishness and thought of ever more reasons why she should stay. She listened, but her face was set, enigmatic.

'I hear what you say,' she said at last. 'But it makes no difference. When you go? I go, too.'

18

The next day confirmed my foreboding. Tam McGregor brought news from the outside world. He went often to Port Royal, or Kingston, posing as a smallholder with goods to sell. In this way he collected information and gossip, as well as the currency to purchase needs such as cloth, gunpowder and shot, which we could not supply ourselves. He had come back from his last trip with a grave face. I was hunted, he said. A reward had been offered for information about my whereabouts and that of the slaves who had abducted me.

Abducted. That was how it would appear. I had not thought . . .

'Any caught can expect worse than hanging.' Tam grimaced. 'That Brazilian bastard's got himsel' involved and there's no stopping him. He's putting up a big reward for any or all who are captured. It's a mighty amount. Enough to tempt any man.'

He scratched his beard and looked about. The people here were among the poorest on the island, the poorest any-where. The sum offered would test any man, no matter how honest and loyal. Even if we were not betrayed, it was only a matter of time before the village was dis-covered. The Brazilian had bloodhounds and was going to use them.

The news was bad enough to bring deep concern to the faces of Tam and Hero. They set extra guards and watches, but the village was suddenly full of fear and appre-hension. People could see their whole way of life heading for destruction. All because of me.

'We must go to Phillis,' Minerva said. 'She'll know what to do.'

We went to her hut to find her, to ask her to use her gift for divination. Since we had come to the maroon village, she was consulted frequently and treated as a re-spected oracle. I told of my dream. She rose without a word and fetched her things. She spread a cloth on the hut's beaten dirt floor and sprinkled palm wine. Then she took out four bright vermilion parrot feathers and placed them carefully at the points of the compass. In the space between them, she cast shells and seeds from a polished gourd, passing her hands over them and scanning the scatter, her eyes darting across the random pattern as if it spelt out the future in letters that could only be read by her.

At length, she looked up at me.

'You already know the answer,' she said. 'You must leave. Your dream is true, he is coming. There is no escaping him. If he finds you here, he will kill every living thing.'

'If she goes, I go with her,' Minerva said. I began to protest, but she put up her hand to silence me. 'I have decided. So we need to know, Mamma. Where should we go? What should we do?'

Phillis rocked back on her heels, hugging her knees.

'I see this, too.' She turned to her daughter, and to me. 'You two are bound together. Do you know that?'

We both nodded. Although we seldom spoken about Duke and that night in his stinking room, we did not pretend that it had not happened. It was always there, and always would be. We had witnessed things, each about the other, that we found hard to look at even in ourselves. She'd seen me kill a man, seen his blood spatter over my face, seen me smear it away with the back of my hand. I'd seen her threatened with violation. How could we speak of these things? But they brought us close together, as close as sisters, closer.

'It will break my heart to lose you.' Phillis touched Minerva's cheeks and cupped her chin, as if memorising the curves and contours of her face. 'But I know this village is not the place for you. I know you feel that, too. When they come, they'll come for both of you.' Phillis rose to her feet. 'We wait for a sign.'

We turned to go, but Phillis called me back.

'Have you still got that thing he gave you?'

She meant the necklace. I shook my head, embarrassed to admit that I had disobeyed her.

'Don't lie to me now,' Phillis said, her dark eyes searching mine.

'I'm not!' I began to protest.

'Even if you are,' she said, and I could see by her eyes that she knew that I was, 'I'm telling you again. You must get rid of it, or it will draw him to you like a lodestone.'

I did what she told me, or at least, I left the hut full of that intention. There was a place near the camp where deep holes opened up in the ground and plunged hundreds of feet down. I took the rubies from my belt, fully intending to cast them into one of these pits. But when I looked at them, I found I could not do such a thing. I failed the test that Phillis had set me. I was still under the spell of their worth and their beauty.

19

'Pirates coming! Pirates!' A little boy ran pell-mell into the village, yelling, followed by another. They were quite out of breath, having run all the way from the beach, but the pirates moved fast and were not far behind them.

They were a fearsome-looking bunch, bearded and sunburnt, wearing a bizarre collection of clothes and festooned with weapons. Some were in regular sailors' rig: trowsers and shirt, with a scarf about the head or a woollen monmouth cap; others were sporting fine hats with feathers in them and were tricked out as gentlemen in silks and satins. They were all armed with knives, cutlasses and pistols, and hung about with swinging bandoleers weighted with shot and cartridge boxes. The pirates formed up into a wedge, their captain at the head, as they marched into the village.

They had come straight up from the sea, scaling the sheer cliffs that led up from

Cutlass Bay. That shore was guarded by treacherous coral reefs. The villagers would not anticipate an attack from the sea. I expected the men to dash for their weapons, for the women and children to make for the caves as they knew to do if the village came under attack, but no one moved. Everyone waited until the pirates were in the central clearing of the village, then Hero and Tam stepped out to meet them. They stood unarmed and showed no signs of fear. I was thinking how brave they were, when Hero stepped forward, arms outstretched, to welcome the strangers into the village.

The coming of the pirates was a cause for celebration, not conflict. Phillis saw my reaction and laughed.

'*You* see pirates, and you think one thing,' Phillis observed to me. 'You got to learn to see differently. Only regular folk be afraid of them, and you ain't one any more. You living outside the law. Outlaw folks stick together. They come to trade. Can't sail into Port Royal with the Navy tied up to the docks, so they come to us.'

The pirates traded for fresh fruit and vegetables, smoked pork and goat meat. In return they offered sacks of rice, lengths of cloth, a chest containing items of clothing, boxes of thimbles and buttons, balls of thread, tools and implements, including scissors, and a quantity of knives and hatchets.

By late afternoon the bargaining was over, the goods exchanged. Both parties seemed well satisfied. Hero emerged from the council hut, declaring that there would be a feast, a boucan. Beside him stood another man. The captain of the pirates.

I had failed to recognise him under his broad-brimmed hat with its dancing feather cockade. When I'd last seen him, he had been fastidiously clean-shaven and altogether the most mild-mannered of men. Now, a newly-grown beard and moustache served to disguise him further and add to a fiercesome appearance that had me thoroughly fooled. His plain broadcloth had been replaced by apricot brocade and he wore dark crimson velvet pantaloons tucked into the folded tops of a fine pair of shining black boots. I'd never seen him armed, other than with his officer's sword; now he was wrapped around at the waist with a wide cummerbund stuffed with weapons. Pistols hung at his side, slung from his shoulders on red and pink silk ribbons.

'Do you know him?' Phillis whispered.

'He was the mate on the ship that brought me here.'

'That is your sign,' she said.

Before I could ask her more, Captain Broom was standing in front of me. My skin was brown, my hair dishevelled, and I was wearing a shapeless shift all stained from gardening. I thought it doubtful that he would recognise me, but he swept off his hat and bowed low to the ground.

'Why, Miss Kington! What an unexpected pleasure!' We could have been meeting in the Bath Assembly Rooms. He took my hand and kissed it with a flourish. 'I hardly thought to find you here under these . . .' he cleared his throat, '. . . unusual circumstances.'

'I could say the same for you.'

'Our ship was taken by a Captain Johnson, just after we set out for home. We were given a choice: to be turned off the ship, or go on the account. As you see, most chose the latter course.'

'What about Surgeon Graham? And the captain?'

'Oh, Graham is with us. The captain refused, but Johnson is a humane man. We put him off on New Providence, within walking distance of Nassau. I'm sure he arrived safely, if a little footsore.'

'I didn't know pirates were so merciful.'

Broom gave me a look as though there was much I didn't know.

'What made you join them?' I asked. 'You and Graham?'

'Money,' he said simply. 'I could make a lifetime's wages from just one prize. Don't always happen, of course.' He pursed his lips. 'Can't pick and choose; you have to take what's on offer, so to speak. Hence the thimbles and buttons and such. If it don't work out, we can always set up as haberdashers.' He laughed. 'We're free to sail as we please and there's always the chance of treasure. And look at me!' He flourished his hand and gave a mock bow. 'I'm captain now and it's taken months, not years. Or,' he laughed again, 'maybe I just didn't fancy the tramp to Nassau. Now, may I introduce you to my companions. Mr Vincent Crosby, and Mr Ignatius Pelling.'

Vincent Crosby, the mate of the ship, was a handsome young mulatto of about five and twenty with skin the colour of dark honey, a high forehead and wide cheekbones. His nose was straight, flaring a little at the nostrils, and his black eyes had an upward tilt as if he found much to amuse him. He was medium height for a man, not much taller than Minerva, but well built with broad shoulders and a narrow waist. His breeches were as white as milk and he wore a splendid coat of midnight blue with deep bars of scarlet on the facings and cuffs. The ribbon tying back his long curling hair was of the same shade of red. He was quite as much of a dandy as Broom, although he showed rather more taste and discernment.

In contrast, the quartermaster, Ignatius Pelling, was barefoot, in striped shirt and canvas trowsers. He barely came up to Vincent's shoulder; a wiry little man with muscles like knotted string, and skin so quilted and creased it looked as if he'd been pickled in brine.

Broom bowed to me, introductions completed.

'I'm pleased to make your acquaintance again, Miss Kington, and there is much for us to discuss, not least how you came to be among this crew, but I think it's a tale for after dinner. All I can attend to now is the growling of my belly.'

Fires had been started, animals butchered, fish skewered. Pirates had come up from the ship rolling barrels of rum before them. Meat was now roasting above beds of glowing embers. Bark and twigs stripped from spice trees gave off aromatic smoke and added a sweet pungency to the smell of cooking drifting across from the fires.

'The man is right,' Phillis said to me. 'Eat first, then we talk. Men don't think too well on an empty belly. When you finish,' she turned to Broom and his two men, 'you come to Nancy and Minerva's hut. Try some of my palm wine.' She kissed her bunched fingers. 'It is sweet and good. Not like that rot-gut rum you brought with you.'

The sun went down, replaced by the velvet blackness of the warm forest night. Frogs took over from the chirring insects, and bats flickered in and out of sight, swooping on the white-winged moths blundering towards the fires.

The deep belling hoot of a conch announced when the meat was ready, and the night was given over to feasting. The men from the ship stuffed themselves, gorging on the roasted flesh until the fat ran down their chins. The food was washed down with drafts of rum until the whole company was merry.

The pirates had a couple of fiddlers with them, and there were musicians among the maroons who had fashioned instruments from the materials that they found around them, transforming wood, gourds, animal skins and gut into drums, reed pipes, flutes, lutes and harps. The instruments were perfectly pitched and sweetly resonant; the sound coming from them could be softly melodic, or powerfully strident.

Once the feasting was over, a space was cleared for dancing. The players came together, striking tunes off each other, until the music flew up, swirling into the air like sparks and motes from the fire, travelling through the air, drowning out the cries and calls of the forest creatures and echoing back from the hills.

Phillis said I'd had my sign. Now a plan was forming. I took Minerva aside. A smile lit her face as I explained what I had in mind and her eyes grew wide at the audacity of it. We watched and waited. At last, Broom slipped away and came to our hut, bringing his quartermaster and mate with him. Phillis brought palm wine, sprinkling some of it to bless and purify, and poured little cups for them to drink. Minerva set out bowls of fruit for them to eat and I lit small oil wick lamps. We sat on mats woven from palm fronds and I put my proposal to Broom. I told him of the Brazilian and what had happened at Fountainhead; how danger followed me and how I needed to get away, my very presence putting the maroon camp in jeopardy. I told him that Minerva wanted to come with me and pleaded our case the best I could, begging him to take us on board.

Broom listened to all I had to say, and then sat for a while, deep in thought.

'I'd like to help you, Nancy. I'd like to say "yes", truly I would. But it's not for me to decide. I'll have to put it to the men. I'll call a ship's council in the morning.'

'Can't you just tell them? You are the captain.'

Outside, the uproar was increasing by the minute. Several fights had broken out. Through the open door, I could see bodies reeling about, accompanied by a great deal of crashing and shouting. Judging from that racket, the ship's company would not be in a state to decide anything in the morning.

'We're not on one of your father's ships now,' Broom grinned. 'Everything's decided in common. We have all sorts on board. All colours and nations. But as yet —'

'As yet no women.'

'No.' He rubbed his newly-grown beard. 'Not as such. No women at all. There's some think women unlucky. That aside, they can cause trouble for reasons that are obvious, pirates not exactly being gentlemen.'

'Calico Jack had women on board,' his quartermaster spoke up. 'Dressed as tars, served their watch and carried out their duties, same as the men.'

'We could do that!' I seized my chance. 'Dress as men, I mean. We'll use clothes from the chest you brought up from the ship. We can serve our turn. We can work. We're both strong and I've been around ships all my life. What we don't know, we can learn. If you'll give us the chance.'

'We'd have to be straight with them.' Broom frowned. 'Got to be clear who you are, right from the start. That said —'

Broom and the quartermaster looked at each other. The quartermaster shrugged.

'Very well.' Broom's brow cleared. 'I'll put it to the company.' He leaned over, shaking first my hand, then Minerva's. 'Here's my word upon it.'

They left us, and we settled down on our mats. The noise from outside had died down to the occasional yell and yelping laugh. The pirates had drunk themselves into a state where they sounded like calling monkeys. The night stretched towards dawn, but I could not sleep. Neither could

Minerva. I could hear from her breathing that she was wide awake.

'Are you sure that this is what you want to do?' I whispered, reaching for her hand. 'You can still change your mind and stay here with Phillis. You don't have to do this.'

'But I do. I want to go with you. The more I think, the more I'm sure about it. Phillis likes it here; she says it reminds her of home, but I have no home.' She did not count the plantation.

'Broom says his home is the sea.'

Minerva thought for a moment. 'There are people of all nations sailing there. That suits me. I want to see the world. Find my place in it. Not stay here, bound in by forest walls, living all the time in fear, wondering if this will be the day that they find me and take me back to slavery.'

I propped myself up to look at her. She sounded sure and determined, but there was a roughness in her voice and in the dim light her face gleamed wet with tears.

'Are you certain?' I asked again. 'It is easier for me. I have no one. Nothing to keep me.'

'A girl has to leave her mother sometime.' Phillis spoke from the darkness. 'That's the way in life. Can't stay together for always. You go with Nancy. I will be fine here. Hero's a good man. He look after me. I look after him. One day, maybe, you will come back to me . . .' Her voice wavered and broke, as if the uncertainty had sucked the air from her throat and made her choke.

'I will,' Minerva whispered. 'I vow it.'

The vow would likely prove impossible to fulfil, but it was bravely made. It carried us through the moment and we clung to the empty promise, whispering of what surprises we would bring to that unlikely homecoming.

In the morning, we would tie back our hair and bind our breasts. We would pull on our shirts and button up our trousers. But we were not bold pirates yet. We both clung to Phillis and wept. Mother for daughter, daughter for mother. It was as if they already knew that they would never see each other again. I thought of the mother that I had never known and cried for her as well.

Female Sailors Bold

20

'What have we here?' Broom exclaimed when we presented ourselves at the ship in the morning, our bundles slung over our shoulders. He walked around, inspecting us. Then he tipped back his hat. 'Damn me, if I don't see as likely a pair of lads as ever went on the account.' He clapped me on the back and put a fatherly arm around Minerva. 'Let's see what Surgeon Graham thinks of you.'

I squinted, shading my eyes against the glaring white of the sand and the glitter from the water in the shallow curving bay. The whole beach shimmered with activity. The ship lay like a stranded leviathan. Men were swarming over her, scraping away at the weed and barnacles that collect below the water line and slow a ship down. Others went behind them, caulking and tarring, replacing rotting or worm-ridden planking, making the ship sound and sea-worthy. I recognised some of them from

235

the *Sally-Anne*. Gabriel Grant, the carpenter, had set up a workshop under an awning. He was busy planing and shaping, his feet lost in shavings, the air around him fragrant with the smell of freshly worked wood.

'Old Gabe's a clever fellow,' Broom grinned. 'A good shipwright's worth his weight in guinea pieces. I don't know what we'd do without him. I took care to take the best with me from the *Sally-Anne*.' He walked on, going closer to inspect the work being done. 'She's a good ship right enough, but she needs to be changed for our purposes. New gun ports, and get rid of some of the upper deck to make her lighter, more manoeuvrable. Gabe's even promising to heighten the masts so we can get that extra breath of wind.' Being a pirate was all about taking the advantage and keeping it, being able to outrun and outgun any other vessel. Broom was clever, he learned fast. 'We'll be a match for anybody, excepting for the Navy, but we can get places they can't, because of our shallower draft.'

I listened to him talking and watched the men working. We hadn't set foot on the ship yet, but I felt as though I was already on the account. The fear and dread that I'd felt in the maroon camp were receding. To be wearing a sailor's rig, to know that we would be leaving on that ship, it all felt most liberating. I had to force myself to rein in my growing excitement and remind myself that we were on probation. Our joining had to be put to ship's council and the vote would not be taken until the end of the day.

Surgeon Graham was under another awning made from a sail. He had a number of men resting on pallets in a makeshift hospital.

'Ah, Broom,' he looked up as he saw the captain approaching. 'Moved these poor devils off the ship. Fresh air is good for them.' He swilled blood from his hands in a pewter bowl. 'I wondered when you'd be back. How was the maroons' camp?'

'We had some fine entertainment, and I got the fresh food you requested. They are bringing it down now.' He paused. 'I managed to find a pair of new recruits.'

Broom pushed us forwards, but Graham barely glanced at us.

'Good. I could do with some help.' He looked at me, but with absolutely no recognition. 'You'll do. Roll your sleeves up and come with me.'

He turned on his heel. Broom shrugged

and signalled for Minerva to follow him. I watched as they walked off together. She made a handsome lad. Loose-limbed and long-legged, she had always been graceful, but now there was an ease and freedom about her. Wearing boys' clothes suited her.

'Hey, you!' Graham thrust his head out from the awning. 'Don't just stand there a wool gathering. Get in here! I haven't got all day!'

The sun struck through the canvas, bathing the interior in a yellowy light. Up to a dozen men lay on low pallets set out in neat rows. One or two of them groaned and tossed, as if gripped with fever, but most lay still and listless in the growing heat of the day. The sides were open to the air, but there was little or no wind, so it was stifling and smelt of sickness.

'Come over here.'

Graham led me to a table set a little apart from the pallets. The sailor lying there turned his head when he heard us coming. His hands balled in fists at his sides and his eyes opened wide, big dark pools brimming with fear. He was just a boy, younger than me. I recognised him. Joby Price from the *Sally-Anne*. He shut his eyes tight now, and lay quiet, biting his lips bloody to stop himself from crying.

'There, lad,' Graham patted his shoulder. 'Soon be over.'

Graham moved about the table examining the boy's legs. One was much thicker than the other, as fat as a young tree trunk. It was swathed in layers of soiled bandage which Graham was gently cutting away. As he did so the smell of the decay grew so thick I had to cover my mouth. From the knee down, the flesh was a mottled blackish grey and purple. A thick yellow discharge oozed from an elongated wound dimpling what had been his shin, and the whole of his foot was swollen and discoloured, the toes showing like a row of black fruit.

'Give him this.' Graham thrust a bottle of rum into my chest. 'Get as much as you can down him, then stick this in his mouth.' He gave me a gag of plaited leather, darkened and matted, pitted with teeth marks. 'Then hold him.' He took in my relatively slight build. 'Lie across his chest if you have to, but hold him tight.'

I poured rum down the boy's throat until he choked and gagged, then I poured some more.

'Ready?' Graham asked, a long bow-saw in his hand.

'Ready.' I thrust the leather between the boy's teeth and threw myself across him as he grunted and bucked.

It was over in a second. I felt a sudden lightness and the boy's body went limp, his head falling to one side.

'He's fainted,' Graham muttered. 'That's a kindness. Quick now, bring me the hatchet. In the brazier. Over there!'

The haft of the axe was scorched black, but was cool enough to carry. Graham took it from me, and applied the glowing flat of the blade to the stump of the leg. The flesh hissed and smelt of barbicue.

'Don't faint, and don't vomit,' Graham snarled. 'I need you. Bring me the pot from the fire.'

A little pot of tar bubbled on the coals. I was grateful for its cleaner smell. I used a cloth to carry it to Graham. He dipped a brush into the molten tar and daubed it over the wound.

'There.' He stepped back to inspect his handiwork. 'That should do.'

The boy was still unconscious. Graham left him and went to wash his hands in the pewter bowl, the water clouding with blood. He tipped the contents into the sand.

'Go and fill it up with sea water.' He

looked up at me. 'You did well.' He smiled. 'Thank you.' He shook water from his hands, drying them on his stained shirt front. 'I didn't expect to see you, Miss Nancy. Not under these circumstances. But I'm sure I'll hear your story soon enough.'

'The boy. Will he be all right?'

Graham shrugged. 'Who knows. Another day, that leg would have killed him. Now, I dare say he'll live for Gabe to fashion him a new one. He was up aloft repairing a sail torn at the luff edge when he fell from the rigging, hit the deck and shattered his shin bone beyond any repairing, but I dare say he'll brag how he lost his leg in a fearsome fight. 'Tis a shame to lose a limb, and in one so young, but at least he won't be turned off. He's due £150, according to the Articles, and can stay in the company for as long as he wishes.'

'Articles?'

'We have our own rules. Laws that we live by. Everyone has to swear to them.' He laughed. 'You'll find a pirate ship is quite a little Commonwealth.' He went back under the awning, charging a large syringe with some viscous liquid. 'Mercury. For the pox.' He waved the curving spout. 'I don't suppose you want to help me administer that. Off you go and get fresh water. You acquitted yourself well. You'll get my vote, for what it's worth.'

Down by the shore, Minerva was undergoing her own tests to prove her worthiness to join the ship's company. Several fork-tailed frigate birds floated headless in the shallows, their long wings spread. Vincent, the mate, presented her with a reloaded pistol. A coconut exploded from a palm at least a hundred paces away, the remains of it tumbling to the sand.

'She's a good shot,' one of the men exclaimed. 'By damn if she's not!'

Vincent clapped his hands by way of compliment. When Minerva made to return his pistol, he smiled and thrust his hands in his pockets.

'No, no,' he shook his head. 'It's yours now. It pays to have a weapon handy on the account.'

We set about making ourselves useful, working on the ship. After the changes had been made they would rename her *Deliverance*, in the way that was common to all pirates, transforming the ordinary and everyday to something more exotic, which gave justice to their intention. *Mary, Mercy, Greyhound* became *Revenge* or *Rover, Success* or *Fortune*, as if there were a magic in names. After that the black colours would fly from the mast and proclaim to all that the newly-named ship was a pirate vessel, and strike fear into the hearts of all she approached. Or so they hoped.

We worked alongside, but the men kept their distance. Our fate was yet to be decided, and until then we were not to be treated as part of the company, but rather as oddities, as if a pair of monkeys had suddenly appeared from the forest and snatched up tools and fallen to scraping and sawing.

The ship would put to sea in the morning. The crew would spend one more night on shore. As the sun sank further, fires were lit, and food was prepared. There would be no rum drinking, by Broom's order. At least, not until the council was over. The decisions about to be made demanded clear heads.

We were not invited to attend the debate. We sat some way apart, our backs against a fallen tree, and watched as the sun sank deeper, turning the sea a deep bloody orange. Darkness fell and the sun disappeared with one last flash on the horizon, like a red eye winking out. Someone threw more wood on the blaze, sparks flew up in firefly showers and flames roared, streaming in the wind like torn scarlet flags.

We could not hear what was being said, but it was clear from the length of discussion that not everyone was happy for us to join the ship. Broom was a flamboyant orator with a taste for the dramatic, pacing and gesturing like a courtroom advocate. The opposing voices were quieter, more sullen, but from the muttered 'ayes' and nods of agreement, their arguments seemed to be gaining. Then Graham stood up. It was obvious from the men's faces that they respected him, and he was listened to in silence. He moved the motion to a vote. The quartermaster took a count on a show of hands. It was a close thing, but we were in the company.

Vincent came over to ask us to join them. A rough table had been put up, set out with a Bible and a hatchet. Captain Broom would read out the Articles of the company, and we would have to sign to them, as all there had. A pirate ship is a Commonwealth, as Graham had said, ruled by laws agreed by all.

These were the Articles of the newly-named *Deliverance*.

1. Every man shall be given a vote in af-

fairs of moment and every man shall obey civil command.

2. The captain shall have one and one half shares in any Prizes, the mate, quartermaster, surgeon, carpenter and gunner, one and one quarter, all the rest one share each. All have equal title to fresh provisions and strong liquors seized. These to be enjoyed at pleasure, except in times of scarcity when it may be necessary to vote a retrenchment.

3. If any man shall board a Prize and not declare a find of gold, silver, plate, jewels or money above the worth of a Piece of Eight and so seek to defraud the company, he shall suffer marooning, landed in some desert place with one bottle of powder, one bottle of water, pistol and shot.

4. No person to game at dice or cards for money.

5. None shall strike another on board but every man's quarrel shall be ended on shore with sword and pistol.

6. Every man to keep his piece, pistol and cutlass clean and fit for engagement. Any man failing in this shall be cut off from his share and suffer such other punishment as captain and company see fit.

7. He that shall be found guilty of cowardice or desertion in time of engagement to be punished by marooning or death.

8. No man is to talk of breaking up our way of living until each has shared £1000. If any man lose a limb, or become crippled in our service, he shall have the sum of £150, and remain with the company as long as he shall think fit.

9. Any man snapping his arms in the hold, or smoking an unlidded pipe, or carrying a lighted candle without a lanthorn shall be punished as captain and company see fit.

10. No boy or woman to be taken to sea. If any man seduce a woman and carry her to sea disguised, he is to suffer death.

This last had been a sticking point, and arguments threatened to break out afresh, with voices declaring that Broom was breaking his own Articles. The captain replied as smooth as any lawyer, his argument running thus:

Firstly, the women in question (us) were not being *carried* to sea by any one person for any immoral purpose.

Secondly, everyone there knew perfectly well what sex we were, so we were not *disguised,* as such.

Thirdly, women on board could be useful, he added for good measure, and better than any set of false colours. For if we were up on deck in our feminine attire, who would take the ship for a pirate?

Broom stood back and let that sink into them, with the confident air of a man who knows that he has found his mark.

'There's been female pirates afore,' Pelling spoke up in support, just in case Broom needed it. 'Mary Read and Anne Bonny. Bold pirates both. As bold a pair as ever went on the account. Served with Calico Jack.'

'Aye, and look what happened to him,' a voice joined in. 'Hung at Gallows Point, along with the rest of his crew. Excepting those two. Pled their bellies while Rackham swung. That's women for you.'

There were cackles of agreement and cries for Broom to get on with it. There would be no grog until this was finished and the crew were getting restive.

11. Any man offering to meddle with a prudent woman without her consent shall suffer present death.

'And how likely be they to go a meddlin'?' a voice from the back jeered. 'What's the point of makin' 'em swear to that, Broom? Where's yer sense?'

'They might go a meddlin' wi' you!' someone remarked, to much ribald laughter.

247

'They can meddle wi' me any day!'

The comments were flying thick and fast, the council threatening to collapse. Minerva seemed calm, and was even smiling, but I did not like the turn the proceedings were taking. We would be on board ship with these men for weeks, months. I looked at her in alarm.

'Never fear,' she patted the pistol she now wore. 'Any of them come near either of us and I'll stop him with this.'

'Easy, mates.' Broom put up his hands, trying to quell the commotion. 'All have to swear to the same Articles and these two have been invited to join the company. I thought that much was decided.' His manner remained mild but, as he looked around the assembly, his brown eyes turned hard and flinty sharp. 'If any man has something to say, let him step up. Say it out loud, not behind his hand.' He rested his palm on the hilt of his cutlass and no man moved. 'No? In that case,' he turned to Minerva and me, 'are you ready? Right hand on the Bible, left on the hatchet. Now, do you swear before God, your maker, to keep these Articles unto death?'

We stood facing each other, arms crossed, her hands warm under mine.

'I swear,' we said together.

'Now, you must sign.'

Broom took a knife from his belt and pricked our thumbs. The quartermaster offered a quill, first to me, then to Minerva. We signed our names one above the other, my blood running into hers.

A ragged cheer went up, but I could not tell if the huzzahs were for us, or for the great two-handled silver cup being filled to the brim with rum. The mate offered it to the captain first, then to us. Minerva drank without spilling a drop. It was all I could do to lift it up, and the strength of the rum made me want to cough, but I choked it down and passed the cup on without spilling. It went round the company to be brought back and filled again. By the time the fiddlers struck up, we were all but forgotten.

We slipped away to find somewhere to sleep at a distance from them, Minerva setting sticks to warn of any approach.

I was used to sleeping on the ground, but I woke stiff and chill on the cold sand. The cook fire was already alight, so I went over to warm myself. Abe Reynolds had exchanged his steward's job for ship's cook. He gave me a dish of strong black tea and a bowl of porridge and seemed glad to see me again. I asked him how he liked life as a pirate. He replied with a grin, showing his tusky teeth, and said if there was a better one, he'd not found it. I sat on a tree trunk and broke my fast while he talked about how different the ship was now, and all around us the pirates slept on, lying where they had fallen, like an army cut down by drink.

The sun rose, heating the day, and the men were soon sweating off the rum, harnessed in teams like horses to haul the ship off the sand and into the shallows of the lagoon. Once there, it lay listing on its side, waiting for the tide to lift it further. When it was more or less floating, teams of rowers laboured at their oars, towing it to deeper water.

I was sent to help Jan Jessop, the sailmaker, with the black hoist that would fly from the main mast and instil terror in any merchantman we cared to approach. The device was of Broom's own designing: a skull over crossed bones, flanked by an hourglass and a curving cutlass.

'The meaning being that time is running out and it will be death to resist,' the sailmaker explained, without much conviction. 'Leastways, that's what the folk on the ships is supposed to think.'

Jessop was a doleful little man with a long sorrowful face and big mournful eyes. He was good with a needle, but bad at drawing. Earlier attempts had been rejected and Broom was getting increasingly impatient.

'What's that supposed to be?' he had bellowed at Jessop's last effort. 'A painted pig's bladder over a couple of sticks? What are they going to think? That I'm some fool at a fair come to beat them over the head?' He thrust the flag back at the sailmaker. 'Ship's cat could do better than that.'

I worked on a fresh piece of white cloth, drawing the skull from the ones I remembered from the memorials in St Mary's. The cutlass I borrowed from a passing pirate. I was soon surrounded by a group of admirers, nodding approval.

'That's more like it!' One of them clapped me on the back. 'Scare 'em shitless, that will! Oh,' he stopped, suddenly remembering who I was. 'Sorry, Miss. Begging your pardon.'

'I hope you're right.' I smiled as I carried on with my work. 'That's certainly my intention.'

Jessop stitched my design on to black cloth. Now we were truly ready to go on the account. Broom was delighted. He ordered the new colours raised, to signal our intent, and the sails set. The tide was at the full, just starting to turn, and a fair wind had sprung up to take us out of Cutlass Bay. Broom was setting a course for the Windward Channel between Cuba and Hispaniola. We would hang in the sea roads there, waiting for a fat merchantman sailing to or from the Islands. They were as common as chickens in a hen yard and moved about as fast, according to Vincent, so it would not be long before we took our first prize.

An invisible line divides the outlaw from the law abiding. Just being on the ship did not put us beyond it, but once we took part in an engagement, that would change everything. I put it to Minerva that we could still leave if we wanted, that the Articles were not binding upon us. She did not answer, but set her gaze resolutely seaward. Our piratical lives had begun.

21

You never forget the first attack. I was cotton-mouthed and terrified, standing at the ready, waiting to hear the two ships grind and splinter together. The waiting is the worst of it. I've seen strong men turn pale as porridge, and dash to the heads to relieve themselves, or vomit over the side. No one makes any comment. No one mocks or jeers at them, even these men who seem to laugh in the face of death itself. They stare straight ahead, gripping weapons and grappling hooks, half pikes, axes and hatchets. Sometimes, Broom ordered drums and cymbals to add to the clamour, or the cannons fired, filling the air with the reek of powder, so we boarded the prize through blinding billows of smoke. Once on the ship, then it was different. Our own fear did not compare with the terror we instilled in the ordinary crew and passengers. We would board with reckless boldness, and if the prize offered resistance, it was kill or be killed.

I stood with Minerva as our first fight came, pistols primed and slung about me, my cutlass honed sharp as a razor, my axe hanging heavy from a loop on my belt. I could not keep my legs from shaking, and my knuckles were white from gripping the rail, but Minerva had a stillness about her; her features remained calm and expressionless. I'd seen the look before, on the faces of Phillis and Thomas and the other slaves when confronted by Duke in his fury. It was not resignation, more a refusal to show any reaction to whatever fate was about to enfold her.

I was green and sick with nervousness. She put her hand on mine to steady me, whispering through the cannons' roar.

'We will watch out for each other. We will not be afraid.'

We leaped the gap between the ships together, ready to fight and die for each other, but the fight was soon over. We had barely engaged, when the company surrendered to a man. The ship was an ordinary merchant vessel and those aboard her had not signed on to fight with pirates.

They offered no resistance, but after they had laid down their weapons, I barely reached the rail. Minerva found me spewing over the side.

'Are you all right?'

'Fine.' I wiped my mouth. 'I was frightened, that's all. And . . .'

'And?'

'One of the officers looks a little like William.'

'Oh?' Minerva regarded the captured group with renewed interest. 'Which one?'

'The mate.'

Minerva grinned and nodded approvingly. 'He is handsome.'

'It's not funny, Minerva.' I turned away from her. 'What if it had been him? What would he think of me? Dressed like this? A pirate? And there is more . . .' The bile rose in my throat again at the thought of it. 'He would be an enemy. He could be killed. By me.'

My words sobered Minerva. 'But he is in the Navy,' she said after some thought. 'Broom would not attack a Navy ship.' She looked at me. 'It is more likely that they would attack *us*.' Her words brought little comfort. I had not thought of that. 'Let's hope it does not come to it,' she added. 'The sea is wide. There is no reason why we should encounter his very ship. You must put all this out of your mind. This life is new to us, but we have no choice but to follow it. It's best not to worry about tomorrow, but to live one day at a time.'

Each attack took the same pattern. I tried to follow Minerva's advice. I put all thoughts of William out of my mind and, as one attack followed another, I lost my terror and became as fearless as the rest of the men. We sailed under false colours, a painted canvas dropped over our gun ports. Once a ship was sighted, we would make for her as a dog runs down a sheep. Sometimes Minerva and I would walk about the deck, wearing our women's apparel, so as not to alert the captain and crew of the other vessel as they viewed us through their spyglasses. We would close rapidly, being quicker in the water than most merchantmen, and as soon as we were within gun range, the false colours were hauled down, the black flag hoisted. A warning shot was fired and the gunners made ready to load chain shot to bring down the sails and rigging, grape shot and canister shot to cut through the crew. They rarely resorted to a broadside because that would damage the prize. Merely the sight of us was enough for most captains to strike their colours. To resist was to invite wholesale slaughter, that everyone knew.

Broom watched us to see how we performed. Minerva and I could expect no special treatment, he made that very clear, but he was a good captain and a canny one. He knew how to get the best from his crew. Minerva swarmed up the rigging as though born to it and her agility and balance made her as sure-footed aloft as she was on deck. Her fearlessness in attack and her marksmanship singled her out from the ordinary. Broom made her a sharpshooter, and when the attack came she would be hanging in the rigging with Vincent and the others, ready to shoot out the captain, officers and helmsman on any ship that saw fit to resist. I feared for her, for the sharpshooters were clear targets, and I dreaded seeing her tumble to the deck like a broken gull, but I learned to put such thoughts away and concentrate on the fight ahead.

Broom did not set foot on the prize until the vessel was secured, the captain and his officers disarmed and guarded, the rest of the crew and any passengers herded together on another part of the deck. Once this was done, he came aboard as if his visit were a courtesy, enquiring of the captain as to his port of origin, where he was bound and what he was carrying. Then he asked if there were any valuables, in the way of money, or bullion, adding in a quiet voice that if the captain lied, it would be the worse for him, his crew and his ship. Broom was mild compared to other pirate captains, but his outward show of affability could be far more chilling than displays of fiercesomeness.

The ship was thoroughly plundered. Every single useful thing was taken off her. Cargo, valuables, small arms, guns, supplies and equipment, personal effects. The most prized finds were gold and silver, jewellery and coin, but the days of treasure ships were long over. We were more likely to find sugar, rum or cocoa, or cloth and household goods, all depending on the direction in which the ship was heading, and whether she was on an outward or inward voyage.

Whatever was found had to be given up to the quartermaster, on pain of marooning, and an inventory was kept. Broom was as strict as my father on that, and since I could read, write with a clear hand, and figure, more and more it became my job to keep these records.

Minerva and I were accepted as part of the crew. We worked alongside them and shared our mess with them, but we slept away from the rest.

'Shipmates they may be,' Minerva said as she slung up her hammock, 'but they are still men.'

So we set up a place apart where we could be private. Jan Jessop rigged screens so we could dress and undress away from prying eyes and we hung sailcloth to catch rain water for our ablutions and to wash our clothes and linen. We stood guard one for the other when we bathed or used the heads. No one offered us any insult; the knives in our belts saw to that. We shared duties and stood watches, the same as any other. We neither sought nor received any favours, but when time on deck was over it was a relief to retreat to our quarters and to our own company.

I had never slept in a hammock before. Minerva took to it right away, but I continued to find it strange. Most of the time, I was so tired that I slept soundly, but one night, try as I might, I could not get comfortable. I eventually fell into a troubled sleep, made fitful by dreaming. I woke, eyes wide, bathed in sweat. It was a hot night, and stuffy below. I began to climb out of the hammock, but my movement disturbed Minerva.

'What's the matter?' she whispered.

'I cannot sleep. I'm going up on deck.'

There was a soft thud as her bare feet hit the floor. 'I'll come with you.'

'I had the dream again,' I said, as we gained the deck.

'About the Brazilian?'

I nodded.

She led me away from the watch, up towards the starboard bow. The night was clear, the air cooling to my sweating skin. The ship held steady in a gentle westerly, cutting her way through the black sea. Above us, a great spangle of stars filled the sky from horizon to horizon.

'He will come after me. He could be putting to sea this minute.'

'How can you be sure?'

'I heard the ship in my dream. The rattle of the anchor chain. The hush of her moving through the water.'

'But you don't *know*. "Don't fear tomorrow, till today's done with you." That's what Phillis would say.' Minerva paused. 'Did you do what she asked? Did you put the necklace away from you?' She looked at me. 'You didn't, did you?' I shook my head. 'Phillis is wise. What she says comes to pass. You should heed her.'

'But it is so *valuable*.' I turned away to hide my guilt and anguish. 'This new life is uncertain. Full of danger. Who knows when we might have need of it? It seemed foolish to cast it away in such circumstances.'

Minerva nodded, as if she could see the wisdom of that. 'Where is it?'

I put my hand to my waist. 'Here in my belt.'

'Perhaps you are uneasy because you wear it so close to you. Give it to Broom for safekeeping. Then it may cease to trouble you.'

I felt better straightaway.

'That is what I will do,' I said. 'First thing in the morning.'

Minerva smiled. Sometimes, she showed as much wisdom as her mother.

'I'm not as brave as you, Minerva,' I confided. 'Some things in this new life frighten me.'

'I am not brave.' Minerva gripped the rail. 'I feel fear as much as you. But when we attack, I think that they have come to take me back. That makes me fight the harder.'

She was silent for a while, as though she had other things to say, but when I turned to her expectantly, she just smiled and suggested that we go back to our hammocks and get some rest, or we would be too tired to work in the morning.

* ★ ★ ★

I did as Minerva said. Broom's eyes widened as he accepted the necklace from me, but he made no comment as he took it into his safekeeping.

At first, Minerva and I were hardly apart, the life being strange to us, but gradually we found our places on board. Minerva soon earned everyone's admiration.

'She's a born sailor,' Vincent remarked to me, his dark eyes following her progress aloft.

Minerva's natural sense of balance meant she could run along the top of the yards and then drop down on to the foot ropes when sent to loose or furl sail. It made me sick to look at the risks she took, but her tricks aloft earned her the regard of the men. She had an easy way with them, even joining in their rough humour, her quick tongue turning the joke back on any who sought to mock her or make fun. They were more wary of me, and I of them. Their teasing always made me blush, however much I tried to join in with their sporting and joking. My blushes made them laugh the harder, but they were less easy with me than with Minerva. She was much more accepted, treated as an equal and made welcome. Although she made one enemy.

Vincent had taken her in hand, as if she were his midshipman, teaching her the ropes, how to manage the sails, and how to navigate, by sextant and compass, by the stars at night. Vincent certainly spent a lot of time with her, but he treated her like a younger brother. It was as if he'd forgotten she was a woman, although I don't think Minerva had for a minute. She would admit to admiring him for his skills as a sailor, his bravery in action, and for being a man of mixed blood who had won the respect of everyone, but she blushed and laughed when I pointed out that he also cut a dashing figure and was undeniably handsome. His generous praise of her and the attention he gave to her did not make her popular with Charlie, the ship's boy, who had been the mate's erstwhile favourite.

Charlie was a surly lad, given to brooding, and no one took much notice of him, but he was like a leak beneath the water line that is easily overlooked and can, with time, bring a ship to grief as surely as a great hole in her side.

While Minerva was scaling the rat lines and walking the yards, I was given more mundane tasks. Assisting Broom with his logs and inventories, or helping Graham in his sick bay or surgery. Graham was adept at getting to the root of what caused pain. When he had seen to his other patients he turned his attentions to me.

'How are you taking to the piratical life?' he enquired, looking up from his mortar and pestle. 'Minerva seems happy enough, but what about you?'

'I live for the day,' I replied, repeating Minerva's advice.

'Really?' Graham grunted. 'How long can that go on?'

I shrugged. 'What other choice do I have?'

'Does the life not suit you?'

'It is not the danger, I am getting used to that. Or the work.' I looked at my chapped and callused hands. 'Although I fear these would never pass muster in my step-mother's drawing room.'

'What is it then? What is it that makes you unhappy? Apart from the fact that if we are captured we all might hang?' Graham gave a hollow laugh.

'It is, indeed, related to that.'

I confided my fears about William.

'Ah, William.' Graham smiled. 'We sent your letter to him. I gave it to the bo'sun of the *Sally-Anne*. He stayed loyal to the captain, but he owed me a favour or two. He promised to deliver it. Did William receive it, I wonder?'

'He did,' I said. Although the thought did not cheer me. 'He thinks me lost to him,' I went on, 'but I'm not! I risked everything to stay free for him, but in doing so I've become a pirate!' I put my head in my hands, hardly able to believe the tangled mess that my life had become. 'What if he finds me out here! What if he boards the ship? What will I do?'

'You worry needlessly, my dear.' Graham shook his head. 'Broom would not attack a Navy ship. If he sights one, he'll take to his heels, and this ship is swift. They would be unlikely to catch us. You are more likely to meet him in port, and then you'll be dressed as a lady and how will he know you are a pirate? Unless you tell him?'

'Perhaps he will find me too changed!' I felt for his ring, safe round my neck, heavy on its chain, and clasped it like a talisman.

'Perhaps,' Graham agreed. 'Perhaps you will find him so too. Perhaps he will find you changed for the better. When I look at you, I still see the girl that I met on the *Sally-Anne* — not much different.' He smiled. 'Her eyes still brighten when she talks about her sailor lad, like sun striking on water. She is still a little given to melancholy, and somewhat given to worry, but she has a heart that is kind and true, and a brave and generous spirit, all the better for having been tested. I also find her a little more knowledgeable about how other people live in the world, rather less given to self pity, and a great deal less selfish. Do not fret so, my dear. Any man would be lucky to have you as a wife. Pirate, or no pirate.'

I took comfort from Graham's words and began to feel a little more settled. Apart from when we were on the attack, the time on board was spent in the same way as on any other vessel. Merely keeping the ship afloat and moving through the water took constant work and effort. There was little time for idleness — Broom liked a tidy ship — but there were quiet times when the men gathered together. They would collect just at the fall of evening, as the sun was sinking, and sit about on the deck, taking a pipe or two, drinking their ration of rum or a flagon of beer, and yarn until full night came and the watch was set. Minerva and I were welcomed, shipmates like the rest, and the stories would begin.

Everyone had their own tale of how they came to be on the account. Vincent was Malagasy. He had been born on the island of Madagascar, the son of a native woman and an American pirate named Flood who had served with Captain Every. He had left the island when he was twelve years old, joining a passing merchant ship that had stopped in for fresh water. He called himself Crosby, the nearest English tongues could make of his Malagasy name. He had served on one ship, then another, until eventually he had been taken by pirates and had chosen to go on the account.

'So, I wind up following my father. Something as a boy I swore that I would never do. Swore to my mother, too. Yet here I am.'

The men would nod, recognising the vagaries of life at sea, its unpredictability. For none there had planned to go on the account. They had all started out as ordinary sailors.

Vincent would tell stories from his home, of the pirates who had settled there and the tales that they had told in turn of the fabulous Moghul wealth taken by Every: gold and silver, emeralds and pearls, diamonds as big as a fist. The men liked to hear about this. They liked tales of treasure. Dreams of such wealth cushioned the risk of being on the account and made the dangers seem worthwhile.

Others would talk of treasures they'd seen, captains they had known, but no one could match Ignatius Pelling. He had served with the best of them, so he said, the greatest pirates who ever sailed the seven seas. He'd been on the *Queen Anne's Revenge* with Edward Teach, whose heart was as black as the beard which gave him his name, and he'd been bo'sun to Stede Bonnet, who couldn't sail worth a damn, but had been a real gentleman. He'd even sailed with Black Bart Roberts.

'Dressed like a lord, he did. Give Broom a lesson or two. Legend in my own life, lads. That's what I am,' Pelling would grin, exposing a row of tobacco-stained stumps. 'Would you like to hear of it?'

Of course they would. The men sat and listened, quiet as children, while Pelling spoke of the *Queen Anne's Revenge* and how Teach sank his own ship, running her aground on a sand bar and abandoning his crew to their fate.

'Worst of the lot he was. When they caught him, he took twenty cuts and five pistol balls, and he still weren't finished.' Pelling would drop his voice then, as if other presences were gathering to listen in the growing darkness. 'Weren't natural. "Let us make a Hell of our own," said ol' Blackbeard. I heard him say it, mates. Heard him with my own ears. There's they that do believe,' Pelling's voice dropped lower, as though he sensed the phantom eavesdroppers moving closer, 'that the Devil himself were aboard Blackbeard's ship. Did I ever tell you that?' He did not wait for a response. The men nodded for him to go on. 'We were cruising off the Carolinas when the rumour spread that there was one man on board more than the crew.'

'Anyone seen him?' Charlie asked, with a note of scepticism in his voice. 'What did he look like?'

'He was seen all right. Up on deck and down below. He looked like any other fella. Sometimes like this one, sometimes like that one; but no one could give an account of who he was, or where he was from. Just before the ship was took, he disappeared.' Pelling paused. 'Queer story. But everyone on board that ship would have swore it was true.'

This story usually silenced the company. Many were new to the account and had yet to encounter captains of such legendary fury as Edward Teach, who made a friend of the Devil and defied the laws of both man and God; but this time someone spoke from the darkness.

'I heard that story before,' he began in a sibilant voice, that I didn't recognise. The speaker's English was heavily accented, as if he were Portuguese or Spanish. He must be new to the crew, I thought, from the French ship that Broom had just taken. 'A long time ago. They tell it about a privateer. A Brazilian, called Bartholomeo. He had the Devil on his ship, that's what they say, and the Devil sail with him all over the Caribbean until one day he leave. Can't stand it no more. He say the captain worse than him!' He gave a little laugh, like rusty hinges creaking. 'It is an old story, I think.'

A chill passed over me, although the night was hot. Minerva felt me shiver and looked up. At her suggestion, we searched out the man after the company broke up for the evening, wanting to know more, but there was little else he could tell us.

'He dead, for all I know. He retire from the sea many years ago. I heard he buy plantations, make a comfortable life for himself on land. Why go back?' The little man gave his creaking laugh again. 'He have no reason. Not like me. He keep his money.'

'It's just a tale,' Minerva whispered, as we lay in our hammocks. 'You know what sailors are for stories.'

I hardly heard the rest of what she was saying. I knew she was trying to lessen my fears; and her faith in the ship, and in the ability of Vincent and the others to repel any attacker, had grown a great deal since we had spoken of this before. But to me the ship's bells that tolled the hours towards morning sounded a warning, like a tocsin. We had been on the account for nearly a month, cruising about the Windward Channel, taking ship after ship, but we were hunting over the same ground. We had been laying a trail a mile wide. The sudden thought chilled me again, even though it was close below decks. Every ship taken added to Broom's reputation. He and his crew were becoming known. How long before it was also known that there were women among them? The Brazilian was far from stupid, and he had once been a buccaneer. How long before he picked up our trail? How long before he found us?

That night, when sleep eventually came, I had the dream again. I heard him laughing on the quarterdeck. I heard the crack of canvas in a freshening wind. I heard the hiss of a ship moving fast

271

through the water. I did not see the ship. It remained indistinct, a black shadow moving on the dark sea, but I could see its bow wave and its wake.

I woke with the certain knowledge that he had put to sea, and that someone had betrayed us.

I wanted to urge Broom to move to another cruising ground, but I feared that he would not agree, and neither would the council. We had done well, changing the *Deliverance* for a large French vessel that had been heading for Martinique. Renamed the *Fortune*, she had been joined by two sloops: smaller, swifter vessels that allowed us to hunt as a pack. All three ships were stuffed to the gunnels with plunder. Minerva could not see why Broom would change course on the say-so of a dream of mine, and I had a feeling that she was right, but I was determined to ask him.

I found him in his cabin with Pelling, going through the manifest of what was on board the three vessels.

'Rum, sugar, molasses, spices.' He ran a finger down a column. 'What's the use of that? We might as well be shipping coals to Newcastle. Cloth, combs, buttons, thimbles, scissors, shoemakers' knives. It reads like the contents of a peddler's pack.' He threw his quill on the table. 'I did not go on the account for that.'

'I got an idea, Cap'n.' Pelling stepped forward.

Broom looked up, expectant. The quartermaster on a pirate ship holds a special position. There is no one like him on an ordinary vessel. He is chosen by the men and stands between them and the captain, bringing their grievances to his attention. Pelling was held in high regard, not least because of his experience. He had been a pirate for longer than any on the ship, ten years by his counting. To have escaped hanging for so long was enough to compel the respect of everyone. Being new to the account, Broom relied on Pelling. The crew had made Broom captain, but they could just as easily be rid of him. Pelling had come to say that the men were getting restless. They wanted paying, and in gold and silver. Broom had to find a way of turning the cargo into money and quick. The men would not wait much longer.

'I was thinking,' Pelling went on. 'About the time when I was in the Carolinas, with Teach and Bonnet . . .'

Broom looked impatient. He did not enjoy Pelling's stories as much as his crew did.

'Well, it's just we did a deal of trading while we was there. All along the seaboard, in fact, from Charlestown to Baltimore.'

'Hmm.' Broom leaned back, considering.

'Avid to buy, they are, and just as keen not to pay a penny to the revenue. We could sell the lot, no trouble at all, and at good prices. Got another idea,' he thrust a thumb at me, 'relating to her and t'other one . . .'

'Go on.' Broom was all ears now. 'I'm listening . . .'

Pelling's idea appealed to Broom. Not only did it offer a way to turn a profit, but it gave him a new role to act and, showman that he was, he liked that. It appealed to me, too, seeming the perfect way to give the Brazilian the slip, but I was not sure how it would be received by Minerva.

22

Pelling's plan was simple. All we had to do was take what we had acquired so far, sail up the eastern seaboard as regular merchantmen and sell our cargoes to the Americans. When that was done, we would go to New York, divide up the profits and break up the company. To make our pose as honest traders all the more convincing, Broom ordered the name of the ship to be changed to the *Neptune*. He changed his own name to Abraham, shaved off his piratical beard and moustache, laid aside his silk and satin in favour of plain linen, woollen vest and breeches and a sea coat of blue broadcloth. Minerva and I had a vital part to play. We would revert to women's clothes and take up our roles. I would be Broom's niece, Minerva my companion.

The crew had got used to seeing us as men, so when we stepped on to the quarterdeck dressed in female apparel we were greeted with hoots of laughter and a good deal of ribald comment.

'Enough of that!' Broom bawled down at the crew. 'That's my niece and my ward, an heiress from Barbados. I'm taking 'em back to England to finish their education, and I'll have 'em treated with respect!'

It had taken a great deal of persuasion before Minerva would consent to take on this role. Pelling's original idea was for her to play my slave. She utterly refused, and I could not blame her. She'd risked death without a second thought; but to go back to being a slave, even as a pretence, would be a death of a different sort. Broom persuaded her in the end by telling her about a Barbadian heiress who had taken passage on one of his ships.

'Very rich, she was. Going to England to finish her education. You'll be a lady. Equal to Nancy, here. Superior, in fact. She can act as *your* companion.'

Pelling's plan worked better than we could have dreamed. Women on board added credence to Broom's claim that we were honest traders, sailing in convoy out of fear of attack from the pirates who lurked off the coast. In Charlestown, the crew roistered in the inns and drinking dens, no different from sailors anywhere, while Captain Abraham, his niece and his charge, Surgeon Graham and the other ship's officers were entertained by the finest families. Charlestown held a promise of elegance, and the people were generous and hospitable, although they did not know quite what to make of Minerva. They treated her with the utmost politeness, but drew away when she moved among them, as though a panther walked in their midst, which served to make her distant and haughty. She spoke little, but when she did, she sounded like me, which they found even more confusing. None of them expected a person of her colour to sound like a lady.

We joined in with Broom's play-acting for the business we were doing, but I could see it made Minerva unhappy, and I was ever more aware of the risk we were taking. Broom wanted me to dress very fine, and even urged me to wear the ruby necklace. This I refused to do. I had developed a deep superstitious fear of it; the very feel of it on my skin set me shuddering. The middle stone was larger than the others. Smooth and rounded, slightly darker at the centre, like a great crimson eye. I know it was foolish, but I began to fancy that he could watch me when I wore it, so I would not put it around my neck. Broom persuaded me into the earrings, however, and I consented to wear those, since they were rich enough to excite admiration, but not so ostentatious that any might take us for thieves or sea robbers.

Pirates were hardly welcome here.

Blackbeard's head had been brought into Bathtown hanging from a bowsprit and Major Bonnet and his crew had been hung at White Point. The people of Charlestown were proud of the part that they had played in bringing these men of blood (as they saw them) to justice; they were prouder still of the fact that the famous female pirate, Anne Bonny, had begun her career out of the Carolinas. I duly gasped and threw up my hands and did my best to express my amazement and horror at behaviour so unnatural, while wondering what the town's good people would do if they knew that they entertained just such another.

We did brisk trade wherever we went. Not just in the towns, but with the plantations which were growing up along the creeks and inlets of the coast of the Carolinas. The planters were no less hospitable, inviting us to dine with them and attend their parties and balls. Female presence, and Broom's gentlemanly appearance, were enough to prevent any from suspecting who we really were, and allowed us to command the highest prices for our stolen chattels.

We cruised on to Baltimore and New York. Both proved more workaday ports than Charlestown, like to my own town of Bristol, although their streets and docks were not crowded in by the past. There was a newness here which held promise. I had a feeling that it was possible to arrive as one person and swiftly become quite another. For pirates, such places hold possibility.

When we reached New York, Broom broke up the company. The spoils were divided, each man receiving his share of a hoard that was considerably more than the £1000 agreed in the Articles. After the share out, the crew dispersed as fast as rats from a ship on fire. Some, who had a mind to become lubbers, headed off up the Hudson, for there was much land to be had in America and their money would buy them a fair acreage. Others left for the north: to Rhode Island, or the ports of New Haven, Boston, Salem, Nantucket and New Bedford to carry on a seafaring way of life: fishing, whaling, honest trading, or going back on the account.

Most, however, went no further than the New York waterfront. They would be back with us after spending their money on drink, or losing it in some gambling den, or having it stolen by the New York whores who plied their trade on Petticoat Lane.

23

We took lodgings with a widow woman in a fine big Dutch-gabled house on Pearl Street. Broom needed time to negotiate the sale of the ships he no longer required, he said. Besides, he had business to conduct. Pelling grumbled. Staying in one place made him nervous. I was tired of the play-acting and shared his nervousness. We'd had no word about the Brazilian, and Broom had roundly dismissed my dreams and any threat from him, but I did not share his complacency. He was out there, prowling the coast somewhere, I was sure of it. For all I knew, he could sail into New York any day and tie up in the berth next to ours. And if I was weary of keeping up the pretence, Minerva was nearing mutiny. She hated the stares and whispers she attracted, saying she felt as though she had been taken from a menagerie and was being led about on a chain by me. There were many people of colour, both slave and free, but they were all treated as inferior in New York — as much as in the colonies to the south.

'I'm tired of this,' she told me. 'I could buy this house and everything in it, yet that woman treats me as if I were a servant, although she knows very well that I am not. I'm thinking of going back to the ship.'

She was staring out of our window at the ships moored on the river, concentrating her gaze on the sloop tied up just below us.

'What will I tell Broom?'

'Tell him what you like. But that's what I'm going to do.' She turned and gave me a brilliant smile, suddenly more cheerful than I'd seen her in a long while.

'I'll help you pack.'

'Don't need to.' Her smile broadened. 'You don't think I'm going like this, do you?' She spread the wide silk skirt of her dress. 'There are plenty of clothes on board. And if I'm in need of finery, then Vincent can lend me some of his.'

Vincent lived on board the sloop. He was captain of the ship in Broom's absence. She was going to leave me and go back to dressing as a man. I sat down on the bed, feeling suddenly lonely. I'd be on my own for the first time in months.

'I wish I could come with you.'

'Well, you can't. Broom would never

allow it. Besides, the landlady might recognise you — we're moored right outside her parlour window.'

'What about you?' I was piqued, and not a little bit jealous.

'I'm safer than you are. She wouldn't look twice at another mulatto tar. Don't look like that!' She took me in her arms and hugged me to her. 'Will you miss me?'

'Of course I will!'

'Chin up.' She tipped my chin with her finger. 'Now smile. That's better. I'll miss you, too.'

But if she did, I noticed no signs of it. The next time I saw her she was dressed as a sailor, an old acquaintance of Vincent's newly met in a tavern, his good friend, Jupiter Jones. They both gave me a wave, blowing kisses up to my window as they went into the port. They were of a height and looked well together, matching stride for easy stride. They both dressed alike and wore gold hoops in their ears, their long curling hair tied back with red ribands. Minerva had borrowed Vincent's blue coat with the gold shiny buttons and scarlet bars and looked very handsome in it. I watched them go into the town, heads bent together in easy conversation, and I longed to join them.

But I was left behind, as lonely and confined as a princess in a tower. On the deck of the sloop, I could see Charlie, the ship's boy, gazing after them with brooding devotion, waiting for Vincent's return like a dog tied up at a rail.

The year was turning. In the day, the heat was oppressive, the stink from street and river all but overwhelming, but the mornings had the breath of winter, mist curling off the river. On the deck of the sloop, Vincent looked chilled, his skin tinged with grey. I went with Broom on one of his daily inspections and we found the mate shivering, hugging his coat around him. He had been on deck half of the night and he was not made for these climes, and nor was Minerva. They were anxious to go back on the account, and I feared they might go off on their own if Broom stayed much longer in New York.

'You will make a good captain one day, my lad.' Broom clapped him on the shoulder after his inspection. 'None better at keeping a ship in order, and none better in a fight. Best marksman I've encountered,' he turned, linking him to Minerva, 'apart from this lass here. You look after the ship better than I do myself. Loyalty like yours, what captain could ask for more?'

As Vincent looked at Minerva, a wide smile lit his handsome features. I doubted his loyalty was just to his captain. Broom needed to get a crew together as quickly as possible, or he might wake to find his sloop gone.

Broom was sailing close to the wind, according to Pelling. Sooner or later someone would be on to him, but the captain would not move yet. He was acquiring a new schooner, and when he was not at the boat yard, he spent his time in the taverns on Wall Street, drinking rum punch and smoking Long Island tobacco, talking business with various new associates, negotiating to buy land as the town expanded north up Manhattan Island towards Niew Haarlem. He advised us to invest our money, too, or at least to leave our share with a Dutch banker, Fredrick Brandt.

'No good burying it in the sand like Kidd, or carting it about to be thieved, or it ending up at the bottom of the sea.'

That's what Broom told me, and I passed the message on to Minerva. Our shares would be deposited together. Broom told Graham to do the same, but the doctor was undecided. He could see the sense of it, but feared being cheated. When he was done with the sea, he wanted to set himself up in practice in Bath, or London, or Edinburgh. I thought he would welcome any scheme that would keep his money safe. I told him that I judged the idea a good one. My father had deposited money with bankers in London, so that he might draw on funds more easily. Banking was an ordinary part of commerce and trade, a way of keeping money secure and enabling funds to be released as and when they were needed through notes and promises to pay.

We resolved to go with Broom to sound out Mr Brandt. In turn, Broom wanted me dressed in my best, to impress the banker, so that he could see that we were wealthy and that I was a lady. Broom said it made him feel more confident. I needed a new dress and bonnet, and went in search of the best that New York could afford. I would have wished for Minerva to help with the choosing, but I could hardly have taken a young sailor lad along with me. When I presented myself to Broom, he was delighted.

'A picture, my dear. You look a picture. Just put this on and the ensemble is complete.'

He held out the ruby necklace. I took it with reluctance, but I duly obliged.

We met the Dutchman in the private room of a Wall Street inn. He was tall and thin, exquisitely dressed in a dove-grey coat, with matching breeches and high shiny boots only slightly mired by the New York streets. He carried a cane, wore an immaculate, freshly-powdered wig and looked very much the gentleman.

'Appearances are not everything,' Graham whispered to me, but I felt inclined to trust the man. He had the cold eye of one who liked collecting coin and counting it.

He had interests all over the world, he said. Offices in London, Amsterdam and Rotterdam. Connections with merchants in West Africa at Whydah, in Cape Town, Bombay, Madras and Batavia.

'You may say my interests are world wide.' Brandt fixed us with his clear grey gaze. 'As I think yours may be. Your money will be safe with me. My family has acted as bankers for centuries. We accept money from anyone: kings and dukes, merchants and manufacturers, thieves and corsairs.' He laughed, as if he thought that there was no difference between any of them. 'We do not care where it comes from, or how it was acquired.' He spread his pale hands. 'It is all money. If you want to leave your funds with me, then I will take good care of them. Are we in agreement?'

'A moment,' Broom said.

Brandt left us to our deliberations, but the discussion was swift. What choice did we have? It was either leave our money with this man, or bury it in the sand, as Broom had pointed out. He called the banker back again.

'Very well, then.' Brandt extended his hand to each of us in turn. 'I have the appropriate papers already drawn up. I will protect your interests, for now they are mine, too. To that end, Captain *Abraham,*' he beckoned to Broom, 'I would have a private word with you.'

Graham and I waited on the sidewalk.

'Well, Nancy,' Broom said when we got back to Pearl Street. 'Seems I owe you an apology. Brandt tells me that a Brazilian planter and former buccaneer is hot in pursuit of a certain Miss Kington, a pretty young English heiress, late of Jamaica, who has been kidnapped by pirates and is said to be on a ship commanded by a certain Captain Broom.'

'Here. Have this.' I removed the necklace and gave it to Broom. The mere mention of the Brazilian had set me shivering, just like the first time when he had fixed the rubies round my neck. I rubbed my arms and began pacing. 'What are we going to do?'

'What do we always do? Make sail, my dear. Make sail! We have the money on deposit, our business here is concluded. I think it's time we left New York.'

Vincent had taken possession of the new schooner and was already making her ready. He had his own news to tell us and it was not good. Charlie had been acting surly and mutinous, refusing to obey orders, and now he was missing. Vincent feared that he had gone to peach us up to the authorities. I was so sure he was right that I half expected to hear the tramp of militia along the dockside. Even if we got away, our secret was out. Broom was captain of a pirate ship with women on board. We were known to be on the account. The knowledge would spread up and down the seaboard, wherever ships came into port.

We left on the very next tide, and only just in time. There was a dark ship just off Sandy Hook on the Jersey shore. She was waiting for the tide to turn in her favour so that she could enter Manhattan harbour. We spied her at a distance, as we slipped by fast in our new schooner. If she marked our passing, she showed no sign of it, but it was his ship. I knew it. The ship was black. That was why I could not see her in my dreams.

24

I was now very glad that Broom had
swapped the three-masted ship for the
schooner. She was not known to anyone, and
she was fast through the water. Pelling, however, had not approved of the exchange. A
schooner was too small, he said, with too few
guns and not enough room for either men or
supplies to sustain a long cruise. Now he had
to eat his words. The new ship's sleek lines
suggested some powerful fish, and she was
made for the water. Broom had been very
proud of her right from the start. The hull
was American oak with two masts of white
pine, each fashioned from a single tall forest
tree, to give strength and flexibility. Now he
had been proved right in his choice, which
pleased him immensely. No one could believe the speed of her. He called her the *Swift
Return*.

'These ships are going to be the thing,
Pelling. You mark my words. And worth
every penny of any man's money.' He

beamed as he strode her gleaming deck. 'Just you wait and see. This is perfect. Especially now. Let them come after us! Nothing will catch her in open sea.'

We had some new crew members, hired on by Vincent, who had been collecting men even before Brandt's news and Charlie's desertion. He had done the rounds of the dockside taverns, sweeping up those he could find from the old hands and signing up more. Not all of them knew we were pirates. Broom elected not to tell them until we were well under way. Any who did not want to sign to the Articles would be put ashore at our first port of call. In the end, they all signed. Vincent had chosen well.

Different watches kept us apart, but I had slung my hammock next to Minerva's as before. I'd sorely missed her companionship when I was left on shore in New York. On our first night off watch together, we talked long into the night about the lucky escape that we'd had, and all that had happened in New York during the time that we had spent apart. Broom was setting a course for the West Indies and Minerva was glad of that, declaring the climate would suit her better, that it was too cold in the north.

We finally exhausted our store of conversation. We had spoken of many things, but I lay in the darkness, listening to the creaking of the timbers, the sound of the water on the hull, thinking that we'd said nothing at all. I longed to ask her about Vincent and what they had done together on their jaunts into the port. Things between them had changed, I could see that. They were very close now. As close as sister and brother. Closer. Exactly how close, I wanted to know, but hesitated to ask her. There were no walls between us and the rest of the ship, just a flimsy sheet. It was impossible to know who might be listening on the other side of it. Besides, she might not tell me. She seldom revealed her feelings to anybody. I spent too long deliberating. Her even breathing told me that she was asleep. Or else she was feigning, guessing what was in my mind. I turned away from her and tried to get some sleep myself. I would be on watch in a few hours.

We were in the Straits of Florida, Cuba to our south, the weather set fair. Broom had still not declared exactly where he intended cruising, not even to Vincent. The mate was worried. The hurricane season was nearly upon us and that was not the best time to embark on a cruise. Great storms swept out of the ocean, accompanied by winds that could level a forest, rain that could wash away mountains, leaving the land wasted, as though touched by an angry god. I had seen where hurricanes had struck Jamaica. I could not imagine what such a force of nature would be like at sea. There were those on board who talked in hushed dread of bright day turned to darkest night, of waves so high that they looked like green glass mountains, of white water spread from one horizon to the other, of great spouts and towers sucked from one element into another. Any ship caught in open water would be pounded to splinters or swamped like a cockleshell. Whole fleets and convoys had disappeared altogether, with no trace ever found.

I shared the morning watch with Vincent and observed his growing unease. The dawn came clear, promising a fair day, but Vincent stood up at the prow moving from larboard to starboard, studying the water as it disappeared under the bow. The sea was deep green tinged with purple and moved with an odd motion, in great oily slow-building swells that made the ship lurch and judder.

'I don't like this,' he said, looking first at

the sky and then at the sails to check the wind direction.

The wind was brisk, nothing out of the ordinary, but it seemed at odds with the direction of the waves.

'Look up there.' Vincent focused his spyglass upon a flock of birds, flying so high we could not hear their cries. They flecked the sky, wheeling and turning in random confusion, like ash whirling up from a fire.

'We are not far from land,' I pointed out. 'To east or west or south of us . . .'

He shook his head with impatience. 'They are not sea birds. They are birds of passage. Something has disturbed them from their normal course.' He collapsed the spyglass and ordered: 'Away aloft! Shorten topsail! Bring in sail fore and aft.'

Sailors jumped to, scurrying up the rat lines into the rigging, hurrying to roll up canvas, manning the ropes to haul in the yards so there was less sail for the wind to catch. This slowed the ship considerably and brought Broom from his cabin demanding to know what the devil was going on.

'Storm coming, Captain,' Vincent replied.

Broom scowled his disbelief, but before he had time to speak the wind veered and freshened.

'By God. I think you might be right!'

'Look there, Cap'n!' One of the topmen shouted from the main topmast yard-arm. As he spoke, his hat blew off, scudding over the rising waves like a bird. He shouted again, the wind snatching his words, scattering them around us in meaningless syllables. The wind was strengthening by the second, whining and moaning through the rigging like some malevolent spirit. The men aloft clung to the yard-arm and pointed to a long black bank looming on the southern horizon, like a great mass of land where no land should be.

'Topmen!' Broom roared above the rising voice of the storm. 'Shorten sail! You men bring in the yards! Look lively!' He leaned over the quarterdeck as all hands jumped to. 'We'll outrun this. Helmsman! Fine on the starboard bow! Pray to any gods you know, boys. We will see what she can do!'

Broom was to prove his seamanship that day. He might have had his faults, but he knew how to sail. The men might quibble and grumble, but none doubted him. The crew worked with unfailing strength and unquestioning obedience. He would pit himself, and us, against the weather with the same daring and dissembling swagger that marked him out as a pirate, but the storm that threatened was beyond common experience, almost beyond human capacity to survive.

The wind was coming from the south, pushing us like a huge hand. We battled to take in sail, all hauling together.

'Cap'n is heading for the Bahamas,' Vincent shouted in my ear. 'Going for the shelter of the islands.'

I nodded to show that I'd heard. I did not want to waste effort on words. The wind was screaming as if all the demons from hell were loosed upon us and the sky was black as night above us now. The sea was being whipped to a frothing mass of white breaking water, the air about us full of spray. Flashes of lightning illuminated a world turned upside-down. The deck fell away as we mounted one vertiginous wave after another. At the top of each, the great ship seemed to skim, flying like flotsam on the breaking spume, only to be cast down into such a tremendous gulf that our own element was lost from us. We were surrounded on all sides by great cliffs of black shining water, as if we were being thrown into some pit of the deep never to see sky again. Overwhelmed by the elements and paralysing terror, I clung on to the cordage, unable to do anything. It felt as if I were drowning. The very air was sucked away, taken by huge waves that then broke over me in torrents of frothing water. The crowded deck was suddenly empty, scoured of everything that had not been tied down. Full barrels and heavy crates were dislodged and tossed over the side as if they weighed no more than buckets and bird cages.

The strength of the wind and waves bent the huge masts like bows, threatening to snap them in two or rend them from their footings. Minerva was with the men who had been sent aloft to work on yards as slick as glass and ropes as twisting and slippery as live snakes. The ship bucked and plunged under her as she fought with the others to furl sails made many times heavier with water; all the while being torn at by winds which threatened to pluck her from her perch and cast her into the churning maelstrom, never to be seen again. Down on deck, we could not see how she or any of them fared; we could not even hear the cries of any flung down into the deep. She is nimble, she is strong, and she will come back to me. I chanted it in my mind like a litany, praying for her safety and that of the others aloft.

The ship was suddenly hit by a tremendous wave from starboard, which sent her yawing sideways, as if she had been cuffed by some giant paw. I found myself clinging on for my life as the deck fell away from under my feet, and became vertical beneath me. All thought left me as I saw the opposite rail dip beneath the waves. She was going beam-ends. She would be swamped, all would be lost. My heart stopped within me, then slowly, very slowly, she began to right herself. With a great sucking sound the sea released her and she bobbed back as if made of cork.

I waited with dread for the next great wave to tip us over, but although the ship leaned heavily, her side did not touch the water. The storm went raging on, but gradually its grip on us began to slacken, each buffet less powerful than the one before. The ship still pitched and plummeted, but she was riding the waves; even the constant screaming of the wind became less insistent, until it was possible to hear human shouts and cries through the roar.

The men came limping down from the rigging, falling the last couple of feet on to the deck. With them was Minerva. I ran to her, but Vincent was there before me. He helped her to her feet. Her legs buckled and he caught her, holding her in his arms, cradling her head against his shoulder. He wiped the water and spray from her face, pushing back the hair that had escaped her cap. He looked down at her, smiling his relief that she was safe, and I thought for a second that he would kiss her, but he did not. Perhaps he thought that it was not the best moment, surrounded as they were by sailors and crew. He held her away from him, clasping her by the shoulders, gazing at her as if she were some fragile thing delivered back to him unbroken. She looked up at him and my questions of the night before were answered in that one glance. He murmured to her and she nodded. It was as if the world about them were not there any more. The chaos wrought by the storm, the torn sails, the broken spars, the exhausted and injured men, did not exist for them.

'Mr Crosby!' They were roused by Broom's shout from the quarterdeck. 'A moment of your time, Sir! The ship's been through a little difficulty. There's work to do. Miss Kington! Perhaps you could assist Miss Sharpe there!'

Vincent and Minerva looked about them as if they were waking from a dream. Their discomfort raised a weak laugh from the crew around them and I went to help Minerva down below decks.

I took her to our quarters, for we were both soaked to the skin and weak with exhaustion. We were glad of the darkness and privacy that below decks afforded, for neither of us could keep from shaking and we clung to each other, weeping most unpiratical tears of relief and joy to have survived and both be alive. She had been as terrified as I, but had not been able to show her fear, or even acknowledge it. A failure of nerve on the topyards means death. It all came flooding out now. I held her, sobbing in my arms, and scolded myself for feeling jealous, excluded by the closeness that had grown between her and Vincent.

Broom ordered stoves lit below decks to dry bedding and clothing. The men were allowed to rest. Minerva slept. I watched her sleeping face and thought about her and Vincent. That they might be lovers served to remind me of how alone I was, and made me long for William. I had convinced myself that if I could only explain to him how and why I had fallen into this way of life, then he would surely believe me and most certainly forgive me, and

probably love me better than he had before. Deep in my heart, I was not at all
sure that this was true; he might just as
easily reject me. I brooded on that as we
sailed to quieter waters. Abe Reynolds
went the rounds with measures of rum to
warm and hearten the men. I sipped my
tot as I lay in my hammock. Even thinking
of being with William, telling him all the
things that had happened to me, made me
love him more.

We were between Andros Island and
Grand Bahama. The men threw back their
rum and any who wanted it was given another, but all celebration was postponed
until we reached port. The wind had slackened in the lee of the land, but the sky to
the west was still ominous: ragged
streamers flew out from black banking
cloud, like riders trailing banners. If the
wind veered, the storm would turn our way
again. We had to make safe harbour or we
would be caught and driven on to the islands whose shelter we sought.

The nearest safe anchorage was Nassau,
on New Providence.

No pirate would normally set a course
for Nassau. The port had been a pirate
haven, but Woodes Rogers had cleared it
out. Wholesale arrests and mass hangings

made it a graveyard for those on the account, but we had no choice but to go there. The American schooner had repaid Broom's faith during the storm. Even Pelling had to concede that. Anything older, or heavier in the water, would have gone down. Nonetheless, one of the masts was damaged. Sails were torn and wanted patching. There was a leak below the water line, so the ship needed constant pumping, and the men were in need of respite. If another tempest hit us, we would not survive.

We had to find port, no doubt about it, but if any of us had known what fate awaited us, we would have taken our chances on the high seas.

25

The storm had all but died as we sailed into Nassau harbour. We were not the only ship that had run there for safety. The harbour was dotted with vessels of all kinds: frigates, brigantines, sloops and snows, showing the flags of half a dozen different nations. We edged into our berth as day gave way to night. Excitement rippled through the ship. Once we were secured and the watch set, Broom would allow the men into the port. The celebrations would begin.

He rang the ship's bell and called the men to him.

'Any ship is only as good as the men on her. If it weren't for you, we'd have foundered.' He drew a purse from his pocket, chinking the coins together. 'I'll thank you all to join me in sampling whatever entertainment this town can afford!'

Someone called for a round of three, and one deep-throated hurrah followed another. Broom stood, hands on the rail, grinning down at them. He was a fair man and generous. Most of the men had served under captains who gave them nothing but curses, beatings and haughtiness. That was not Broom's style. By rewarding their hard work, he won their loyalty, even their love.

The men changed out of their ragged shipboard rig and into the clothes they kept for a run on shore. Broom donned his finery and went with them, leaving Vincent and Graham and a handful of crew: Jessop the sailmaker, with Joby to help him, and Gabe the carpenter, for there was work to do repairing the ship from the ravages of the storm.

Minerva and I stayed on board. I stood at the rail looking across the black water of the harbour. Lights spilled from the windows and open doors of the straggle of buildings stretching along the dockside, shining in the water as if there were another town mirrored there. I thought of Port Royal and the story my father had told me about how, back in the time of the buccaneers, half the town had slipped into the sea as the result of some terrible earthquake. God's judgement, so some had called it, on the wickedest place in the world. I thought of the drowned town that lay beneath the waves, the church bells tolling in the restless currents. It was as if that town were calling up to me.

'What is it?' Minerva came to lean on the rail next to me.

'I don't know,' I replied. Although I had no name for it, I tried to explain what I felt. We had been brought so close to death, and it had affected me. I could be dead now. At the bottom of the sea. So could Minerva. My initial relief had given way to another stranger set of feelings. A kind of melancholy, laced with recklessness.

Minerva listened, frowning. Then she said, 'Perhaps we should go into town.'

'Dressed as men?'

My male disguise had been confined to the ship. Until now.

'Of course. Why not? When I leave the ship, I go as Jupiter Jones. You can be . . .' she paused before naming me, '. . . Davey. Davey Gordon.'

'But what shall I wear?' I had only working clothes, stiff with salt and smelling of tar.

She smiled and her eyes sparked mischief. 'Come with me. We will raid Vincent's chest.'

'Won't he mind?'

She smiled. 'It was his idea.'

Vincent was quite as much of a dandy as Broom and his trunk was full to bursting with the finest clothes to be found on the ships that he had taken. We sorted through his collection and Minerva picked out a jacket for me and a waistcoat of deep plum velvet, a cream silk shirt and black satin breeches, white stockings, and black shoes with silver buckles.

'You look very well, very well indeed,' she said as I threaded the latchlets of my shoes.

Then it was my turn. I asked her to wear the blue coat with red bars, because it was my favourite, matched with white breeches, a snowy lace-fronted shirt with long trailing cuffs, a stock of white satin, and a black silk waistcoat.

'How do I look?' She peered into the cracked glass of the small round mirror that Broom used when he shaved, trying to see her reflection.

'I've never seen a *man* more handsome,' I grinned at her. 'You lack only one thing.'

I went to my trunk and took the ruby earrings from it.

Minerva took them, fixing one in her ear. The earring glowed against her skin, swinging as she moved her head, distilling the light to a deep rich brightness. A man would never dare to wear such a thing. It made her look even more handsome. The Brazilian had been wrong to think that white was the colour to show off the jewels' perfection.

'Handsome? I'll show you handsome.' Minerva held up the other earring for me to wear. She turned the mirror for me to see and smiled. 'We make a handsome pair.'

When we appeared on deck, even Vincent was lost for words. He opened his mouth and closed it again, staring, looking from one to the other. We asked his permission to leave the ship, and I thought for a moment that he would not give it.

'I know I said dress up, but —' He spread his hands.

'Why?' We looked at each other. 'What's the matter?'

'Nothing's the matter. Not the matter as such.' Vincent spent so long with Broom he was beginning to talk like him. He started to pace up and down. 'I wish I could come with you, that's all.'

'What for?'

'To protect you, of course.'

'From what?' Minerva parted her coat. 'We're well armed. What man is going to give us trouble?'

'It's not the *men* I'm worried about,' he said, laughing, and gave us permission to leave the ship.

As we walked along the quay, I felt a little unsteady, as if I were half drunk, although I had hardly touched a drop of liquor. Out in the harbour, the ships rocked on their moorings. The swell washing in from the open sea made their bells ring and their swinging lanthorns set little reflections dancing across the blackness like will o' the wisps. I thought of the mirror world and melancholy tugged at me again. The wind had died now, the night air was warm about us. White stars blazed across the sky. I looked up at them, reading the constellations, wanting to set a course that would take us far away from everyone and everything, to a place where we could live together without danger and be free.

'What are you thinking?' Minerva asked.

'Oh, I don't know.' I thrust my hands in my pockets. 'I was thinking of a song. About a magical ship with ropes of silk and sails of silver and a mast made from the rowan tree. I was thinking how good it would be to set sail in her and steer for the sun and the moon and the stars.'

Minerva looked away from me. To the harbour.

'Do you regret the turns your life has taken?'

I didn't answer, because I didn't know.

'We're set on a strange course,' she said. 'There's no denying it. We live lives that are not ordinary and never will be.'

'Sometimes I feel alone,' I began. 'I've cut myself off from everything I have known. Everyone I cared for, or who cared for me. It frightens me.'

'How are you alone?' She turned to me, her face silvered by the rising moon. 'You have me. I love you, Nancy. You are more than my friend, you are like a sister . . .' She stopped suddenly and looked at me. I thought she would say more, but instead she put her arm round my shoulders and pulled me towards the tavern door. 'Come on, tonight is not a night for melancholy. We should find our shipmates.'

26

'Welcome, young sirs.' The young woman looked us over. 'Welcome, indeed!'

She caught us both by the shoulder, steering us to an empty table. She was tall, with fine fair hair, and the face of an angel, but there was devilry in the tilt of her blue eyes and the curve of her smile.

'I'm Alice. Alice Castle. This is my establishment. Polly!' She sat down with us and called to another young woman. 'Bring us something to drink here! Make sure it's the good stuff!' She leaned back, her stare both bold and appraising. 'We'll have a drop to drink, then we'll keep company. I haven't seen fellas as fine as you two for a very long time.'

Polly brought rum and sat down to join us. She was younger than her friend, with thick dark curling hair, bright blue eyes and a wide smile.

'Now, let's get acquainted, shall we?'

Alice looked to each of us as we introduced ourselves.

'Pleased to make your acquaintance, Davey and Jupiter.' Alice caught Minerva's ruby earring in her hand. 'There's a pretty bauble.' Her finger traced the line of the jaw down to the lips. 'Suits you very well.' She leaned closer. 'No need to be unfriendly. What does a girl have to do to sit on your knee? That's better.'

Minerva moved to accommodate her, put her arms round the girl's waist and whispered in her ear. Alice giggled and gave her a friendly cuff. Minerva ducked her head and smiled back. The earring caught the light as it swung, and I wondered what she'd said. She was much better at this than I was, but then she'd had more practice.

'My, what fine skin you have.' Polly touched my cheek. 'And so smooth! What most girls would give to have such skin!'

She leaned closer towards me, her arms going round me, under my coat. I turned my head away, putting my hands on hers, to stop them roaming further.

'Don't you like me?' she asked.

'It's not that,' I said. 'It's —'

'Perhaps,' she glanced over at Alice and Minerva, who were looking at me now. 'Perhaps you would prefer someone else.'

'No!' I shook my head, drawing away from her. 'It's not that, honest! It's just that we . . .'

'. . . are promised,' Minerva said quickly. 'We both have sweethearts waiting for us.'

'Now that is a pity.' Alice looked over at her companion. 'Both promised in marriage. And so young and handsome. That's a shame for the rest of us, eh, Poll?'

Polly nodded. 'It's what I call a real waste.'

'But we'll pay,' Minerva said, taking a bag of gold from her pocket. 'Escudo. Louis d'or. Silver dollars. Pieces of eight.' She rolled the coins across the table. 'For conversation. And your company.'

'This'll be an easy night, and no mistake.' Alice smiled as she stacked the coins. 'You off that schooner that just came in?'

Minerva nodded.

'Thought so,' Alice winked. 'Dressed like a dandy with money burning through your pocket. I can always tell.' She refilled her own glass, then Minerva's. 'Terrible storm this morning. Played havoc with the ships in the harbour and flattened a row of houses on the edge of town. Died down now, but there'll be another one behind it, I shouldn't wonder.'

'That's what brought us in here. We had to find shelter.'

Alice smiled. 'Not the healthiest place for you, if I might say so.' She looked round at the rest of the company. 'Still, it's nice to see gentlemen of fortune in again. It's not been the same since they left. Calico Jack, Black Bart Roberts, even old Blackbeard himself. They all used to call here. Business has fallen off something chronic. We're thinking of moving on. Ain't we, Polly?'

But Polly wasn't listening. 'Do you hear that?'

From outside came the rhythmic tramp of men.

'It's the Navy,' Polly said quietly. 'No one else marches like that.'

Alice listened for a moment, then nodded. 'Now, Poll, with the Navy coming, we'll need a new barrel. Take these young gents down to the cellar with you . . .'

'There's a tunnel,' Polly whispered, 'out to the quay . . .'

She rose to take us out, but before we could go anywhere, the door was booted open. Chairs scraped back and tables fell over as a dozen men got to their feet, looking around for a way to escape. A hammering of musket butts shattered the shutters. A troop of marines was marching into the room, bayonets fixed.

At the head of them came William. My confusion was complete.

'They might just be pressing men,' Alice whispered. 'Leave it to me.'

She walked up to William as if he were just another customer.

'Why don't you bring your boys in, Sir? There's plenty of room.' She turned to the grim-faced marines lined up in twos behind him. 'What will you be having?'

'We are not here for refreshment, Madam,' William answered. 'We aren't a press gang, neither.' He looked around. 'We come in search of pirates and, by God, I think they're found!'

Men from the ship reached for their weapons, grabbing for pistol and cutlass, but before they were half out of holster or scabbard, a volley of shots rang out, filling the room with smoke, cutting men down where they stood. One man crumpled, clutching his belly, another man's arm hung by a string. Peter, the Dutch gunner, fell back in his chair, a hole in the middle of his forehead.

'Weapons on the table.' William holstered his spent pistol and took out another. 'Hands where I can see 'em.'

The marines began moving through the room. Anyone slow to comply received a musket butt in the face. His Majesty's forces meant business. We did what we were told, just like everyone else.

The gunfire brought Broom to the top of the stairs, pulling on his breeches, the whores he'd been entertaining craning over the balcony to see what was going on. All eyes turned to him and William's gaze flicked upward, just for a moment. Minerva reached down, slipping out a short-barrelled flintlock from her boot top, keeping it under the edge of the table, angled upwards to catch William under the chin. I heard the hammer click, as loud in my ears as a shot. One step nearer . . .

William moved towards the stairs.

I knocked Minerva's gun sideways, so it discharged into the floor. We were immediately surrounded by marines, muskets trained upon us.

Minerva stared at me, furious. A barrel jab in the back brought her hands slowly on to the table, fingers spread.

I put up my own hands. 'I knocked the gun off the table! It discharged by accident!'

The marines were reluctant to believe us. More of them cocked their guns.

Broom had turned tail, hoping to escape by an upstairs window. A crash and cursing from outside the building indicated that he had not succeeded. He was brought in to be lined up with the rest of us.

'Round 'em up!' William said to his troops. 'I want 'em alive so we can hang as many as possible, so no more shooting unless strictly required.'

The marines began collecting weapons into a sack and forcing men from their seats.

'Sure you couldn't do with a wet? This here is thirsty work.' Alice smiled at William. 'Once these rogues are rounded up, I'm sure your boys will want a drink. I got some excellent Barbados.' She brushed away William's protests and addressed the officer of marines, who was looking interested. 'Take a barrel back to the mess with you. My compliments.' She called the pot boy to her. 'I want you to go and get some rum for the officers, Sam. In the cellar, far corner. *You* know where. Swift return!' she added in a whisper. 'Now off you go!'

The pot boy was no fool, and had obviously seen this happen before. He nodded and scuttled out before anyone could stop him.

'Slip down and get a barrel up,' Alice whispered to Polly, 'There's a good girl.'

We were ordered to line up, facing the wall. Minerva stood slowly, refusing to be hurried, despite the muskets trained on her. She stopped in front of Alice and dropped something into her hand.

'For you,' she said.

The ruby earring glittered, bright as blood, in the woman's closing palm.

We stood, arms behind our backs, wrists manacled, ankles shackled. We were no longer a danger, but were told to watch the wall as the marines took their rum. They drank quickly and spoke in grunts to each other, ignoring Alice and Polly and the other girls' attempts at flirtatious chatter. I stared at the rough-grained planking. The wood was unpainted, unfinished, the edges bordered with thick reddish bark. Behind me, boots scraped on the sand-strewn floor and the room was heavy with the buzz of flies drunk on spilt blood and rum.

'I could have had him,' Minerva murmured next to me. 'We should have fought 'em while we had the chance.' I looked sideways. Minerva's face glistened with tears of rage. 'That whore has more courage in her little finger than all of us put together.'

I realised then why she'd given Alice the earring. She had tried to get us out. When that hadn't worked, she had sent the boy to warn Vincent on the *Swift Return*. Even now, she was causing delay, giving our ship time to get away. Alice had acted with bravery and resourcefulness. In Minerva's eyes we were all white-livered cowards compared with her.

'Why did you stop me?' she hissed. 'I had him in my sights!'

'I couldn't have you kill him. It's William.'

She had never seen him before. How could she have known?

My revelation temporarily silenced Minerva, but her brows were still knitted with anger, her fists curling and uncurling with frustration.

'Even so, we could have done something!' she hissed. 'Instead we allowed ourselves to be taken without any kind of fight!'

'They outgun us,' I said. 'We could have all been killed!'

'For me, it is better to die than to be captured,' Minerva stared at the wall. 'Perhaps it will be different for you.'

I knew what she was thinking. As a slave, she might not receive the same treatment accorded to us. At least hanging was quick. Death more or less instant.

'You do not know —' I began to say, but was silenced.

'Shut it!' a marine roared close to my ear. 'Or I'll shut it for you!' He caught me a blow across the side of the face with the butt of his musket to show just how he would do it.

We were herded together, shuffling in our chains between flanking lines of marines, loaded into long boats and rowed out to the waiting warship. The *Swift Return* was no longer at her moorings. Sam, the pot boy, had managed to warn them. She was already slipping away to lie in the darkness outside the harbour. There was no point in the ship being taken as well as half the crew. She might even be able to come to our rescue.

Any spark of hope was soon extinguished by the size of the warship looming above us. The *Eagle* was a naval third rater with seventy guns on two gun decks. The schooner would be no match for that.

27

We were assembled on deck. The captain emerged from his cabin and inspected us in flaring lanthorn light, his face twisted into disgusted disdain, as if the rats on his ship had been rounded up for inspection.

'Lock 'em up!'

He turned back to his cabin and we were hurried down the companionway and through the decks until we reached the hold. It was well below the water line, dark and cold. Here we were chained to benches, the hatch slammed down upon us, and left in blackness, listening to the water suck and slap against the hull.

We thought that we would rest in the harbour until morning, but from above came the dull thump of a drumbeat and singing, full-throated and disciplined, many men in chorus together. A groaning sound accompanied, slowly building to a rhythmic grinding creak.

'It's the capstan!' Halston, the gunner,

shouted out. 'Well, I'll be damned! They're hauling anchor! Hark at that!'

Everyone listened to the winding capstan, the drag of hemp on wood as the huge anchor cable passed through the hawser holes. There was a splash as the flukes left the water.

'They must have seen the *Swift*! They must be going after her! It's not just us. They want the ship, an' all!'

The man of war began to move, slowly at first as the boat's oarsmen manoeuvred her through the harbour, then more quickly as the wind filled her sails, taking her into the open sea.

They could not leave us down here for ever. Sooner or later someone would come to check upon us. As soon as the hatch was thrown back, I knew what I would do.

A lanthorn swung, throwing light into the blackness.

'Hey, you there!' I shouted up to the sailor above me. 'I want to see the captain!'

'Oh, aye?' he sneered. He was young by his voice and what I could see of his pimpled cheek. 'What business does the likes of you have with him? What if he don't want to see you?' he snickered, seeming to find that amusing.

'I think he might.' I moved so that the

light shafting down through the hatch fell full upon me.

'And how do you reckon that then?' He snickered some more.

'Because I am a woman!'

I held my two hands together and pulled my jacket open, rending the shirt beneath so that he could see my breasts. The effect was dramatic. His eyes grew wide and his face paled. The light wavered, swinging wildly around, the lanthorn shaking so much in his hand that I feared that it might fall down upon me. I pulled my coat across my chest to cover myself.

'So go and tell someone.'

He'd already gone, screaming for the lieutenant and running pell-mell as if pursued by the ghosts of every pirate who'd perished at the hands of His Majesty's Navy.

'Which one?'

The sailor pointed.

William squatted in the hatchway, frowning down on me. I'd asked to see the captain, but had got the lieutenant, as I hoped I might.

'Get her up. You two go down with him. Keep an eye on the rest of them.'

The two guards stared at me with interest, while their mate approached me warily, as if I were some dangerous animal. He undid the manacles, releasing me from the running chain that linked us all together. The men stepped back, so I could ascend the ladder first.

'What is all this?'

I held my coat tight around me. 'I'm a woman.'

'Gi's a look then!' one of the marines leered, trying to part my lapels.

I looked to William, appealing to him. 'Please, sir! I must speak with you privately.'

'That's enough of that!' William glowered at the marine. 'Come . . . er . . . Madam. You had better follow me.'

He sent the others away and took me to an empty storeroom, closing the door behind us. Before, I had just been one of a hoard of pirates. Now, he held up his lanthorn, studying me more carefully, searching for what had been missed before. I could not bear his casual curiosity; this stranger's scrutiny.

'Do you not know me, William?'

'Nancy?' He turned as white as the young sailor. 'Is it you?'

I took out the ring I wore around my neck as proof and token of my identity.

'Do you still wear yours, I wonder?'

His hand strayed to his neck, showing that he did.

'Oh, Nancy!'

His reaction astounded me. I'd expected shock, surprise, even disapproval, but instead he hung up his lanthorn and came to me, his dark eyes moist with tears, and put his arms around me, hugging me to him.

'You're found! Thank God for it!' He cupped my face with his hands and gazed down at me, as if at some precious possession lost and found again. 'When it was given out at Port Royal that you were kidnapped and taken by pirates, I thought that I would never see you again.' His face showed the shock he'd felt at the news, his fear for me. 'We've been out on patrol, searching for the desperate crew who would do such a thing. And by God, we found them!' His eyes narrowed. 'Hanging's too good for what they've done! Making you dress in men's clothes! Perfidious rogues! But you're safe now.' He held me to him and kissed me with all the passion he'd shown at our last meeting. Then he let me go. 'I must tell the captain, straightway, and then we must see if there are any women's clothes to be found.' He surveyed my garb. 'You should not have to endure such humiliation and such discomfort for a minute more.'

He turned towards the door, but I caught his arm.

'Hold up,' I said. 'Hold up. Just a minute.'

'What is it?'

'Before you take me to the captain, there is something you must know . . .'

I told him everything. About my brother's duplicity. The marriage that had been arranged for me. About Duke, and Minerva, the maroons, and Broom. How I'd begged to be taken by the pirates. While I spoke, he paced about. Then he came back to me, shaking his head.

'I cannot understand. How could you allow yourself to fall into a way of life that goes so utterly against nature? Against all the feelings and instincts of your sex!' He spoke rapid and low, his face flushed, his voice hushed as if it shamed him to speak such shocking things out loud. 'Dressed — like this. Living with these men, going with them freely, staying with them under no duress. They are pirates! The scum of the sea.'

'I had no choice! Pirates they may be. But none have offered me any disrespect. Dressing as a man is not some whim. It is sensible and practical. It keeps me safe.'

'Even so . . .' He struggled with what I had told him. 'When we found you, you were consorting with whores!'

'What about it? Have you never done it?'

'I am a man!'

'They are women. I was talking to them. It's not as if I am some country miss who does not know of their existence. I grew up in Bristol. Why can you not see! I'm still the same Nancy! I still have your ring. I wear it constantly. I've thought only of you through all that's happened to me.'

He studied me intensely, as if trying to see beyond my male disguise. Gradually, the horror and loathing faded from his eyes. He stepped towards me, searching my face, looking to find my old self there.

'Well,' he sighed, and gave the ghost of a smile. 'You always were different, Nancy. I'll grant that. And loyal, and honest, and true. Not just to me, but to others, too. To Robert and the urchins we played with about the port. That's what I have always loved about you. I still have your ring. And my feelings haven't changed for you, whatever rig you wear.' He smiled at me then, and I thought that I had won him, but then his face clouded. He began to frown and pace again. 'Even so, I'm astonished at what you have told me. Broom. And

Graham, too.' He shook his head. 'I knew them as good men! I'm shocked that they have chosen to go on the account.'

'Perhaps you have not been listening,' I said. 'Or you don't understand.'

'I own I don't, Nancy.' He sighed again, more deeply. 'All I know is I am a naval officer, and you have all been arrested for piracy. I can only do my duty.'

Maybe I would have pleaded with him more, but we were interrupted by a furious banging at the door.

'Lieutenant! We found another one! She's been took to the cap'n.'

'Let me speak to him,' William said to me, as we went towards the door. 'Take your lead from me. It might go easier for you, and your female companion, if he does not know that you chose to join Broom's pirate crew.'

'Piratical women!' The captain stared at Minerva and me in disgust. 'God's teeth! As if we didn't have enough on our plates. What next? A captain in petticoats?' He steepled his fingers and regarded us with eyes as cold as a winter sea. 'Kidnapped, you say?' He turned to William. 'Forced to go with them? I've never heard the like.' He threw up his arms. 'Well, I've no time to get to the bottom of it now. I'll leave that for the judges in Port Royal. I've got a ship to command and the rest of the rogues to round up. Take 'em below and lock 'em up. But keep 'em separate from t'other rabble.'

With that, we were dismissed. The captain's brow creased and he went back to poring over his charts without giving us another glance.

'I don't know who he wants least on his ship,' Minerva whispered as we were taken away. 'Women, or pirates.'

We were delivered to the orlop deck, a level above the hold where our shipmates were chained.

'What do you think will happen?' Minerva asked. 'To us? To the rest of them?'

I sat on a barrel with my head in my hands. 'I have no idea.'

Suddenly, the whole ship juddered and took on a sideways shift, throwing us against each other and causing the lanthorn we'd been left to swing wildly. Minerva and I clutched on to each other as the erratic motion worsened. The ship was out of the captain's control. She was being driven by wind and tide on to rocks, or a reef. From above, came the sound of the fast running of cable and the rapid rattle of the descending anchor. On a ship this size, the anchor was twice as tall as a man. We waited to hear the great splash as its weight hit the water, holding our breath, as anxious as any above decks for the anchor to slow the ship in its sideways drift.

From below us came a muffled thumping.

'The anchor's dragging!' Minerva's eyes were wide with fear. She meant that it could get no purchase. It had landed on smooth sand, or flat rock or coral. From above us came faint cries and shouting and the sound of feet running. There was the sound of another, lighter, chain running and another splash.

'They've thrown down the sheet!'

We listened.

'That's not taking either!'

There was the same bump, bumping as the sheet anchor dragged over the sea bottom. If neither took, the ship was done for.

'We have to get out of here!' Minerva rolled over to the door, trying to take the canting angle of the deck into account. She meant to hammer, demand release, but she'd barely raised her fist, when the door opened and William was standing there.

'I've come to get you out of here. The

330

ship is like to founder. Captain is so set on chasing the pirate that he's sailing into waters too shallow for his ship's draft!'

We were sailing south, following Exuma Sound, threading through an archipelago of islands and cays, some no more than lumps of coral rock surrounded by reefs. Vincent had set a trap and the captain had fallen right into it. He was leading the Navy ship into dangerous waters, the schooner skipping in front like a dipping gull.

'Come with me and I can save you. Your . . . er —' William looked at Minerva, unsure of her status, or how to address her, '— companion, too. But you must come with me now.'

'What about the others?' Minerva spoke up. 'Broom and his men, down in the hold?'

'There is no time. We are being driven towards an island. The ship could hit at any second. They have let go the anchor, and the sheet; both are dragging. Each surge of the surf takes us closer to the reef.'

'I won't go without them.' Minerva folded her arms, her face set and determined. 'I will not save myself and leave them all to drown!'

'Please, Madam!' He turned to me. 'Nancy! Tell her. There is no time to lose!'

I knew it was no good pleading. Nothing would shake Minerva from her resolution, and I would not go without her. He looked from me to her, and back again, and seemed to despair, recognising that we were two of a pair for stubbornness.

'Give us the key to their chains.' I held my hand out to him. 'We will go and free them.'

'I cannot wait, Nancy!' William's face creased in anguish. 'I have my duties. My own men need me!'

'Then you must do your duty. Do not wait for me. I would not expect it of you.'

'If we are separated this day,' he said, 'and if we survive it, don't doubt that I will find you. I will search the world over, I promise, but now I must go.'

Muffled by the hull, a dull roar sounded and then a lull, then the dull roar again. The noise of surf breaking. We were on a shore. Or a reef. From the deck came the screaming screech of winding gear.

'The davits are out,' William looked in the direction of the sound of the boats lowering. 'I must supervise the loading of my men . . .'

'Go, then!'

He led us to the companionway and, with a swift kiss, he left me. As he went up to the deck, we went down towards the hold.

'What's that?' Minerva held my arm. A squeaking came from all around. Tiny red sparks showed part of the darkness to be moving. A shadowy carpet undulated about us, pouring over our feet with a tiny skittering scrape of claws and a sudden brush of fur.

'It's the rats. They always know.'

The rats were gone as swiftly as they had come. There was a sudden silence, eerie and odd in a world where noise is constant.

'D'you hear it?' Minerva whispered.

A scraping, as if the ship had grazed something, merely glancing off it in a way that was of no consequence. But there are no innocent encounters between a solid surface and a ship at sea. We knew that.

'We must hurry!' We stumbled on towards the distant cries of desperate men left and doomed to die.

'There she goes!' One voice carried above the others, and the next surge brought a rending and tearing, a creaking groan followed by a series of sharp cracks.

Wooden boards being torn from each other.

'She's stove!'

There came a sudden rushing surge, a sudden coldness and the smell of salt in the fetid bilge-water stench of the ship's depths.

The single voice became the shouts of many men as every surge brought more breaking. Our feet slid from under us. The ship was heeling over; settling on to a resting place that was likely to be final. The water was pouring in now. From above came the cry of: 'Every man!' The ship was being abandoned.

The movement of the ship had sent us sprawling, but we were near to the trapdoor now. We went on, crawling on hands and knees, feeling for the bolt hole.

'Here it is!' Minerva hauled up the trap. 'We're here!' she shouted below. 'Hold on lads!'

We dropped down among them. The water was above our knees and rising. Men were on their feet, sliding into the water, dragging at the chains, wrenching until their wrists were bloody, shouting for help, some pleading for mercy from man and God, others cursing, thinking that they had been abandoned by both.

28

It was a frantic race against the rising of the water to free the men from their chains and some still wore their manacles as we struggled through the overturned world of the listing ship. It was dark below decks, and what had been wall was now floor. The sea poured down the companionway in such a gushing roar that we could not climb against it, so we had to find another way up.

'This ship might well prove our coffin yet,' Broom said as water poured over him. 'Come on, lads! This way! Follow me, boys!' he shouted as he found a different way to the deck. 'The Navy rats have run, let's follow 'em down!'

The deck dropped away almost sheer beneath us. Phillips, the gunner, found an axe to strike off the last of the manacles, and Broom and Halston used all their cunning and knowledge to get us off the stricken ship. We climbed and cut our way through the tangled mess of ropes, shrouds and sails, and used the main mast as a bridge to take us away from the buffeting surf and over the lines of sharp coral into the lagoon on the other side of the reef. Once we had gained calmer water, we swum and floated, clinging to jetsam, helping each other, until we reached the shore.

Not all had survived the desperate flight from the wrecked ship and, if there were no food or fresh water to be found, we would be counting those who had already perished lucky beyond measure. We were on a rocky island, a comma of coral on the blank blue ocean. Broom sent out searching parties, while the rest of us wandered the foreshore, driving the scuttling crabs from the corpses that littered the white sands.

I, for my part, could take no pleasure in my own survival. I did not know what had happened to William. Had he got away in one of the boats when the ship was abandoned, or was he lying dead on the shore? I steeled myself to look at each body. I did not find him among them. But how could I be sure? Pirate or sailor, there was no telling between them. Most were unrecognisable even as men: their clothes torn to ribbons as if slashed away by razors; their flesh shredded by the vicious coral. Many had not made it to the shore at all. Sharks threshed in the waters of the reef, driven to frenzy by the blood in the sea.

The dead were buried together: pirate, sailor, marine. No longer on different sides. All made equal by death and the sea. Pirates are superstitious, like all seamen, and they did not want to be haunted by wandering souls or spirits, so we scooped a pit above the high water line, using driftwood as spades. After we had finished, Halston bound two pieces of wood together in the shape of a cross and Broom said a few words.

'Lord receive the souls of those buried here and have mercy upon them. There but for Your grace go we.'

The searching parties came back. No water.

We were marooned.

We all stood together as the sun sank lower in the sky and bowed our heads to pray for the dead, and for the living. We prayed for delivery, for a ship. For if one did not come and take us off the island, it would not be long before thirst took us, a day or two, three at the most, and we'd be following those we had just buried into the unknown. The only thing left would be a nest of bleaching bones.

I stayed there after the others had gone to find a place to rest among the dunes. I sat watching the sun set, the wrecked ship standing in gaunt silhouette against its great red circle. The sea turned from crimson to purple, and all the time I prayed that a boat would come to take us off this island, and I prayed for William, hoping that he had got the boats away, and that he had taken a place in one of them and had survived.

29

Vincent had not deserted us. By noon the next day, a sail showed on the horizon, small as a lozenge, flickering in and out of sight, lost in the glare and glitter of the sun on the water. As the ship grew larger, we could see by the rigging that she was a schooner.

The *Swift Return* sailed into the bay on the other side of the island where the water was deeper. A few questioned where she'd been and grumbled that she needed re-naming, for we were all mighty thirsty and hungry by the time she was sighted. Vincent explained that he had been playing ducks and drakes with the Navy. He had sighted a flotilla of small boats, sails hoisted, the men hauling for all they were worth. By that, he knew that a wreck was certain and had come in search of us. But William's ship was not the only one in the vicinity.

'So there's a good chance that those in the boats would be found?' I asked him.

'Aye,' he replied, giving me a curious look. 'Drinking grog and eating biscuit right now, I shouldn't wonder. The Navy ship changed course to pick 'em up. That's how we managed to slip past. Why should you care?'

I did not answer, but left him with Minerva. He was glad enough to see her safely returned.

'Only sips of water!' Graham knocked a bucket from the hands of a guzzling pirate. 'And eat sparingly. Too much water and food all at once will cause you to swell like gourds and go off like grenadoes.'

Not all the pirates heeded the doctor's advice. Although none actually exploded, they were soon lying in their hammocks groaning with bellyache.

The schooner left the bay, searching for a deserted cay out of the Navy's way, where we could hold up and call ship's council, for Broom to declare his intentions and say where our next cruising ground should be.

The crew assembled in the fo'castle.

'It's my opinion,' Broom began, 'that the Caribbean is getting a little too *active*. Navy don't look kindly on those that wreck their ships from under 'em.' A cackle went round at that. 'So we have to set a fresh course, boys. To somewhere new. Some-where different. Where we ain't known. And I'm proposing,' he looked around, 'I'm proposing, mates, that Africa might prove a suitable destination.'

'Africa?'

It was as if he'd thrust a marlin spike into a hornet's nest. The council grew rowdy. Everyone was entitled to his say and was determined to have it. The wrangling did not die down until Vincent shot a pistol in the air.

'Hear the captain out, boys. Hear the captain out!'

It took a couple more reports to bring them to silence, but at last they all settled down. Whatever the uproar, Broom'd get my vote. Anything that would take us away from these waters. I wondered how long it would take for the Brazilian to hear of our adventures with the Navy?

Broom stepped into the centre of the circle and looked around him, waiting for complete quiet.

'What do you want, boys?' he asked them. 'What do you want from this piratical way of life? Why did you go on the account?'

Broom's questions set off another storm of shouting. He stood, legs apart, feet square on the deck, right hand grasping his cutlass hilt as he did in the face of a gale.

'Freedom!'

'No masters!'

'No mad captains to take us to rot on the Guinea coast!'

That last remark brought laughter, and Broom laughed with them.

'Aye,' he said, 'that's right enough. But what else, boys? What else?'

The crew looked at each other, puzzled, like schoolboys found slow at their lessons.

'Well, I'll tell you then, shall I? Gold, my boys. Gold. Wealth and treasure.' He looked around. The mention of gold had got their attention. 'Ain't that the truth of it?'

'Aye.' There was a ripple of agreement. 'That's true enough.'

'Course it is! That's why we all signed on!' Broom began walking up and down, sure that all eyes were upon him. 'Now, we could stay here in these waters and risk the Navy's wrath, for they are after us, boys, none doubt it. They don't take kindly to ships lost, like I say, so after us they'll stay. We could remain in these waters, dodging His Majesty's finest ships. We could lead them a dance. I'm sure we could. But they'll likely get us in the end, and then there'll be a different style of dancing. The kind that happens at the end of a rope. Many a good crew and captain have done that jig, boys.' He looked up. A shiver went around the company, as he knew it would. 'And for what? Boxes of buttons, bolts of cloth, barrels of sugar and molasses. Cargoes we're lucky to give away for the price of a tot o' rum.' He gestured, arms wide. 'The ships sailing *these* waters ain't hardly worth the trouble and risk of boarding. That's a fact. I didn't take up this way of life for that.' He looked them over. 'And I'll warrant you didn't, neither. I wanted gold and silver, to make my fortune. I'd wager you did, too.'

He looked around them. He had them in his hands. They were listening quiet as mice before a cat.

'I know where to get it. I know where there's gold and silver held in great store. Coin and ingot, as much as a ship can carry.'

His eyes were as bright as the gold he was describing. The crew stared up at him, their eyes wide, as if the hoard were already before them, as if they could feel the weight of the bullion, the cool slippery coins running like fish through their fingers. He smiled, and his eyes narrowed, reflecting the men's own greed back to them.

'Trust me, boys and I'll lead you to it.' His voice grew quiet, inviting them into the conspiracy. 'All you got to do is trust me and you'll never live in want again. Neither will your children, or their children after that, I shouldn't wonder. Now, what do you say? Who's for, and who's agin?'

What choice did he give them? All doubts were swept aside. Broom's plan was passed unanimously. He did not normally encourage drinking on board, but that night was given over to celebration. A great punch bowl was set up, Broom mixing it himself with sugar, rum and brandy from his own cabin. When that was finished, fresh barrels were breached. No one went thirsty that night. The fiddlers struck up and the decks were cleared for dancing. It was near dawn before the last pirate keeled over on the deck. They slept where they fell, no doubt dreaming of the gold that their captain had promised them. I only hoped that Broom could deliver those dreams to his men. If he could not, he would not stay captain for long.

We Lived and Reigned
as Masters of the Sea

30

The *Swift Return* was a small ship to undertake such a crossing. Pelling was as keen as any on gold and riches, but he was a worrier, and it was his job to look after the interests of the crew.

'What if we run out of water, or victuals?' he asked, his wrinkled face creasing further.

'The *Swift* might not be large,' Broom pointed out to him, 'but she's fast. We'll reach Cape Verde in no time, no time at all. We can always pick up supplies on the way, if we run low.'

By which he meant we could take a ship or two, but these were not the normal sea lanes. Merchantmen were few. The only ships that we were likely to meet would be slavers on the middle passage. No slavers. Broom was adamant. Either here, or on the coast of Africa. They carried little of any value, except their human cargo, and that was nothing but trouble. Broom was not alone in wanting to avoid them. Slave ships were rarely attacked. Their foul smell travelled on the wind for miles. They were universally avoided.

It wasn't until we were approaching the coast of Africa, that Broom decided that we definitely needed another ship. The lookouts were instructed to keep their eyes peeled for a merchantman. Pelling's ears pricked up at that. When he asked why, he was told that it was all part of the plan.

' 'Ere,' Pelling called to me. 'You're close to 'im. What's he up to?'

I shrugged my shoulders and told Pelling what the captain had told me. When I'd asked what the exact plan was, he'd invited me to 'wait and see'.

'Even if we find a ship, I don't know how we're going to man it,' Pelling said gloomily. 'We're under strength as it is.'

A number of the crew had fallen sick during the voyage across the Atlantic. They had been left at the Cape Verde Islands, Graham fearing a spreading contagion if they were left on board. A Navy ship in the harbour had kept our stay short. There had scarcely been time to take on all but the most essential supplies. Perhaps that was why Broom was going in search of a merchant vessel.

Later the next day, the man at the masthead shouted, 'A sail! A sail!'

She was far to starboard, almost on the southern horizon. She looked big, a three-masted merchantman. Broom smiled as he trained his spyglass upon her.

'She is perfect!'

His eyes held the gleam of coins again as he folded his spyglass, ordering the sails set to catch every scrap of wind and the helmsman to steer two points to the starboard bow.

We came upon the ship rapidly. She turned, hauling in sail and tacking across the wind to meet us. As she neared, the ensign went down and she hoisted a black flag.

'She's a pirate!' The call came down from the masthead.

'What colours?'

'Can't see for the flapping.'

Pelling was up the rat lines fast as a monkey.

'Red skellington on a black ground. That's Low!' He scampered back down to the deck. 'I thought he was dead! He's a devil, he is. He's cowardly, what's more. Not to be trusted at all . . .' He ran off to tell the captain, who ordered our flag hoisted.

Our colours were answered by cannon shot across our bows. Broom ordered returning fire and the two ships came on towards each other, each manoeuvring for advantage, trying to show the least side towards the other. The red skeleton danced in the wind, while our own skull and crossed bones glared from the mizzenmast.

Stories about Low spread up and down the ship like St Elmo's Fire.

'He don't give no quarters, puts whole crews to the slaughter.'

'Cut off the lips and ears of one captain, so I heard, and fried 'em up in front of 'im.'

'He cut the liver and lights out of another poor bugger and made his mates eat 'em.'

'I heard it were a heart he cut out.'

'He rammed his gun in the mouth of some other luckless bastard and fired straight down his gullet.'

The two ships were now within hailing distance of each other.

'Pipe down there!' Vincent growled. He watched the men carefully, trying to measure their mood. Such tales of terror can serve to stiffen the sinews of resistance, or they can strike such fear that the ship is lost before it is even boarded.

'Where from?' A voice from the other

ship shouted over the water.

'From the sea.' Broom gave the answer of all pirate captains.

'And you?'

'From the sea also. Don't believe I know you.'

'Captain Broom. And you?'

'Edward Low.'

'I heard you were dead.'

Low's laughter rang out, made loud and hollow by the speaking tube he held in his hand.

'Well, you heard wrong. Though many wish me so.'

They were close enough now to speak man to man. The crews lined up to face each other. Their swivel gun was trained upon us. Phillips turned ours to match it.

Low had left his quarterdeck and stood, arms folded, in the body of his ship. He was tall and handsome, with long fair hair falling down his back. He was as fond of ribbons and fancy clothes as was our captain. If it were not for the weapons bristling about his person, it would have been easy to take him for a gentleman.

'Nice rig you've got there, Captain. She has a colonial look about her.'

'Made in Baltimore,' Broom countered.

'Thought so,' he nodded. 'I was quite of

a mind to attack. I can't abide Americans, being at war with them for insult done to me.'

'He's at war with the whole world! Said it himself!' Pelling muttered under his breath. 'Americans particularly. Vowed to destroy any he came across. Could've blown us right out of the water. We was lucky!'

'I hate Yankees,' Low said again. 'Like their ships, though. Now I know that you're not one of them, we can be friendly. Come aboard, Broom, why don't you? Share a bowl of punch with me.'

'Be glad to, Captain.' Broom ignored Pelling, who was shaking his head and hopping about as if bees were stinging him. 'We're in want of supplies. I wonder . . .'

'We have plenty.' Low smiled. 'And will be happy to share with you. Come. Bring your officers.'

When the ships were grappled together, Pelling wouldn't go, so Broom beckoned Vincent to him and Halston, who was now second mate. At the last minute he added me to the party as a kind of midshipman.

'A pretty one, too,' Low winked at me. He was not so handsome up close, his skin pocked and turned to leather by the sun and weather, his hair thinning under his tricorn hat, and his blue eyes bleak and cruel. He led us under the quarterdeck into his cabin. It was spacious and well appointed, with a line of windows looking out over the stern.

The table was set with a great silver punch bowl. Low bade us sit down.

'Your health, Captain.' He took out a pistol and cocked it. 'Drink,' he said, holding the gun to Broom's head.

Broom took the bowl in both hands, sweat popping on his forehead.

'All of it.' Low smiled.

Broom glugged down about a quart, before choking and coughing. The rest of it slopped down his tunic.

Low laughed and discharged his gun in the air, before grabbing for another. It must have been the signal for a general attack. From outside came a roar and the booming of the swivel gun. Our gun answered. Wood splintered as part of the quarterdeck was shot away. The outer deck exploded, shrieking turned to screaming as men scattered or fell where they stood, limbs shattered, blood showering over the deck. Grenadoes followed, sending smoke billowing into the cabin. We threw the table over and reached for our weapons. Low fired into us, but Broom pushed his arm upwards, causing him to miss his mark. We drew our cutlasses and we fought our way out of the cabin and on to the deck.

The fighting was fierce on both ships. Low's men had swarmed on to the *Swift Return*, while our men had come on to his ship to attempt our rescue. We were heavily outnumbered, our men spread thin on both vessels. The fight was hopeless. We were bound to lose. But who thinks of that in the thick of battle?

The deck swirled with smoke; it was like fighting in a fog. There was no time to draw a pistol, and guns are useless at close quarters. We had to slash our way back to our own ship. In the confusion, I found myself being pushed backwards by Low, in the wrong direction. I fought as hard as I could, but he was too strong for me. It was all I could do to parry his blows. His blade was longer and heavier than mine. One powerful cut caused sparks to fly and sent my weapon spinning out of my hand. I jumped back, but the sword caught me, slashing down from throat to navel, cutting through my coat and shirt to the skin.

I thought I was done for, but Low drew back.

'My, my! What have we here?' He came towards me. His blade whispered past my cheek and he plucked a lock of hair from my shoulder. 'You *are* a pretty one, and no mistake.' He rubbed the hair between his fingers. 'As golden as guineas. Who would have thought that Broom would have such a prize on board that tub of his?' He parted my shirt with his sword and stared. 'No need to rush things. A dish to be consumed at leisure.' I spat at him and swore. His sword was at my throat again. 'You will learn some manners, Madam, or I'll share you with my crew and then feed you to the fish.'

He dragged me to a companionway, booting me in the back to force me down the stairs. Once at the bottom, he took me by the scruff of my coat, pushed me into a little storeroom and slammed the door. I heard him hauling boxes of shot, piling them up to stop me getting out.

I put my back against the door, pushing and shoving, but I could not budge it. I looked down and wondered at all the blood smeared about me. I looked up, thinking it must be coming through from the deck. I put my hand to my chest, and it came away red. My shirt was soaked, and my coat. The sight made me light-headed. I sat down suddenly, as if my legs had been kicked from under me, and I remembered nothing more.

31

I opened my eyes to the sound of the boxes being pulled away and the door opening. I was sure that it would be Low back to finish what he had postponed. I was gathering what I had left of my strength to punch him in the face.

'Hold up.' A hand wrapped itself round my fist. 'Steady now.' The hand was small, not much bigger than mine. I was looking up into Minerva's brown eyes. 'Who put you here?'

'Low.'

'Did he . . . ?'

I shook my head. 'Saving me for later.'

'I've been searching for you all over the ship.' Minerva helped me out of my place of confinement and on to the deck.

'What happened?'

'We put up a harder fight than they expected. They came on to board us and we hit 'em. Things began to go badly for 'em and they cried quarters.' She shrugged.

'Suddenly it was all over. Low's ship is ours now. His pirates are dead or with us.'

'Where's Low?'

'Broom put him in an open boat to shift for himself, along with any of his men who chose to go with him.' Minerva hooked her thumbs in her belt. 'Not many did.'

I was glad that we'd won the day, but sorry that Low had got away. They should have made him eat his own ears, that was my opinion, but Broom always was soft-hearted — for a pirate.

Low's was a big ship. Men scurried like ants to repair the damage she'd suffered during the recent fight. Besides the captain's cabin, there was a ward room for officers, and a dining room, even cabins. Minerva helped me to one of these.

'I think we'll claim this one,' she said, and laid me in a cot slung from a beam. She stripped away my clothing, and fetched water and a cloth to see what wounds I had under the caked layers of dried blood.

She frowned. 'Perhaps I should go and fetch Graham.'

'No!' I caught her hand. 'He will have enough to do. There must be much worse cases than mine. I want you to look after me.'

'Very well. But you do as I say and no complaining.' Minerva went away again and came back with fresh water, strips of linen for bandages and a bottle of rum.

She bathed me all over. Her gentle touch and the feeling of being clean again made me almost forget my wounds. There were cutlass slashes on my hands and arms. She sewed the worst of them with button thread. There was a nick under my chin where Low had forced me back and a long cut starting at the hollow at the base of my throat, travelling down my breast bone and ending at my navel.

Minerva swabbed the wounds with stinging rum and dressed them, then she wound me round with bandages. After that, she made me drink a cup of brandy, heated and laced with spices. The spices reminded me of Phillis, and I went to sleep thinking of her.

Graham came to see me and congratulated my nurse on her care. My wounds were healing cleanly and I would be left with only a little scarring, although I carry the marks to this day: a white crescent under my chin and a line running the length of my upper body like a silver thread.

My bodily hurts were mending, but I

was having the nightmares again. The dream ended with his mocking whisper:

I know where you are going.

I jerked from sleep, and lay in my cot in the rocking ship, as though in some double cradle. It seemed that he knew about our run to Africa. But how could that be so? Perhaps there *was* no escaping him. I truly believed that he would follow me to the ends of the earth. A yawning pit opened inside me, a chasm of despair. I could hear Minerva's hammock creaking, hear her breathing in the darkness of the cabin, but I felt alone on the ocean vastness. Beyond the steady rush of our ship, I seemed to hear another, her bows cleaving the sea, quietly whispering through the water, coming after me.

I tried to imagine the ship, with him upon her. In my dream I seemed to glimpse her, as if through a grey mist, but awake I could not recall her. Instead, I saw other ships sliding by us, packed with people whose lives had been stolen from them.

We were sailing the African coast now, and it fairly bristled with forts and castles, their dungeons full of people: mothers, fathers, wives and husbands, children. More, and still more, were being herded down to

359

the coast in coffles, chained together at the neck. Next to the stumbling columns, I saw the neat lists of figures in my father's ledgers, some in my own hand.

'What is the matter?' Minerva whispered out of the dark.

I could not answer her. To my very great surprise, I began to cry, and once I had started I found I could not stop.

Minerva swung her legs out of her hammock and came to me. She lay down in the cot beside me and comforted me, stroking my hair as she held me in the hollow of her shoulder. I soaked her shirt with my tears. Lacking a mother, I had never been held by a woman like that before. I felt the roughness of the fabric under my cheek, the warm skin beneath it. I thought of the mark that marred its perfection, and cried more. Minerva rocked me, hushing me as if I were a baby, and eventually I quietened. Nights on the Guinea coast are hot and close. We did not sleep again, but lay talking.

'Your heart's got to lay down its burdens,' Minerva whispered to me. 'That's what Phillis would say.'

If my heart could lay down its burdens . . .

'I had the dream again.'

'About the Brazilian? Is it the same one?'

I shook my head. 'I see the ship clearer, with him upon her. Up on the quarterdeck. That great diamond cross swinging from his chest. He's still after me.'

'How can he know where we are? We are not in the Caribbean. How will he know to come here?'

I shook my head. 'I don't know. I just feel that he does.'

'But you don't *know*. Not for sure. Remember what Phillis used to say? "Don't fear tomorrow, till today's done with you." It's a true thing.'

'I know. That's just it. I *still* get frightened. When Low came at me . . . when I thought of what he would do to me . . . when he said he would give me to his crew . . .' I bit my lip, fighting off the tears that threatened to come again as I gave my secret fears to her. 'I belong nowhere. To no one. I have cut myself away from my family, from everyone except William. And he's probably disgusted with me for turning pirate and will find some proper girl to be his wife.'

'Ssh! Hush!' Minerva held me closer. 'You still have me.'

'But for how long? You have Vincent . . .'

'I do *not* have Vincent!' Minerva tried

her best to sound indignant, but I could tell by her voice that she hoped it was so.

'You could if you wanted, I've seen the way he looks at you. And you like him, you can't deny it. And then I will truly have no one. Nothing. No home. No family . . .'

'You will still have me. You will always have me.' Minerva made me listen in turn. She had burdens of her own. 'There is something you must know.' She wound a lock of my hair round her fingers. 'Something I should have told you a long time ago.'

'What is it?'

'You are my sister. Your father was my father, too.'

Minerva was my sister. I was so stunned, that I could not speak. We had been through so much together and she'd never said a word. I half rose to look at her, to search her face for a clue as to how she could keep such a thing from me, and for so long.

'Why did you not tell me?'

'Phillis made me promise not to.'

'But why?'

'Your father made her promise to tell no one. She gave her word and he never released her from it. For Phillis, his death bound her to silence.' She paused. 'You are not angry, that I did not tell you?'

'Oh, no!' I marvelled that she could even think it. 'It is strange to me, that's all. So many things make sense now, that did not before.'

The way my father spent part of every year in Jamaica; his special care of Phillis and Minerva. The way that sometimes, when I looked at her, it was like looking in a mirror. The differences between us had blinded me to the similarities. The likeness was there clear enough: a certain way of standing, the arch of the brow, the tilt of the chin, our stubbornness. Even William had noticed how alike we were in that. I was astounded that I had never recognised what it truly meant.

Things were becoming clear to me and, in that moment, much of my fear left me. I had found one safe haven in a seething sea of threat and uncertainty. Men's love might change, prove fickle, but Minerva was my blood sister. I would always love her, and she would always love me.

32

A pirate ship is its own wooden world where
each man depends on the other. Discontent
and dissatisfaction among the crew can
bring a ship to ruin, as sure as teredo worm
eating through the hull. The *Swift Return*
and the *Deliverance* before her had both been
happy ships. Broom had renamed Low's
three-master the *Fortune,* but that had not
changed the atmosphere upon her. Tempers
grew short, frustrations began to surface.
Quarrels flared, as quick and ugly as fire in
the hold.

'Only takes one bad apple,' Pelling observed. 'And we got a barrelful.'

Vincent was now captain of the *Swift Return,* Broom taking the *Fortune.* I knew Minerva missed him. She would not say so,
but was not above staring towards the horizon to where the *Swift Return* shadowed
us, hoping for a glimpse of her mast and
sails. I caught her climbing down from the
topgallant crosstrees for the second time in

one morning and asked her why she did not go with him.

'I would not leave until your wounds are healed,' she said. 'Besides, Vincent would not allow it. He says for he and I to be together would make difficulties for both of us and have an unsettling effect on the men.'

She missed him the most, but we all had occasion to feel the lack of his strong presence, and his influence upon the men. Although we needed as many hands as could be mustered to run two ships, the men taken on from Low's crew were surly and quarrelsome. They behaved like dogs who'd had a bad master, fawning one minute, snarling the next. One in particular, Thomas Limster, seemed intent on causing trouble. He'd had ambitions to be Low's quartermaster and now thought to take Pelling's job, making himself busy among the crew, trying to win them over to his side. He boasted Low's careless cruelties as the methods of a 'real captain'. Broom was weak, he said, leading us nowhere and passing fat prizes every day. Why leave slave ships when we could get a good price for their cargo further up the coast? Rumour whispered of a round robin to get rid of the captain. Limster was careful who he asked to sign, each one writing his name as part of a circle so none could be picked out as leader if the conspiracy were discovered.

That I was a woman wearing man's clothes was generally known. Up until now, my sex had provoked little comment, but Limster changed all that.

It was evening, the idle time before the night watch was set, when most of the men were on deck, smoking pipes and drinking.

'Duck in drake's clothing,' he sneered as I passed by him. 'A whore's a whore, whatever she's wearing.'

It was not the first time he'd made a comment, and before I'd let it go by. This time, I begged his pardon and asked him to repeat what he had just said.

'You heard. Let's see what you got, then.'

His lips curled as he spoke and I could see his scurvy-blackened gums, smell his rotten breath as he pulled me towards him, grabbing at my jacket. He was a big man, with hands like ham hocks and wrists as thick as hawsers.

'Get your hands off me!'

I wrenched at his fingers, but I might as well have been trying to pull apart a Turk's head knot. He was forcing my coat apart, ripping off the buttons. It made me furious to be manhandled in this way; to stand in nakedness in front of my shipmates would be more than I could stand. I took my head back, meaning to butt him in the face, when the steel of a blade came between us and a voice said, 'Unhand her!'

Limster released me when he felt the cutlass across his throat. Minerva smiled as she sheathed her weapon and took my arm.

'I know what this is about,' Limster jeered after us. 'Want to keep her for yourself, ain't that the way of it? Why don't you let us all have a piece!'

Although he recognised me as a woman, he only knew Minerva as Jupiter and thought that she was a man. No one had seen the need to inform him otherwise. Now a word in his ear disabused him. Laughter gusted around him but, like many of a mocking nature, he did not like the joke turned upon himself. He let off a volley of the vilest curses that could be aimed at womankind. His slanders had Minerva walking back to him.

'You have a bad mouth, Mr Limster. As foul as any I've heard. You'll take that back.'

'Or?' Limster sneered down at her. 'What will you do?'

'I'll consider myself insulted.'

Limster snorted. 'Pox take the both of you!'

Minerva took a step back from him and delivered a stinging slap.

His hand went to his face. He rubbed his leathery stubbled cheek slowly, as if he could not quite believe that she had struck him. Then his fist went back.

'Hold up!' It was Pelling. 'No fighting on board ship.'

We were all summoned to the fo'castle where Pelling kept court.

'Who struck first blow?' the quarter-master enquired.

Minerva stepped forward.

'Fighting's against ship's rules.'

'We know that,' I said. 'But he insulted us.'

Pelling ignored me. He unfolded a dog-eared sheaf of papers that he had retrieved from his sea chest and studied them.

'Item Five of the Articles states: *None shall strike another on board but every man's quarrel shall be ended on shore with sword and pistol,*' he read, as prim as a clerk in a court of law. He looked at Minerva. 'You understand?'

'Aye. I do.'

Limster grinned, obviously thinking that

he could overmatch her. She was only a girl, after all.

'And don't you be thinking to save your skin by going to Broom,' Limster jeered. 'Cap'n has no jurisdiction in quarrels of this nature. Ain't that right, Pelling?'

Pelling ignored him. 'You will be put ashore tomorrow morning, accompanied by myself and the doctor,' he said. Pirates are as nice about the points of their duelling as any London gentleman, their rules very similar. 'You may choose your own seconds to attend you.' He hesitated for a moment. 'May the best man win.'

Pelling was meant to be neutral, but he had no love of Limster, so that night he came to our cabin and gave Minerva much good advice as to how to conduct herself in the morning.

'Do not be afeard of him. A pistol is a great equaliser, and since you be the smaller, try to finish him with your one shot. But be prepared, he's a shifty bastard an' like to cheat by turning before the count is finished, dodging so you can't get a bead on him, feinting to the side likewise. Beware of that. If it comes to the blade, keep your back to the sea, that way you're against the light and are harder to see. Push him back toward the softer sand,

369

that'll tire him an' make it harder for him to move around. He'll likely be a might slow in the morning. There's rum going round, and for once I'm turning a blind eye. Sleep well, my pretty.' Pelling put his callused hand out to Minerva, clapping her lightly on the shoulder. 'I'll come for you at first light.'

Minerva seemed to fall fast asleep almost as soon as she had climbed into her hammock. I stayed awake, listening to the bells sound the hours until morning, my mind flooding with fear for her, and guilt that I'd caused this fight to happen.

33

The sun was just above the horizon, turning the sea to silver, when I rose to help Minerva to get ready. I was her second, and she allowed me to dress her in a fine white linen shirt, white stockings and blue breeches. I wound a crimson scarf about her slender waist, fixing her sword belt above it.

'This duel is my fault,' I said. 'I should be fighting him. If you hadn't stepped in . . .'

'You would have butted him. I stopped you. You're too weak to fight. Your wounds are only just healed.' She picked up her pistol, sighting along the barrel. 'That's what he wanted. Now he has me to contend with.'

She seemed supremely confident, and I hid my fear for her, knowing how fast it can flow from one person to another, as she checked her weapons, rising the hammer on her pistol and letting it fall, click and thud. Click and thud. She took up her cutlass, testing the blade on her thumb, plucking a hair, cleaving it in the air.

There was a knock. 'Ready to board!' Duffy, the bo'sun, called.

Minerva stepped down, as seemingly light and carefree as if we were taking a run on shore. The boat crew held their sweeps aloft, dropping them at the command of the bo'sun, as neat and smart as any naval boat in Portsmouth harbour. We took our place on the thwarts. Minerva sat with Graham and me. Limster sat opposite with his second and Pelling. They did not look at each other and nobody spoke. The only sound was the splash of the blades in the water and the working of the oars between the tholepins as the men rowed towards the shore.

Long lines of curling rollers made beaching the boat difficult, but the bo'sun had chosen his shore party well. The lead oarsmen leaped into chest-high surf, taking lines to tow us ashore. At command, the others shipped their sweeps and more jumped out to pull the boat up above the water line.

Our feet marked the firm, wet sand as we walked up the beach. The sea surged forward and back, washing our footprints away as quickly as we made them. We went on towards a dense line of trees, Pelling casting about for the right spot.

'Stop!'

We halted. Pelling stepped forward, turning the duellists back to back.

'Seconds!'

We came up with the weapons. Minerva's eyes met mine as she took the pistol from me. Then she lowered her gaze and her face became expressionless, as impossibly distant as in the old days, when she was my slave. She would not let me see her hope, or her fear.

Limster's second and I moved away to stand at a distance with Graham, who stood fidgeting with his doctor's bag, clasping and unclasping the fastening, his face pale beneath the freckles and etched with lines of worry and disapproval. He would dearly have loved to stop this from happening, but no one could intervene now. Not even the captain; Broom had kept well out of it. Such things had to be decided in the manner laid down in the Articles. They were our laws. Ours was a world turned upside-down, where normal rules did not apply. To lay our own code aside would be to jeopardise what little order there was upon the pirate ship.

Pelling held the duellists back to back, and then stepped smartly away as he began to count. Limster was at least a head taller than Minerva, his bulk dwarfing her. They stepped from each other, pistols held at the shoulder, measuring their tread. Pelling calling the numbers sounded like a tolling bell. We were all listening for the pause, quicker than a pulse beat, when the counting would cease.

Limster did not wait. Pelling was still counting when he turned. Pelling stuttered and Minerva must have heard the swish of Limster's feet in the dry sand, for she leaped round, only to find herself staring down the barrel of his gun. There was a crack and white smoke puffed out. The ball went past her, bedding itself in the tree behind her. Now, it was her turn.

She raised her pistol, but Limster broke the rules again, diving sideways so that she would miss him.

He was coming at her, low to the ground, cutlass drawn. She threw away her pistol and drew her blade. A cutlass is a clumsy weapon made for slashing, not sword play. My own arms and hands twitched to be fighting for her. I was better with a sword than Minerva, but she was quick on her feet, dancing about Limster, dodging rather than parrying his blows. She was following Pelling's advice, pushing him towards softer sand with her back to the sea, the rising sun on the water making it harder for him to see her clearly. The morning was warming. Limster was coxcomb red, sweating from the heat and exertion, and the rum of the night before. Beads formed on his forehead, dropping into his eyes, making him shake his head like a bull bothered by flies. Minerva kept skipping in and out of his line of vision, keeping him off balance, turning him around and back again.

'Keep still, damn you!' He was losing his temper. 'Stand and fight like a man!'

Wait, wait your moment. I mouthed the words. Get under his guard. Wait. Wait.

He lunged and missed. She leaped away, but he came back at her, sweeping his cutlass in a great arc. The edge caught her shoulder. Blood bloomed, soaking her sleeve in seconds. I could feel the numbness in my own arm.

'First blood! That's an end to it,' Graham shouted, stepping forward, bag in hand.

The fight ended with first blood drawn. Limster had won. Those were the rules, but the big man showed no sign of laying his weapon aside. He came at a run, cutlass raised, ready to cleave Minerva in two.

'I'll kill him!' I was screaming, reaching for my own weapon.

Graham dropped his bag and reached for his pistol. 'Hold!' he yelled. 'One step more and I'll shoot!'

Limster was like a bull charging: he had no intention of stopping; but our shouting distracted him and then he stumbled, catching his foot on a root, or piece of driftwood, half hidden in the sand. It was the chance that Minerva wanted. He twisted, trying to save himself, but he was off balance and pitching forward. She lunged, catching him under his raised cutlass arm. Her thrust met his weight falling towards her, pushed the blade up to the hilt, right through to his heart.

Graham cut Minerva's sodden shirt sleeve away, stanched the blood and cleaned the wound with rum, before stitching the gaping edges together and binding her arm with strips of linen. Minerva did not cry out once. She was carried from the beach between Duffy and one of his crew. Graham gave her a draft of rum, which she choked on, but which seemed to revive her, and she leaned against my shoulder as the oarsmen pulled away from the shore.

Pirate justice is swift and final. Limster had behaved without honour, so he was left where he lay, his blood seeping into the sand.

34

'It's a deep cut. To the bone,' Graham said as we laid Minerva in my cot in the cabin. 'But it's clean and I dare say she'll live. I'll give her opium to make her sleep. If you could help me?' I held her up while he dropped the tincture on to her tongue. 'Now she needs to rest. She does not need you hovering over her. Come.'

He led me out to the great cabin and bade me sit down there with him.

'You laid a heavy duty on me today, you and Minerva. How d'you think I would feel if I had to attend either one of you, dead or dying?' He sighed. 'I went to Broom, but even he could do nothing to stop the fight you got yourselves into. This is no life for you. You should not be having to do with scum like Limster. Belonging to nowhere, and to no one. A life of endless wandering that's all risk and no gain, with a rope at the end. What is the point of it?'

He did not need an answer. He was

talking as much about himself as he was about us.

'I'm thinking of leaving the account,' he went on. 'I'm tired of seeing young men killed and maimed, of patching up torn bodies only to watch the wounds corrupt, knowing there's nothing I can do. I have more than enough now to set up a practice. In London, Edinburgh. Anywhere. Somewhere I can start anew and where no one will know me, or my history. It is only loyalty to Broom that keeps me here. And you.' He turned to me. 'Come back with me, Nancy. You can pass as my daughter.'

'I cannot. I will not leave without Minerva. Especially not now. She risked her life to save mine. I cannot desert her.'

'She could come with you.'

'What as?' I looked at him. 'My slave? My servant? She would not do it, and I will not ask her. You know what life would be for her in England, the slights and insults that she would suffer, the assumptions people would make. I fear we are destined to roam for ever.'

'I hope not. Truly, I do. What of your young man, William?'

'After what happened on the *Eagle*?' I shrugged. 'He thinks me a pirate. I've given up all hope of him.'

'But he knows the circumstances, the reasons for you taking up this way of life?'

I nodded.

'Well, then if he really loves you, that will make no difference.'

'He might be dead for all I know.'

'And he might not. Never give up hope, my dear.' Graham leaned forward and put his hand on mine as if he really were my father. 'Never give up hope. I told you that before.'

'When will you leave?' I asked, wishing to change the subject away from William and me.

'As soon as I can.'

'Have you told Broom?'

'Not yet. But he knows my thinking.'

I could see Graham's mind was made up, so it would be no good pleading, but I had grown very fond of him and I would sorely miss his company. I was about to tell him as much, hoping to persuade him to stay a little while longer, when Broom came in with Pelling, as out of temper as I'd ever seen him.

'See this.' He snapped his fingers and Pelling handed him a piece of paper. 'It's a round robin.' He flattened out the folds to show names written down in a circle. 'A craven compass of cowardly conspiracy.'

380

He turned the paper round with his finger. 'I'll have every bastard on it off this ship.'

He called ship's company and held up the paper to them.

'This here is a round robin. So designed so none can be found out as leader.' He looked around. 'Well, you can forget all that. Every jack who signed it, every name upon it, can sling his hook. With the exception of him lying dead on yonder shore.'

'Vote!' a few desperate voices called.

'Vote! Aye. Let's vote on it!'

'A vote! A vote! Oh, by all means!' Broom grinned. 'Oh, most certainly! Who votes to keep these scumsters on board?'

Not a hand was raised.

'Now! Like I said — haul your gear or, by God, I'll throw the lot of you to the sharks!'

The men who had put their names to the round robin withdrew. Pelling was all for getting rid of Low's whole crew, but Broom did not agree, and neither did the men. We needed them. Fewer men meant more work for everyone else. Pelling had a particular aversion to the band of musicians who had sailed with Low, and argued that they were the least necessary.

Their leader, Hack, stood up, much aggrieved. He was a tall, gangling, saturnine man with an easy way about him. He always had his fiddle by him. It was part of him, like an extension of his arm.

'How fair is that, shipmates?' he asked the company. 'We ain't put our names to no round robin, and who don't like a little entertainment in the evening when the work is over, or a little tune to ease the graft of the day?' Hauling on ropes, turning the capstan, were all done to a rhythm. Music made this kind of labour much easier. Hack plucked the strings of his fiddle, letting the instrument speak for him. Croker, another of the musicians, joined in on a tin whistle which he kept in his top pocket. The duet earned them a round of applause.

The men voted for the musicians to stay. The ship's company had spoken and the jigs and reels started up in earnest. Pelling muttered that no good would come of it, but there was nothing he could do about it.

'Business ain't finished!' Broom roared over the ruckus. 'These men can stay, if that's what you want, but there has been enough irregularity on board this ship. You,' he turned to me, 'and Minerva will revert to female attire. Carry out no more duties. And you keep out of the sun. I want you looking like a lady, not a Barbary pirate. The rest of you,' he looked them over. 'Smarten up! Officers should look like officers, men like sailors, not harbour scum!'

'We don't have no officers!' someone shouted.

'We do now. Mr Halston, Mr Duffy, Mr Phillips, you are now ship's officers. You will all remove to the ward room and keep to the quarterdeck. And that lad there. What's your name?'

'Tom Andrews, Sir.' He stepped forward. He was in his early twenties, but looked younger, with a cap of bright curly hair and fair skin. Being singled out had brought the colour up into his cheeks.

'And what's your history?'

'I'm a navigator, Sir. Taken by Low off the *Hopewell*, an East Indiaman, on my first voyage out for the company.'

He gave a rueful grin and received a rippling laugh of sympathy. He had been kept by Low for his skills.

'Well, you'll do,' Broom said. 'At least you *look* like a gentleman, and we need a young 'un. So you'll join 'em.'

Eyes went to Pelling. He wasn't named and he was normally quick to feel a slight, but he was standing by mild as milk. It meant that Broom had a plan, another scheme up his sleeve, and Pelling was in on it; but they weren't telling the rest of us yet.

'Mr Pelling, you will get this floating midden shipshape. Look at this!' He kicked at a pile of badly-coiled rope, and scraped a fingernail at the crusted salt of the rail. 'This ship should be clean. Tidy. You should be able to eat off the deck.' He looked us over. 'Anyone want to try it?'

The planks were sticky with tar and salt, whiskery with caulking popping out from between the planks. No one volunteered.

'Thought not. I want that deck holystoned until it's as smooth as satin. Get to it as soon as we are rid of these mutinous bastards.'

The men groaned. Holystones were so called because they were roughly the size of Bibles. They slid on a mix of sand and water and I was suddenly glad that Broom had said I had to be a lady. Scrubbing the decks was hard on the hands, as well as being backbreaking work.

'Aye, aye, Cap'n.' Pelling took his orders as meek as a midshipman. 'What are you going to do with them lot what signed the round robin?'

'They got a choice. They can go and join their mate on the shore and shift for themselves, or they can join the sharks overboard. It's more choice than they'd have given us. Make no mistake about that. We've wasted enough time on them already. Make sail!'

All the gold and the silver too,
that ever did cross the sea . . .

35

Now a respectable merchant ship, we continued along the Guinea coast towards the Bight of Benin. Vincent came aboard for a consultation with Broom and Pelling and to see how Minerva was doing, but after that, we hardly saw him. We could not be seen to be sailing in convoy, so Vincent had been told to keep his distance. We put into several places to trade for supplies and that was a chance for us to meet up again.

Native traders drove through the surf offering slaves, just as bumboats row out in a harbour to show their wares. Broom was not there to buy slaves, but he did not dismiss the traders out of hand. He questioned them, and he bought one man, a big Kroo called Toby who spoke many languages and knew the shoals and currents of that treacherous coast. He was freed as soon as the trader disappeared and became very close with Broom. They spent much time closeted together, poring over charts and hatching plans.

Vincent was trading on his own account. Men had been taken from the *Swift Return* to replace the mutineers on the *Fortune*, so he had to find a crew. He began to buy from the slave traders. Many on our ship thought he was sun-touched. Most of the blacks had never even seen the sea before; what kind of sailors would they make? It would be better to sell them off to the next slave ship that passed.

'He'll never teach 'em!' Spall, one of the topmen, summed up the general opinion. 'Easier to teach a monkey!'

'Oh, I don't know,' Minerva replied smoothly. 'Sailing can't be that hard. You learned, didn't you?'

Minerva's arm was healing well, helped by our new idleness. We kept to the main cabin and set about making ourselves into women again. I softened my hands with a kind of rich nut butter Toby had bought from a native trader, and Minerva put the pulp of pineapples on my face, a beauty treatment used by black servants to keep their mistresses white in tropical sun. It was strange to wear women's clothes again. Skirts caught round my legs, and when Minerva tightened my corset, I thought I would not be able to breathe. Minerva groomed my hair for hours, combing out knots and tangles, and I did the same for her. My hands softened and my nails grew so that I could shape them.

The men became used to the new ship's rules. They had all been regular sailors once and remembered how to behave as such. The officers went about their duties, smart and sober. Broom hoisted English colours, and as we sailed on we gradually became what we appeared to be: an honest British trading vessel, out of Bristol, bound for India, but doing some trading along the way.

We cruised the coast, passing the forts held by different nations to protect their own interests and to act as centres of trade. Slaves were brought there from inland to await collection, along with elephants' teeth, gold dust, gum and spices, the produce of the country. The forts were stuffed full of riches, according to Broom.

'And gold.' His brown eyes glinted as if he were already seeing it. 'Gold is kept there to pay for goods coming in, goods going out, and everyone using the fort is taxed.'

His plan was bold and ambitious. With Toby's help, he'd chosen his target carefully: a fort made of mud and brick which lay on an island in the mouth of one of the great rivers that flowed into the Bight of Benin. Toby was well acquainted with the place, having traded slaves there and acted as interpreter, and having been tricked by the governor and sold down the coast as a linguist. He knew the layout of the fort and how many men would be guarding it. He knew the nature of their lives: their fear of the hundreds of slaves kept captive in barracoons, their equal dread of disease that breathed from the tangled mangrove swamps, creeping across to them on cold clammy fogs. Many of the white men sent there were dead within months. The rest tried to fight off malaria and guinea worm by spending their time drinking and seeking the company of native women.

The fort had changed hands many times, but it presently flew the Union flag. A new governor had been sent by the Royal Africa Company to restore order and prosperity, but seemed intent on trading on his own account and lining his own pockets.

'It will be clear sailing, gentlemen. And ladies,' Broom grinned at Minerva and me sitting prim in our dresses. 'We will just go in there and take it. The fort is stuffed with gold, according to Toby, and poorly manned. No match for two well-armed pirate ships. Not that we'll be presenting ourselves as such, of course.'

We sailed into the small harbour, making fast under the fort. Broom ordered most of the crew below. Too many men on deck might proclaim us a pirate. The schooner had passed us in the night and was already at anchor, but no signal went between us. It was important that we seemed strangers to each other.

Broom ordered out the boat with six men in her, all dressed in ordinary blue jackets. Meanwhile, Halston, Phillips, Duffy and Graham joined the captain on the quarterdeck, all arrayed in their best.

'Mr Andrews?' Broom called out. 'Care to help my niece down into the boat?'

Andrews escorted me to the side of the ship. I had put on a fine gown that I had worn in New York and Charlestown, long enough in the sleeve to hide the cutlass scars on my arms. Minerva dressed plain, as a slave. She had agreed to play the part. Just this once, she was clear about that; but to see the fort fleeced of its wealth and all the captives freed, she was prepared to submit to the insult. She would follow behind me, head down, staring meekly at the floor. As far as Broom was concerned, the gold was ours already. A woman with the party, a lady, would fool them completely.

We were met at the landing place by a file of musketeers and escorted to the fort. The governor, Cornelius Thornton, met us with all civility. He bade us sit and share a glass with him. From his complexion I judged that this was not his first of the day. He asked us where we were from, and where we were bound, sipped his brandy and listened as Broom rattled off our story.

'Captain Broom, Sir, out of Bristol. May I present my niece, Miss Danforth? We are bound for India to join my brother. He's setting up in business there. We are doing some trading along the way for gold and gum and elephants' teeth and suchlike things.' Broom regarded the governor in a speculative manner. 'I was wondering, do you have anything of that sort here?'

Broom can seem the most affable fellow in the world, if not a bit of a fool. Thornton's small colourless eyes narrowed and his pale lips twisted into a thin little smile. He was the kind of man who thinks he knows everything, so he never doubted a word that was said to him. Broom strolled about, gesturing with his hands, talking all the time. The governor stroked his greying beard, his mouth quirking further. He clearly thought that the captain was something of a booby. He asked what wares we had to trade, and Broom told him everything that he thought the fort might be needing. When Thornton asked the price, Broom told him a figure just short of stupid. Thornton nodded and allowed himself a private smirk of triumph, satisfied that he could get what he wanted for as little as possible. He was happy to show us about the fort and did not notice Broom's brown eyes taking in everything, from the number of men on guard, to the weapons on the walls, the wind of the stairs and the disposition of the cannon. He saved the strongroom until last, obviously hoping to awe us with his personal wealth and the fort's importance.

The vaults were deep under the ground. The air here was cool; draughts flickered the flames of the torches the soldiers held, throwing shadows up the wall. We were close to the trunks, the underground caves that held the slaves, near enough to hear their groans and the clinking of chains. Thornton cocked an ear.

'That's where the real gold lies. Better than the yellow kind.' He smiled at Broom. 'I've just had a choice consignment from the Congo. They'll fetch an excellent price. I like you, Broom, and I'd be willing to come to an arrangement. Sure I can't tempt you? You wouldn't lose by it.'

Broom shook his head.

Thornton shrugged, as if to say it was his loss.

'Here we are!' He stopped before a wooden door. He selected a long key from the bunch he wore at his hip, turned it in the great black iron lock and the door creaked back. One of the soldiers held up his torch to show the soft gleam of gold from bars stacked to the ceiling. Against other walls stood great chests of oak, and two of red and green leather, bearing a coat of arms on the front and bound in silver gilt. These had belonged to a Spanish nobleman, but now contained Thornton's own fortune.

'Very stout, Sir, very stout.' Broom patted the red wood of the door. 'Very secure.'

'Camwood. Four inches thick. See that?' Thornton put his hand on the surface of the wall. 'Carved out of the solid rock. It would stop Black Bart himself.' He laughed, and we all laughed with him. 'Gloomy down here for a young lady.' He offered me his arm. 'Why don't we take a turn around the garden?'

Thornton's private apartments were kept

cool by the thickness of the walls and were well appointed. They gave out on to a courtyard and beyond to a garden filled with fruit trees and all kinds of plants. Paraquets wheeled above our heads in bright formation, and monkeys chittered from the branches as we walked among orange and lemon trees and the governor pointed out pineapples, guavas, bananas and a nut called cola that the Portuguese use to sweeten water. He was obviously proud of his garden, so Broom and I were quick to admire and praise what we saw. The groves ran down to the harbour. A route of escape if others were blocked.

'It's an interest of mine,' Thornton explained. 'This garden was a patch of hog-trampled mud when I first came, but it's coming on. I mean to take seeds and cuttings and send 'em to Gleeson.'

He was speaking of his country house in England. He was getting it ready for when he returned after his tour of duty. Much of the wealth he made here was being spent on improvements to the house. He told us all about them as he led us back to his residence, where he ordered tea for me and poured more brandy for the gentlemen. Minerva, of course, was offered nothing.

The room was furnished in the way of an

English drawing room, but the fittings from an English country mansion looked strange here, unsuited to the place, or the climate. Damp was attacking the books on the shelves: the pages were thickened and swollen, the covers eroded by mould and insects. The veneers were springing from the surfaces of the furniture and something was eating the sideboard to powder. Black blotches and tarnish marred the mirrors and silverware.

Thornton's talk reverted to Gleeson and his plans for it, but every so often he was forced to leave off his account, afflicted by a wheezing breathlessness. His colour was poor, and he was constantly dabbing at his face with a handkerchief, mopping at the sweat rolling in oily drops down his grey-and-pink mottled skin.

'He's decaying as quickly as his belongings,' Graham whispered to me. 'He won't see Gleeson again. Are you quite well, Sir?' The doctor rose to go to him, but Thornton waved him away.

'*Beware and take care of the Bight of Benin; few come out, though many go in.* Is that not what they say?' His bitter laugh brought on another fit of coughing and wheezing. 'Damned climate!' He drained his glass. 'I usually rest in the afternoon.

Perhaps you would like to join me this evening for dinner. It generally cools somewhat after sundown.'

'We would be delighted.' Broom stood up. 'And we will impose on you no longer.' He looked around. 'I see you are a man of taste, Sir, and discernment. I have a couple of bottles of very fine French brandy; I wonder if you'd care to share 'em with me?'

'I'd be happy to, Sir.' Thornton rose to see us out. 'What say you return about eight o'clock or thereabouts?'

Back on the ship, we were all told to get ready for the evening party. The officers were to dress in the best uniforms they could find, and Broom selected a gown for me, a low cut, fine silk dress that he'd bought for me in New York.

'For just such an occasion. I want you to look particularly fetching. And you will wear this.' He produced the ruby necklace from his pocket and placed it on the table.

I stared at it.

'I thought you had left that with Brandt, the banker.'

'No,' Broom shook his head. 'Why should I? Never know when it might come in useful. Like now.'

'I won't wear it.'

'Why ever not?'

I just shook my head. I could not explain to him.

'You have to Nancy! It's just the touch we need! Thornton won't be able to take his greedy little eyes off it, or you in it. Neither will any of the other men in the room, and I want them distracted.'

In the end, I was persuaded. Minerva fixed the thing around my neck and I gulped at its choking grip. I pulled and worried at it until Minerva told me to stop it. We were rowed back to the fort by six sailors, very smartly turned out, every one with a brace of pistols beneath his sailor's blue jacket. Each pair had a cask of rum with them, to share with their new friends in the fort.

'Don't stint now, lads,' Broom winked as they left us for the guardroom. ' 'Tis our way of showing thanks for all this kind hospitality.'

Broom, Graham and the other officers all had weapons hidden about them. Minerva and I both wore shawls around our shoulders and sashes wide enough to take a pistol. The governor met us and took us to a dining room overlooking the harbour. A glance out of the window would have showed him that our ships had changed position, moving to face the fort.

Dinner was not quite ready, so we were invited to join the other guests and to share a bowl of punch. Broom opened one of the bottles of brandy, much to Thornton's obvious pleasure. The captain of the guard, a battered-faced old rummer with a nose like a strawberry, joined them for a round of toasts. Graham began a conversation about tropical maladies with a pasty young man from the Royal Africa Company. The noise from the guardroom carried, and the captain looked as if he wished he were with them, but Broom plied him with more brandy and Phillips got him talking about his old campaigns.

The rubies did their work. They drew Thornton from right across the room. As Broom predicted, he could not take his eyes off them. I was talking to a weasel-faced factor who traded up-country for slaves, when the governor came towards us.

'Come, Riley, you cannot monopolise this charming young lady all evening. Now, my dear, you must tell me all about yourself.' He led me to a corner by the window, Minerva following, head down. 'That is exquisite!' he said, staring at my neck. 'I'm rather a connoisseur. Beautifully matched stones.' He peered even closer. 'Each one perfect. May I ask where the necklace comes from?'

It was a family heirloom, I explained. Thorton stood with his back to the room. Over his shoulder, I watched Broom approaching. He could tread quietly for a big man.

'Well, it is a very fine —'

He stopped speaking when Minerva jammed her pistol into his side. Broom strolled up and put another at his head.

'You will surrender the fort to me, and everything in it.' Broom's voice sounded loud in the sudden silence. 'Or you are dead.'

Each man turned to find himself covered. Broom nodded to Minerva, who went to the window and discharged her gun. That was the signal to the guardroom. Distant cries and scuffling ended with a single shot.

'The fort is ours.' Broom dragged Governor Thornton to the window. 'See there.'

The two ships had removed the painted canvas shielding their gun ports. Thirty cannon were trained on the fort.

'What do you want?' the governor asked, his face the colour of waxed paper.

'Everything,' Broom replied.

Broom meant what he said. The fort was secured without another shot fired. The soldiers were locked in their own guard-room. The Union colours were struck on the topmost tower: the signal for our men to swarm from the ships to the fort. Broom marched the governor down to his strong-room and made him open his impregnable door. Troop after troop of men weighted down with gold staggered off down to the quay. For once they were not complaining about the loads they had to carry. The boats rode low in the water as they ferried the gold back to the ship. The last things to be taken were the governor's own chests. Once the room was emptied, the governor was put in and the lock turned on him.

Toby led a troop of men to the trunks and barracoons, releasing all who had been taken captive. He was given a choice to come with us, or stay. He chose the latter, so he was given his share there and then.

By morning we were gone.

36

'Pretty, ain't it?'

The gold stood in stacks in Broom's cabin. He could not stop gloating over it.

'Look at this.' He picked up a lozenge-shaped piece all stamped about with seals and coats of arms. 'Portuguese. And this,' he picked up another. 'Spanish. Gold from every nation.' He turned the bars in his hands. 'Each one a regular work of art.' He returned the ingots to their stacks and paced up and down his cabin, the boards creaking under him. 'I swear we're riding lower in the water just from the weight of it.'

Broom was not the only one to be fascinated. Men came just to look at the gold, to touch, even sniff it, as if it had a smell to it, a sort of sweet spiciness. They would ask to hold a bar. It weighed heavy in the hand, slippery as butter. They would hold one piece against another, comparing the colours: burnt orange, daffodil, pale primrose yellow. They would go away, only to return again. No one had ever seen such wealth.

But the nearness of such riches was making the crew jittery. They no longer trusted one another. They grew suspicious. Each one was set with a gnawing worry that he would be cheated, not receive his deserts, get less than his brother. They took to making calculations on scraps of paper, scratching figures on wood with knife point or marlin spike, drawing with their fingers on salt-encrusted surfaces.

The ship grew quiet. The men went about their duties without their usual singing and shouting. They no longer came together in the evening to drink and yarn and smoke a pipe. Joking and laughing had gone from the company. They kept apart, each lying on his hammock dreaming of the riches due to him.

Broom noted the change in his crew and asked Graham if it was the scurvy, which can bring on melancholy, advising the doctor to dose them.

'They're healthy enough,' Graham replied. He tapped his forehead. 'The gold is fevering their brains.' He looked at Broom's anxious expression, his constant fidgeting agitation. 'Yours, too, my friend.'

He sighed. 'Too much gold is worse than too little. Pelling here, says there are new round robins circulating. Everybody is plotting and calculating. I fear mutiny. Worse.' He passed a hand over his eyes. 'I fear a massacre. You, me, Pelling, Phillips and Halston. All who have a greater share. And Nancy here, and Minerva, I don't need to say what fate could befall them. My thinking is that they'll try to seize this ship, then give the schooner the slip.'

'Hmm.' Broom stroked his chin. Graham's words had sobered him. 'It's the idle rogues from Low's crew at the back of this.' Broom shook his head. 'I should have marooned the lot of 'em.'

'Especially them musicians,' Pelling chipped in.

'The musicians?' Broom looked at him with disbelief.

'Hack and Croker and them off Low's ship. Look like butter wouldn't melt. Charm the gulls off the yard-arm. They're the worst of the lot, they are. I seen 'em, screeching and scraping while all around men are being slaughtered or put to the torture, till you can't tell their music from the screams of men dying. Riles the men up, leads them on to madness. That's why Low had 'em on board. You ain't been on the account as long as me, or you'd know. I said at the time, but no one would listen. Should have thrown them to the sharks when we had the chance, along with their fiddles and flutes.'

'That's as maybe.' The doctor's pale eyes creased as he stared out to sea. 'It's too late for that now.' He turned back to Broom. 'It's not just the booty, though that's the bulk of it. They tire of Africa. Once they've taken the ship, they'll set course for the West Indies where they can find punch houses and women. What else will they spend their riches on? They complain that the climate here doesn't suit them. They plan to sail to somewhere more clement in order to whore and drink themselves to death.' He gave a mirthless laugh at his own black joke. 'The gold is inflaming them. My advice is to get it out of sight. Things should calm down once it is out of common view.'

Gabriel was set to build a false compartment at one end of the great cabin to act as a storeroom. It was given out that the hoard would be kept there until such time as it could be divided.

Broom called Vincent over from the schooner to tell him that the ships' companies would be dividing. He did not need to ask why; he sensed a change on the ship as soon as he stepped on board.

'It's the gold breeding greed and mistrust. I saw it on Madagascar.'

We were sailing south for the Portuguese islands of Del Principe and St Thome. It was Broom's plan to land at Annobono, it being the smallest and least frequented. Here he would divide the booty, and the ships' companies if need be. All could take their share and be free to go. Until then, he asked Vincent to stay close and be in readiness.

The mate agreed and left the ship. From now on the ships would sail together.

'They're waiting till we cross the line.' Pelling came to warn Minerva and me. 'I'm telling all I can trust. You two watch yourselves. They'll take advantage of the festivities. That'll be their signal to seize the ship.'

'Why don't we call ship's council?'

'Oh, no,' Pelling shook his head. 'Can't do that. Not a good idea at all. The feeling's so strong that they'd seize the ship from under us. Best to keep our powder dry.' He cocked his head towards the schooner. 'Vincent will be over first sign of trouble.'

37

I'd long felt a prickle of nervousness about crossing the equatorial line that divides North from South. The men teased and tormented any who had not journeyed into the southern hemisphere with tales of all kinds of rites of passage and strange ceremonies of initiation overseen by Lord Neptune. The sailors were secretive about what was involved, but I'd been reassured by Graham that the goings-on were more boisterous than anything, involving a kind of baptism, easily borne by any ready to enter into the spirit. I had a feeling that the rites had a darker side that sometimes got out of hand. The most dreaded of all was keel-hauling, where a man was dropped into the sea and dragged from prow to stern, ninety feet under water, his flesh ripped to shreds by the barnacles that clung to the hull like clusters of razors. Death was almost inevitable. He was like to bleed to death if he did not drown.

We were supposed to be making for the Portuguese islands at all speed, but as we drifted towards the equator, the weather turned as sullen as the atmosphere on board the ship. The sun beat down upon us, melting the tar between the planking, drying the boards to cracking, turning the sea around us to a cauldron of brass. The wind had dropped to nothing; the sails hung drooping and useless. Broom ordered every inch of sail out, but there was less than a breath to stir them. Then the schooner was seized by a contrary current and began to drift away from us. Broom ordered the oars out, but the men rowed with little enthusiasm and we made no headway.

Vincent had no such trouble on his ship. His African sailors were fiercely loyal and only to him. They pulled with a will, but the current was too strong even for them. We watched, helpless, as the schooner dwindled until it was the size of a toy ship, then it was gone altogether.

We were alone.

They did not need to take a sighting. Instinct told the men when we would cross from one side of the globe to the other. Normal duties were more or less suspended. There was a feeling of holiday about the ship. All day the men had been drinking and busying themselves with secret things. Some were up in the rigging, attaching block and tackle to the main yard-arm. Others were making what looked like a cradle or child's rope swing. Still others were raking the hull, hauling up weed and barnacles.

Everyone was ordered below or to their cabin, even the captain. We were summoned by the roll and beat of a drum and there was something eerie and strange about the air of mock solemnity that greeted us as we came upon the deck.

The day was moving towards evening. The sun had lost some of its strength and grown huge in the sky, a great red disc falling into the sea. The deck and everything and everyone on it was bathed in a dusky pink light. Pirates stood in the waist of the ship, lining the rail. Those who had not crossed the line before were hooded and paraded between them towards the fo'castle. Here, we were pushed in the back and made to kneel. Our hoods were pulled off and we looked up to see Father Neptune sitting on a makeshift throne above us, his trident held in judgement. He was naked except for a breech cloth, his body glistening as if he had risen fresh from the sea. He wore a long wig made from seaweed and frayed tarred rope. His face was obscured by a great false beard, streaked brown and green with dripping weed.

We had been told what to expect.

Each of us would be challenged by him: take a ducking or pay a forfeit of a pound of sugar and a pint of rum to make punch. I had a feeling that it wouldn't matter how much rum we proffered. We would still have to pay a forfeit and could expect a dunking. Barrels had been made ready for just that purpose, brimming with a disgusting mix of bilge, tar, rotten greens, old cooking water and whatever else the men had thought to deposit, slopped behind Neptune's throne.

Andrews, the young navigator, was standing next to me. This was his first deep-sea voyage, so he had not crossed the line either.

The smell was enough to make us turn pale and gulp.

'What's in 'em, d'you think?' he whispered.

'I'm not sure,' I sniffed the pungent rottenness, 'but I think I can guess.'

'Barbers' waited with pots of more unspeakable filth to daub on to our cheeks and then scrape off with old bits of rusty iron. I could see by their grinning faces that they could hardly wait to get at Minerva and me, shaving being something new to us. After that was done we would be taken for a washing: put on the makeshift cradle and hauled high up into the rigging. There we would swing above the water, glittering and wrinkling some fifty feet below. Then the rope would be released and down we would plummet, hitting the water at speed enough to take us past the great bulge of the hull, with its waving weed and clinging barnacles, into the muffled silence of the dim green depths where the only sound would be the beating of our own blood. We would be left floating, our lungs near to bursting, and then we would be hauled up for the same thing to happen twice more until we were lowered, dripping and dizzy, on to the quarterdeck.

Broom was willing to go along with it for as long as he could, not knowing who or how many he could trust. He was acting his part as captain, laughing, beaming, clapping us on the shoulder, as all the men cheered from the waist of the ship. I glanced sideways at Minerva. Her face was blank, impassive. As I often had before, I took courage from her.

Below us, the fiddlers struck up and the flutes shrilled. Their playing was loud and frantic, rising higher and higher, faster and faster. Sweat flew from them and the crew crowded in around us, stamping and clapping, setting the whole ship vibrating until the ropes sang and the hull boomed like a giant drum. Then the music stopped, as suddenly as it had begun. The sound ebbed away and I thought that the time had come for the ducking. I readied myself to face the ordeal. Then one chord shattered the silence, echoing and discordant. It was a signal for mayhem.

The fiddlers started another tune, faster than the first, and the stamping and yelling resumed. Crossing the line is a time of misrule, when the captain's orders count for little. On a pirate ship, they counted for nothing at all. We were pushed to one side. Some of the men already on the quarterdeck made to seize the captain instead.

The cry went up: 'Keel-haul him!'

'Steady lads!' Broom tried to reason, still smiling, but it was clear that this was in deadly earnest. Some of the crew were changing the rigging on the cradle, readying it to pass under the ship. Others were cheering them on. All that was wanted was a body. Teams were forming, port and starboard, ready to take the ropes that would drag the victim from one end of the ship to the other. No one could survive such an ordeal. Broom would be taken out lifeless, if the sharks didn't get him first.

'Don't worry, Cap'n,' Croker, the tin-whistle player, winked with his one good eye. The other had been taken out by the end of a swinging hawser. 'You ain't going to be on your own.'

We were surrounded. Men stepped forward to seize Pelling, Graham and the other officers on the quarterdeck.

'Not those two,' Croker pointed at us. 'They've got other uses. Hack don't want 'em messed up.'

Hack looked up and nodded, as if taking a signal to change the tune. He was behind the plot, but it was not clear who was in it, who not. By now, all the men were thoroughly roused. Reason had gone from them. Hack's music was whipping them into a frenzy of blood lust. He was playing like the Devil himself with the crew dancing to his reel.

38

Pelling was being bound to the capstan in the waist of the ship. Gabriel, Jessop, even Joby were similarly trussed. Men were already forming into a circle around them, brandishing knives, cutlasses, tar brushes and marlin spikes, anything they could find to jab and stab. One carried a brand taken from the galley fire. Men were lighting fuses from it, ready to put between toes and fingers. They clearly meant to sweat any who might be loyal to Broom.

We were pushed, pulled, pummelled, mauled and manhandled in ways that left little room for doubt about what they had in mind for Minerva and me. I looked into the faces of men I had known and worked with, and saw red sweating masks leering like jack-o'-lanterns. I nearly gagged on the hot animal stink of them; the stench of rum gusting from their mouths. We struggled and fought, but the struggle was unequal. There were too many of them. Too many hands upon us. Our arms were pinned. We were held fast.

The ship was lying idle in the water. The sails clewed up, rolled tight to the yards. The crew had left off any kind of duty. They were all crowded into the waist of the ship. Even the helmsman had left the wheel. Now, through the danger and confusion, I felt something. A wind had sprung up and, without a helmsman, the ship was turning. Others felt it, too. Sailors are as sensitive as any swinging vane to the slightest change in the weather. The ship took on a shuddering motion as the rudder jammed and there was a violent thudding from under the hull. An unsecured boom swung out, taking a couple of men with it. The rest staggered as the deck tipped and the great body of the ship groaned and juddered under them. They looked around in confusion, but there was no one to tell them what to do.

Just for a moment, the hands that held us slackened their grip. That was all the chance Minerva needed. She twisted like a cat away from her captor and leaped on to the nearest grating, grabbing a flaming brand and a bottle of rum as she went. Her sudden escape brought men clustering around her, their numbers threatening to overwhelm her, but the converging crowd reared back as she swept the brand round. The air was full of the smell of singeing hair and whiskers, then the reek of rum as she emptied the bottle through the grating. Directly underneath her lay the powder hold. The glass smashed, and she held the burning brand hovering over the gaps in the hatch.

'Any closer and I'll drop it! I'll take all of us down to the bottom of the ocean. I swear it!' The men looked at each other, wondering whether to believe her. 'And the gold!'

At the mention of that, they stepped back.

I don't know whether she would have blown us all to kingdom come, or how long she could have held them at bay with the threat of it. Perhaps some of them thought she had, for the sudden boom of an explosion and a billowing of smoke brought a surge of panic.

'Attack! Attack!' someone shouted, and everyone crowded to the rails.

A ship was heading straight for us. A ship in full sail. She had already loosed off one shot, now she let go another across our bows. She was showing a black hoist, with a crudely cut red heart pinned upon it, which meant we could expect no quarter, and she was closing fast.

The captain of the vessel stood on the quarterdeck, his face set and determined. The men forming up for boarding were mostly black. The very ones who some of the crew had said would never be sailors and had wanted to sell back into slavery. They were loyal to Vincent and to him only, Minerva had told me. The rebels could expect no mercy from them.

The fiddlers had ceased playing some while ago. Now they disappeared, making themselves scarce below. Those who had been so brave in leading the mutiny were fast melting away. All the time the other ship was closing. The men looked about them as if waking from a dream, knowing that they should take action, but at a loss as to what they should do.

There were many things that they could have done. Used Broom to bargain for their lives and freedom. Rallied and fought off the boarders. But cowardice and confusion gripped their hearts and they did nothing. The ships ground together. Vincent and his men leaped aboard and the ship was taken with no blood shed and no shot fired.

The rebels were identified and tried for

mutiny with all the solemnity of a court of the Admiralty. The ringleaders, Hack and Croker, were hung from the yard-arm, their bodies cut down and fed to the sharks. The others were cast off in an open boat, with enough food and water to get them to the Portuguese islands, or to the coast of Africa.

The gold that had caused all the trouble was shared among the remainder of the crew. The company was ripe for dividing. It was time for our ways to part.

39

Not all of the men who remained loyal wanted to continue with Broom. Once they had their share, they wanted to leave African shores and go back to the West Indies, the life there being known to them, and more to their liking. They would have been better off staying with us on the *Swift Return*, but there was no way to know what was waiting for those who left on the *Fortune*. Halston was to be captain, with young Andrews as navigator. A great feast was held for them, the last time the crews would be together. The next day they sailed away from us, a tiny dot on the horizon; then they were gone.

The next to leave was Surgeon Graham. It grieved my heart to see him go, but he had long tired of the life. He left us at the Cape of Good Hope. From there he would take ship back to England and begin a new life as a doctor. He begged again for me to go with him, repeating his offer for me to pose as his daughter.

'Why not, Nancy? We'd make a good pair, you and me. We have enough money between us to live in a handsome way. We could settle in any city you please. This is no life for a young lady like you.'

I laughed. 'I'm not a young lady — I am a pirate.'

'And you grow old beyond your years. I fear for you if you persist in this life, with all its violence and danger — and . . . and coarseness. I am afraid it will mark you for ever. You have already seen things no woman should have seen.' He shook his head. 'And who knows how long it will be before you are taken, or killed by some villain? No one lasts long on the account. Come with me, I beg you. What do you say?'

I asked for time to think, but already knew what my answer would be. I could not leave Minerva, I told him, and she would not come with me.

'Why not?' Graham asked. 'She would be free, after all. She would come not as slave, or servant, but as your companion.'

'She might be free in law, but . . .' I tried to explain to him how Minerva felt. 'She says that she does not want to live in a place where she would always have to endure the stares of the curious, the comments of the idle-tongued and vicious.'

'But she would have money. Status.'

I nearly laughed. As if that would make any difference? People would see her as being above her station, and that might even make it worse. Graham was a man of sensitivity and intelligence; why could he not see that?

'I could go into any tavern, in any port,' I attempted to explain further, 'and dressed like this, as a man, I would receive no comment, as long as my coin was good. But if I went in dressed as a woman?'

'I begin to see . . .'

'She wants to live where the colour of her skin is of no more note than yours or mine would be in Bristol, or London. She is of a mind to go to Madagascar.'

'Vincent's country? The old pirate haven?'

I nodded. 'It is our next destination. It is Vincent's idea, and Broom is all for it.'

'And you will go with them?'

I nodded.

'What about that young man of yours, William? We could look for him together. I could explain . . .'

I remembered our last encounter. Over the months, I had gone over it in my mind so much that now it seemed a complete and hideous disaster.

'I no longer think of him.'

'Hmm.' Graham looked at me quizzically, rubbing his chin. 'You expect me to believe that, do you?'

'I mean in terms of marriage. I could not bear the humiliation of finding him with another.'

'Very well,' he sighed. 'If your mind is made up.'

'It is.'

Graham had been like a father to me, and I would miss him cruelly, but my decision was final. He would have to return to England without me.

'In that case, I wish you well and safe from danger.' He kissed me on the forehead. 'I will send news when I can.'

So we watched him sail away.

'Do you regret not going with him?' Minerva asked as his ship left the harbour.

'No,' I said, and meant it.

'You do not stay just because of me?' she asked, worried. 'I would not want that.'

'That is part of it.' I had to be honest with her. There is little hidden between us. 'You are my sister. The only family I have, or want. But it is not entirely because of you.'

I told her of my other reasons for rejecting Graham's offer. If I put on the bonnet and cloak of a doctor's daughter, life would lose its savour, like meat without salt. Life would become insipid, like some floury English pudding, not sweet and sharp to the mouth like the fruits of the south. Graham would have his work, his patients; my prospects would lie in making some kind of marriage. I described a line of whey-faced suitors. My mind would always swing like a compass to William. I still wore his ring. I would marry nobody, if I could not marry him. But he was most likely promised to some nice young woman, a captain's daughter. Even if I found him, I would merely fill his life with confusion, ruin his career when he had worked so hard for advancement. I loved him too much even to contemplate it. So, I would grow an old maid in London, or Edinburgh, or Bath, or Tunbridge, or some other spa, dispensing tea and murmured sympathy to the wives and daughters of Graham's wealthier patients.

'I'd rather stay on the account,' I finished. And I meant it.

The Daemon Lover

40

So we came to Madagascar, the pirate haven.

Vincent guided us into a sheltered deep-water bay, protected from the open sea by two high promontories. A place called Keyhole Cove, the entrance being narrow, not easily seen from the open sea, and protected by long reefs.

Broom stood at the prow, spyglass in hand, casting an eye over the wide white beach and the dark green hills behind. He swung his glass up and squinted through it, taking in the cliff-top heights.

'A couple of cannon up there and this will be tighter than Portsmouth harbour. Well done, Sir.' He grinned at Vincent, throwing his arm round the mate. 'This will do. This will do very well.'

He gave the order to haul in sail and drop anchor. Then he ordered the boat out and we rowed ashore. We trudged along the wide expanse of the beach until we came to a slipway of sorts, made of splintered wooden boards, which led to a path leading up the cliff. It was crumbling now, part washed away by rushing flood water, and all overhung by vegetation, but signs remained of its original formation. The steps cut into the cliff were shallow and wide, their edges reinforced with rough hewn stones and thick planks. We toiled up the slope, Vincent and his men slashing a way with their cutlasses. Vincent knew this place well. He assured us that there was a pirate village above the bay.

At the top of the cliff, the path passed through a high rampart, now partly tumbled down, topped by the remains of a stout palisade. A wooden gate had been thrown aside, but the gap was still so narrow that we could only pass through in single file. The top of the rampart showed a clear view out to the bay. A steady breeze blew in from the sea, pleasant after the heat of the climb, cooling to our sweating skin. A tumbled gun platform rose to our right, and another to our left, topped by corroded cannon which must once have been trained on the encampment's approaches but now lay slumped, pointing at the sky.

I had expected to see huts and buildings

in the clearing that lay in front of us, but it was just an open space, overgrown now with creeping ground plants and sprouting new growth as the forest slowly reclaimed it. There were no signs of any buildings.

Broom looked around, hand resting on his cutlass. 'Any risk from the natives?' he asked, looking to Vincent to advise him, this being his country.

Vincent laughed. 'Hardly. This whole place is *fady*. The people keep away.'

'*Fa-dee?*' Broom frowned. 'What does that mean?'

Vincent frowned in his turn and blew out his cheeks. He had a difficult time explaining. It meant something forbidden, he said, like wearing a hat in church, or a woman whistling on board, but more, something unclean, like eating rat or dog.

The men listened and nodded, looking solemn, as if they knew all about such things.

'Where *are* the natives?' Broom still gripped his cutlass.

'They live a way from here. They come out when they're ready,' Vincent said. 'When they learn we ain't slavers. They're friendly.' He touched his captain's hand. 'Won't be no need for that.'

'But if this was a pirate village,' I asked,

431

'where are their houses?'

'They lived in a solitary way.'

He showed us the points where paths meandered away from this empty centre and wound off into the forest, marked by tall growing hedges long since turned to tangled thicket. Vincent led us forwards, slashing and cutting at the opening of one of the labyrinthine tracks.

'Be careful!' he cried, pointing to the floor and to the sides. It was a long time since anyone had been up here, but long thorns and flint-like stones still stuck out of the ground. Shards of glass and sharp pieces of metal glinted in the thickets that crowded to our shoulders and almost met over our heads.

'What is all this?' Broom demanded. 'Were they afraid of the natives? Of being attacked?'

Vincent laughed. 'They were afraid of each other.'

The pirates had lived singly like spiders, inside elaborate webs of traps and snares rigged to give warning of anyone approaching. They had squatted in their citadels, each guarding his treasure from his fellows.

'What happened to them?'

'Some went back on the account, or

turned respectable, taking amnesty from the government.'

'What about those who stayed?'

'Who knows? Flux, fever, a surfeit of rum — or poison.' Vincent laughed again. 'Not all Malagasy women liked their pirate husbands. In the end, they all died and no one lives here. My father did not live here.' He answered my unspoken question. 'He lived with my mother in her village. The pirates left, or died one by one, until finally this place was deserted.'

We looked about us, thinking of the old pirates, ever more distrustful, listening out for intruders, while death came up the path for them, padding on silent feet, invulnerable to cutting stones and pricking thorns. Suddenly, the woods echoed and clamoured with the most unearthly crying and calling, a sound both plaintive and mournful, as if the lost souls of all those dead pirates were calling one to another, and to us. The noise made us all startle. The men looked around, their faces white and fearful, as voice after voice added itself to the din.

Vincent grinned at our discomfort, although I saw him shiver when the noise started up.

'Indri,' he pointed to black-and-white

creatures flitting high above us through the forest canopy. 'It is a creature,' he thought for a moment, 'like a monkey. We call it father-son.'

He hacked a way through to the dwelling place at the end of the winding path. It was, indeed, a little citadel, surrounded by ditches and ramparts, but still standing, stoutly built and solid. Broom stood on the porch, smiling his satisfaction, brushing away cobwebs in the same brisk way he would deal with any fears of old pirates or lingering superstition. For the houses to be sound and well placed, that was all that mattered.

'If the houses are all like this, we are in business, gentlemen.'

Broom put it to ship's council that the pirate village was a place where we could settle. The bay was deep enough to take a fleet of ships and all the while hidden from the sea.

'This here is a place for us to lay our head in the sand, boys, and rest ourselves awhile,' he said to the men. 'There are cribs up there that can be made snug, and that can't be seen from the bay. If any *do* come for us, we'll have forts set, there, there, there.' He swung round, pointing at the cliff top and promontories. 'Any enemy can be assured of a warm reception. We'll blow 'em to kingdom come.' A ragged cheer went up at the thought of it. 'And all the while we can be living comfortable in proper houses, sleeping in beds, not swinging hammocks. And I dare say the ladies of the country will come calling, once they know we are here.'

The ship was hauled up on the beach and some of the men set about careening her, while the rest toiled up the cliff to cut back vegetation, clear the paths to the houses, root out the hedges, flatten the ramparts and ditches, repair the dwellings and make them sound. Sailors can turn their hands to anything and soon the forest rang with hammering and the central clearing looked like a builder's yard.

Gabriel, the carpenter, scuttled between one site and the other. In a week the ship was clean and seaworthy and the settlement looked more like a regular village. By the end of the second week, we were ready to move into our new homes.

It was a good place to settle. Apart from the anchorage, and the defences, there was abundant sweet water, and we would not want for food. Fruit trees grew all around, native fowl ran about the forest floor and wild hogs were in plentiful supply.

We had seen nothing of the native people, no sign at all. Then, one day, Robbie, a lad who worked with Gabriel, came running from the bush where he had gone to relieve himself, shouting that he'd found a bone yard. It was up on the hillside overlooking the sea, surrounded by a fence to keep out rooting hogs. Crosses and rough stones marked the graves, some bearing scratch carving: dates, places of birth, names, initials.

R. T.
Bristol
D. 1706

Cap'n H. Jones
M'fd H'ven
Dep't this Earth, 1702

The men stood, bare-headed, looking down at the place where their comrades lay buried. Then they set to work, carefully weeding the ground, scraping the moss from the stones to clear the inscriptions. They cut fresh crosses to replace those that had fallen and rotted. They laboured all day on the plot, leaving all other jobs, and finished just as the sun was setting.

They came back the next day to find the

ground planted with a melon vine. After that, the Malagasy came out from where they had been hiding from us. The chief man among them stepped forward in welcome, thanking us for returning to care for our ancestors, meaning our pirate predecessors. They were glad that we were here, Vincent translated, for now those unhappy ghosts would no longer wander, angry and unrequited, causing a disturbance to the living. Now they could be at rest.

The Malagasy are great respecters of the dead, Vincent explained, so much so that they dig up their ancestors and dance with them. The old pirates would remain firmly underground but, as far as our new neighbours were concerned, we were in receipt of their blessing. It seemed to bode well for our settlement.

41

The country was pleasant, we wanted for nothing. The climate was pleasing, the air scented both morning and evening by spice trees and flowers from the forest. The Malagasy were friendly, willing to help and even serve us, for we gave them protection from passing slavers and from other tribes who would take them to sell as slaves.

Vincent went to his tribe, who had moved some way inland to avoid the slavers that cruised the coast, and to live with his people for a while. On his return, he came to see me in the house I shared with Minerva. Our dwelling was a simple single-storey building, with only two rooms, one for sleeping, one for living and eating, but it was light and open, after the confines of a ship, with a wide veranda from where we could see the ocean. I was out there, lying in a hammock, when Vincent presented himself. I thought he had come to see Minerva, and told him she was sleeping, for it was that time of day.

He shook his head. 'It's you I want to see,' he said.

He asked me to walk with him. What he wished to say to me was private and he did not want to be overheard.

We went down the path that had been cut in rough steps to the garden. I was trying to tame the forest by building walls and enticing the plants on to terraces, for never had I seen such beauty and abundance. Ginger, cloves, cinnamon, vanilla, galingale, all grew here. Soft-tongued orchids exuded sweetness to freshen the morning and perfume the evening air. Would it not be wonderful, I said to Vincent, to have them growing all about? Like stepping into paradise.

He replied that paradise was not for taming, nor should I try.

We found a shady corner and sat on a fallen tree. There Vincent opened his heart to me. He wanted to talk about Minerva. He told me of his love for her, how it had grown from the very first moment of meeting, and had gained strength through all that they had done together, until now she was all he wanted, she filled his every waking thought and walked in his dreams. He had told his mother and his people about her, because he wanted to marry her. Did I think that she would consent to stay here with him and give up a life of roving?

I did not answer him straightaway. I had seen this coming from afar, like a sail on the distant horizon. To hear him speak gave me joy and pain in equal measure. I was used to life with her as my close and dear companion. Now everything would be different.

'Why do you ask me, not her?'

'You are very close to her and first in her heart,' he said. 'She loves you above all others. Such love is rare. You are precious to her. Your happiness is her happiness. If you wish to leave —'

'She will come with me?' I shook my head. 'I don't think so. She likes it here. Whatever I decide to do, I think she will want to stay.' I put my hand on his. 'I know she loves you, Vincent. Quite as much as you love her. Her happiness is my happiness, too. Minerva and I are sisters, Vincent. We share the same father.'

'Ah!' he exclaimed, as though that explained a great deal. 'Why did she not say?'

'Her mother made her swear never to tell anyone. She did not tell me for a long while . . .'

'I see! I see!'

'So that is what we are. Sisters. And as her sister, I tell you, you must go to her. And if you do,' I smiled at him, 'I don't think that she will disappoint you.'

He smiled back, his face breaking into a wide grin, but then he was frowning again.

'There is one other thing. Do you think Broom would be willing to marry us?'

I laughed. That was the one captain's duty that Broom had not performed yet.

'I think he would be delighted. Now go. I'm sure Minerva already knows you are here. She will be wondering what is keeping you.'

He took my hand, smiling his relief and thanks, and left me, running up the slope towards the house, leaping walls and terraces, taking the steps two at a time.

I went down to wander the shore, staying away from the house until the sun was setting and night coming on. When I went back, Vincent had gone, but Minerva was happier than I had ever seen her. She fairly glistened with contentment. I did not say that I knew already; that would have spoiled it for her. I let her tell me herself. We sat on the veranda and watched the sun go down and, as the scent came up from the garden, and pale moths glimmered among the flowers, Minerva's joy allowed me to dream again. Not dark dreams of black ships, but dreams of longing and fulfilment. Being here had given us back our youth. We talked far into the night of love and what we hoped life would bring to us, as young girls often do.

42

Minerva's happiness was infectious. The
time of the wedding drew near, the days
were filled with preparations. Broom was
more than happy to perform the offices, as
he put it, and Vincent's people would be
coming from their village to join in the celebrations. Everything should have been perfect, but I had begun to dream of the black
ship again. When I had dreamt of her before,
the ship had been just a vague form. Now
the dreams were more detailed, more fright-
ening, for I was actually upon her deck.

I dreamt that I stood at the rail of a dark
ship, sailing under a black hoist with no
device upon it. I was sailing with the
strangest crew that ever put to sea together: Edward Teach and Captain Kidd,
Calico Jack Rackham and Black Bart Roberts, and we were cruising oceans unknown, navigating by stars that I have
never seen. My ears rang with the roar of
cannon, the screams of the dying and I

walked on decks slick with gore, not knowing if the salt on my lips be water or blood.

I am here.

The words hissed in my ear and I felt his breath, cold on my neck, freezing me as surely as if I had fallen into the black waters of some desolate ice-packed ocean.

I forced myself to wake and lay, eyes stretched wide with horror, utterly unable to move. My skin felt clammy, as though my own death were upon me, and the nets hanging close down made it seem as if I were already sewn into my shroud. I could not even call for Minerva. I waited until the insects were beginning to chirr, the birds and creatures of the forest stir and start their hooting calls and chatter. Then I rose and took the path through the tree ferns that led to the shore. I walked along the cold sand, looking out at the dark ocean, waiting for the moment when the sun would show itself like a great pearl on the far horizon. What did the dreams mean? I shivered and drew my shawl close around me. Was the Brazilian still following me? Would he find me? Was he here?

I had heard stories of a Dutch ship, very like the one I dreamt of, that was said to haunt the Southern Ocean. The captain was a rash and foolhardy man who tried to sail round the Cape of Good Hope in the most dreadful storm. He was deaf to the pleading of his crew and passengers and finally the Almighty Himself appeared on the deck in answer to the prayers of those on board. The captain would not even touch his cap, but fired upon Him, cursing and blaspheming, crying: 'There is but one captain here!' and ordering Him to be-gone. The ship was called the *Flying Dutchman* and she was condemned to sail on until the Day of Judgement. Many have seen this spectral ship, glimpsed through the spray of a storm-lashed sea, or looming suddenly out of the mist, with dead men in the rigging, and dead officers com-manding, and a terrible silence about her sails. It was a good tale to be told with the rum going round and the flames of a fire leaping up into the velvet Madagascar darkness. But it was just a tale, I told myself. Perhaps my dreams were like that. Perhaps they were as unreal as the stories sailors told to while away the time.

Or so I said to myself as I walked back to our house in the morning light. I would not allow any darkness of that kind to shadow Minerva's happiness.

★ ★ ★

It did not take long for Broom to set himself up in a new line of business. Within weeks of our arrival he had established himself as an honest trader again, just like he did in America. He had acquired a fine Dutch East Indiaman which he named the *New Fortune*. He was plying up and down the coast from Cape Town to Zanzibar, dropping into the ports of Mozambique and the islands of Johanna and Comoro, trading in spices, gold, ivory, gems and silks, anything except people, selling to merchants from England, Holland, Portugal, Spain, France. Anyone with money, or the kind of goods that he wanted. The kind that were in short supply here and on the coast of Africa. The bay at Keyhole Cove was turned into a harbour. A jetty extended from the beach into the deeper water. Other ships began to call.

'Look who I have here!' Broom came up to our house one day, bringing a young man with him. 'His ship has put in for fresh supplies. Only happy to oblige.'

His companion was Tom Andrews, the young navigator who had left on the *Fortune*, wearing the badge of the East India Company. I hardly recognised him under the golden beard that he was growing.

We bid him welcome and invited him to join us on the veranda. Minerva went to mix some punch and Vincent offered him a fill from his tobacco pouch. Once he had settled, we asked what news he had.

'Surgeon Graham has hung up his doctor's plate in London and is beginning to build his practice. He will be glad that I have found you. I will let him know where you are.'

'Have you news of any others?'

Andrews hesitated, his fresh face clouding. 'Not good, I'm afraid.'

'What?' We all leaned forward to hear.

'It concerns Halston, and the others on the *Fortune*. They put me off at Cape Verde, and from there I took ship back to England, saying that I had been taken by pirates, but had managed to escape them,' he grinned, 'which is near enough to the truth for the company to know. But not long after I had arrived in London, I heard a report from the West Indies, saying that Halston's ship had been blown out of the water, just after I left them. Almost as soon as they went on the account.'

'Navy?' Broom asked, knocking his pipe out into the garden.

'No,' Andrews shook his head, his golden hair shining in the lamplight. 'Not the Navy. A pirate hunter. He behaves as if he carries a letter of marque.'

'A letter of marque?' I asked. I did not like the sound of this. 'Who from?'

'Who knows?' Broom shrugged. 'His Majesty's government, or France, Holland, Portugal. They all hate and fear us.'

'Perhaps he's in the pay of one of the companies,' Vincent suggested. 'The East India, or Royal Africa.'

'Could be,' Andrews nodded.

Broom snorted. 'They're the real pirates, in my opinion,' he pointed towards Andrews with his pipe stem. 'And I'll say it even if you do work for them.' He took a pinch of tobacco from his pouch, tamping it into the bowl with his thumb. 'The buccaneer's paymasters could be any, or none. Perhaps he just pursues his own pleasure.'

'Whatever the reason,' Andrews looked at us, 'he hunts pirates and gives no quarter. As soon as he spies a black hoist, he attacks with all guns. If he takes any alive, they're killed on the deck and dumped overboard. He's doing for more pirates than the Navy. But the story is, he searches for just one crew, who served on just one ship, under just one captain.'

'Oh.' Broom looked intrigued by that. 'And who might he be?'

'You, Captain Broom.'

The sun had set. Moths were flying out, singeing their wings against the shaded lamp. Broom stared past the yellow puddle of light to the purple blackness of the ocean.

'After us, you say?' Broom turned his attention back to Andrews.

'What manner of man is he?' I asked.

Despite the heat lingering from the day, I felt a shiver, like water trickling down my back. Pirates are used to being hated and hunted, but to be singled out like this? Vincent looked away. I could tell by his face that he would think it *vintana,* destiny, something that could not be avoided, or evaded. I shared his feeling. It seemed to me like a nemesis.

'What kind of ship does he sail?' Vincent asked.

'Big, and bristling with guns, but built in the fashion of years gone by, as if he has sailed out of the past. His ship is black, with dark sails. He has a black hoist —'

'— with no device upon it,' I said.

'Yes.' Andrews stared at me. 'How do you know?'

'I've seen it.'

'Where?'

'In dreams.'

Minerva nodded quickly, confirming what I'd said. Broom gave me a sharp look. I expected him to scoff, as he had before, but he did not.

'Who is he?'

'It is Bartholome.'

I marvelled that Broom did not remember, but then why should he? Although Bartholome had been much in my mind, Broom had probably forgotten all about him.

'The Brazilian?' Broom frowned. 'I thought we shook him off when we left America. I thought he'd give up and go back to Jamaica. The Brazilian! Damn me!'

'Where has he been seen?' Vincent asked.

'He has crossed from Africa to the Caribbean and back again, picking up traces,' said Andrews.

'How is he to find us on all the wide ocean?' Broom leaned back in his chair, describing a globe in the air.

'It's only a matter of time until his mind turns to where else we might be,' Vincent said quietly.

'He's been sighted off the Cape.' Andrews leaned forward, conspiratorial, as if we were in some crowded dockside inn and could be easily overheard. 'Several ships have been frighted, thinking he's the *Dutchman*. Now, I don't believe in those kinds of stories . . .' He drank his punch in a gulp and poured himself another.

Broom frowned. His presence on this coast was known to all and sundry. The Brazilian was bound to find us. He could be but a few days away.

'And after me, you say?'

Broom was a good captain and far from stupid, but sometimes he had the greatest difficulty in seeing beyond himself.

'He's not coming after *you,*' I said.

43

We would not lie skulking and hiding, waiting for the pirate hunter to find us. Broom called the crew together and all agreed. We would go out to meet him, back on the account. We would take our old places. It would be like the old days, with Vincent as mate, Pelling as quartermaster, Phillips as gunner, but we would sail without Minerva.

She was with child. She was in the early stages, and much afflicted with sickness, and although she argued that women have served before in that delicate state, no one would even hear her out. She spoke strongly to go with us, came as near as her nature would allow her to pleading, but Vincent would not countenance it, neither would Broom, and neither would I.

We sailed out on the *New Fortune*. The big Dutch East Indiaman was armed with extra guns, strong enough to take anything that might come against us, or so we thought. The weather was fine and we had fair winds, but Vincent continued gloomy. He leaned over the rail, staring down at the waves folding back from the prow. He was worried about Minerva, about leaving her.

'She will be safe,' I replied to him. 'He comes for me, not her.'

I felt that in leaving we were acting like a bird trailing her wing, leading the fox away from her nest. I thought that she would be safer there on the island than here on the ship with me. But the Brazilian was no fox. He was a wolf of the sea.

Broom set double watches. Every minute of the day and night, to larboard and starboard and high on the topgallant platform, eyes scanned the horizon until they ached with watching, looking to every degree of the compass, seeing nothing, until we all began to question the enterprise, thinking it futile. Perhaps Andrews was wrong in what he had told us. Perhaps the ship that had been sighted truly was the *Flying Dutchman*. Such aimless cruising was pointless; we could wander the Southern Ocean like the albatross and still never find him. We would go back to Madagascar and wait there for fresh news, or none.

He came at us just after daybreak on our fifth day out as we prepared to return to the island.

The night had been calm and there was hardly a breath of wind stirring the sails. I was on watch, staring towards the east, as I always did, longing for the morning, waiting for the first spark of light to pierce the darkness. The day broke with one single beam, as if some great beacon were stationed just below the horizon. The sky began to pale and slowly the tiny dot of light turned into a great wavering orange circle surrounded by clouds shot through with pink and purple.

Dawn brought mist with it, rolling across the sea towards us, and soon we were enveloped. Droplets formed on our faces, our clothes and hair, beading deck and rail, loading the sails with damp. The Southern Ocean can be cold. Men heaved on their fearnoughts, or pulled them close at the collar.

'It's bloody cold up here!' Phillips, who was to take the next watch, came up on deck. 'We could be in the North Sea!' He hawked and spat, lifted a bottle from his pocket and took a nip, offering it to the men shivering round him.

'It'll burn off soon.' Vincent nodded in

the direction of the rising sun. 'It's going already.'

A rosy glow showed deep in the centre of the cloud, like light seen through alabaster.

'Hold up! What's that!' One of the men, Lawson, was leaning over the rail, straining out into the fog. 'There's a ship! Look!'

His finger wavered as he pointed. It was death to be the first to sight the *Dutchman*. The others drew back as if he were already accursed.

A dark shape showed deep in the swirling mist. She appeared in apparent miniature: a ship cut from paper, overlaid with gauze. Then she swung about. She was coming towards us, getting larger and larger, looming out of the fog, standing under a press of sail as though she would run us down.

We stepped back from the rail.

'How is she moving?' Lawson said in wonder. 'And how so fast?' He looked up at our masts. 'When there's not a cat's paw of wind in our sail.'

The black ship was closing quickly. It was possible to see men in the rigging. Once her sails must have been black. Now they were bleached to a rusty hue, like blood dried on to linen. We all knew that something should be happening. Orders shouted. Men jumping to it. There was nothing. No one did anything. The fog sheathed us in silence; the only sound was the hiss of water off the ship's bows.

Vincent broke the spell, yelling for someone to fetch Broom. The captain appeared, stuffing his shirt into his breeches, shouting and bellowing, screeching for men to get up the rigging and put out every inch of sail.

'Turn her! Damn you! Turn her!' he screamed at the helmsman. 'We don't want to meet her beam on!'

The ship groaned and shuddered, as the helmsman strove to do his bidding. Beam on, we presented an open target. We needed to show the attacking ship our stern, or meet her prow to prow.

'Can't budge her,' the helmsman grunted. 'She's dead in the water!'

She was approaching from the windward side. We were giving our whole starboard side to the advancing ship. In answer to every man's thought came the boom of cannon and a puff of smoke from her gun ports. The ball splashed into the water. It had fallen short, but not by much.

'Gunners!' Broom yelled. 'To your posts! Give 'em Hell.' He turned to Vincent. 'They hoisted any colours?'

'Black flag with no device.'

'Well, get ours up there! We'll show the buggers! By God, they'll know what it means to attack the skull and crossed bones!' He turned to yell down the ship. 'Gunners! Prepare to fire!'

'Hold up, Captain! Hold up!' I grabbed his arm.

'Hold up?' Broom looked round. 'For what? She's almost on us!'

'Look there! On the bow!'

Minerva was bound to the underside of the bowsprit, her arms wrenched back. In the eye of my mind, she appears larger than life, as if the ship were named *Minerva*, and she were the figurehead, a carving of her namesake.

The Brazilian's ship was bearing down, threatening to ram us. The wind died as if by command. Except there was no wind. There never had been. His ship's rusty sails dropped in their shrouds as limp as ours. The two vessels came gliding together as sweetly as if piloted by masters.

The mist was lifting; we were in the full light of sun again. The Brazilian stood on the quarterdeck, the diamond cross on his chest breaking the light into a thousand dazzling shards, as he swung round towards us.

'I have found you at last. You have led me a dance.' He nodded towards Minerva trussed under the bowsprit. 'Do you enjoy my little tableau?'

'It's me you want.' I stepped forward. 'Let her go!'

'All in good time.' He leaned over the rail. 'First you must put down your weapons. Throw them on the deck. Any man who thinks to disobey, is dead.'

Sharpshooters flanked him, others hung from the rigging, all with long muskets aimed at us. Pistols, cutlasses, swords and knives clattered on to the deck. As if to prove a point, a shot rang out, then another. Two men fell for fumbling their weapons or being slow at unbuckling their belts.

Already Bartholome's men were streaming down the sides of his ship and over into ours, pouring down the hatches. Some scurried about the deck, collecting the weapons up into sacks. The pirates looked away from them, and from each other; their eyes seeking a stain on the deck, a knot in the planking. I knew that they would be gripped with the shame of having their weapons confiscated, of being taken without a fight. They were just about broken. The Brazilian's men rounded them

458

up with no trouble at all.

We were forced from one vessel to the other, at the point of gun and cutlass, and collected in the waist of the Brazilian's ship. Men went among the pirates, binding them in pairs, back to back, like chickens waiting for market. Minerva was cut down from the bowsprit and brought to the Brazilian on the quarterdeck.

He made her kneel before him and seized her by the hair. He took out a long curving knife and held the blade under her jaw, the point angled into her ear. I thought of her throat cut, the blood spilling like the necklace he'd given to me. I remembered what Phillis had said about seeing my death upon me. What if it had not been me she had seen, but Minerva?

He ordered me forwards.

'What will you do to save her life?'

'Anything,' I replied. 'Anything you ask of me. Anything at all.'

'Very well.' He let Minerva go. 'Remember your promise.'

I was sent below to put on women's clothes. I was trembling with terror, but it was important to show no fear. I kept my voice steady, saying that I would not go unless Minerva came with me. I needed her to help me. She was my body slave;

how could I dress without her? He let me have her without question. He was old-fashioned, rigid in his thinking. He lived in a world where women did nothing for themselves, were helpless without their slaves to attend them. He did not think that I had been living among men, dressed as one of them, for more than a year. What did I do for a woman's help then?

My rooms were prepared: one for living, one for sleeping. I had never seen such apartments given over to just one person, not even to a captain. My own trunks stood against the wall, from Madagascar, even from Fountainhead. One of my own dresses was laid out on a bed bolted to the deck. It was the gown that I'd worn on my sixteenth birthday, when I went to dinner at his plantation.

Minerva was shaking from her ordeal, her eyes wide, her body trembling in every limb. I put my arm round her and led her to the bed and sat next to her.

'They came in the night. Two days after you left. Attacking without warning, on us before any even noticed. They moved up through the village, killing all who opposed them. I heard the commotion, but by then they were already at our house. They held me captive, then went through the rooms, gathering up all your possessions. I had no time even to draw a weapon —'

'Never mind that now. What about the baby? Are you all right?'

She nodded. 'I think. Not that it matters now. He is mad.' I saw the tears start in her eyes. 'He will kill us all.'

A man who would use a living woman as his figurehead was capable of anything.

'That's as maybe,' I whispered, holding her to me. 'But we are not dead yet. Let us see what possibilities this place offers. We need to know our fighting ground.'

The door outside was guarded but, as is common on ships, my quarters were part of a suite of rooms, one opening on to another towards the stern. No one barred our way as we slipped through the folding doors that led to the next apartment. The Brazilian's night quarters. Minerva's eyebrows rose at the proximity of mine to his. We crept past a great carved damask-draped bed, and on towards his day cabin. This was furnished as richly as if the ship were a floating palace. The walls were thickly panelled and hung with antique weapons and armour, badged with coats of arms that were half obscured by a patina of time, as if they had been taken from the walls of some ancient house.

The room was lit by great stern windows, as large as in any admiral's grand cabin. A wide desk stood under them, laid out with charts and flanked by an astrolabe, globe and compass. A great carved chair faced out, as if the occupant liked to gaze at the sea as well as to study the charts in front of him. We had seen enough. We tiptoed back to my cabin.

44

A servant delivered the rubies that had been given to me so long ago. The Brazilian must have gone through all my possessions to find them. It was clear I was to wear the same dress as I had worn on my birthday. It was strange. Puzzling. As if no time had elapsed at all for him. I did not hurry my dressing. We spun it out as long as possible, trying to fathom his mind, pierce into his thinking. If we were to defeat him, we had to outwit him. We were overmastered in every other way. It was our only hope. I had lived in dread for these many months, but now the moment had come, I had no fear of him. It was exactly how I felt before an attack. I would stand trembling and sick as the ships drew together, but once the engagement had begun, I was as fearless as any other.

By the time I was summoned, I had put on the gown. It was low cut at the front and Minerva cinched in the bodice as tight as she could make it. My face was powdered, my lips rouged, my hair dressed and piled high. I was arrayed for battle.

'How do I look?' I whispered to Minerva.

'You look wonderful! He won't be able to keep his eyes away from you. Just like Thornton!'

I fixed the earring in my ear while she clasped the necklace about my neck. The gooseflesh rose on my arms at its cold grip. I slid a finger under the hard edge of the gold, trying to loosen it away from my throat. I felt as if it were choking me.

Minerva took my hands away and held them gently down at my sides.

'Don't touch it in his presence.'

The Brazilian was seated in the great carved chair in the grand cabin, his arms lying along the wide curved arms, gazing out at the view those great windows afforded him. He waved a ringed hand, indicating for me to stand in front of him with my back to the window. The man who had brought me was dismissed.

'Now I have you!' He leaned back against his chair, surveying me. A prize taken at sea.

'I hope you are not disappointed.'

'On the contrary, my dear. I like you all the better for the chase you've led me.'

'What will you do with me now?'

'What I intended all along. I will take you back and marry you. But I do not think that we will return to Jamaica. Too much is known about your history there. No. I will take you to South America. Brazil, perhaps, to São Luís. I have a house there, and my sister will be a companion to you, for I am often away. Or, on the other hand,' he smiled as if he were bestowing some benign golden future upon me, although his dark eyes glinted with cruelty, 'I also have interests in Manaus, far up the Amazon river. Maybe I will take you there.'

So I was to be entombed in a house with his sister, or sent to some Amazonian backwater. His smile grew wider. He knew I would relish neither prospect, but I took care not to react, or show any emotion. I would keep him guessing.

'And what of my companions?'

'The pirate rabble you travel with?' He sat up to reach for a knife that lay on the desk. 'They will go over the side to feed the fish.'

He sat back, straight in his chair, his eyes on mine, playing with the knife he had just taken up. It was narrow, double-bladed, and so perfectly balanced he could hold it on the tip of one finger at the point where the blade met the hasp. He threw it up, catching the hilt and holding it like a drumstick, tapping the needle tip against the palm of his hand.

'The rubies still look magnificent on you, even if your skin is a little tawny. But you lack one earring.' He looked at me critically. 'Remove it. I do not like lack of symmetry. Hold it up.'

I did as he told me. It hung from my fingers like a drop of blood.

'Tell me, my dear. What happened to the other one?'

I kept my eyes on his. His question seemed inconsequential, but I suddenly felt a heaviness within it, as if it were weighted with meaning I could not interpret, as sometimes such questions are in myth and story. The wrong answer meant death.

'I gave it to another,' I said.

'You gave it to a whore. Is that not the case?' He sat upright, his body uncoiling like a snake. 'What a profligate gesture. And quite wasted on her. She was quick enough to tell me how she came by it. Almost as eager to talk as that love-sick cabin boy in New York. The banker was notably tight-mouthed, but the rest? Your old shipmates, the governor of that fort you took?

All happy to tell me as much about you as they possibly could. Everyone has their price, but then you should know that by now.' He paused and looked at the knife balanced on his finger end. 'Put your trust in stones, did I not say that? They are as quick to betray you, my dear. Very like whores, in fact. It's a fine stone.' He focused on the ruby's glow. 'But what's the use of just one earring? I have its pair here.' He fished it from his waistcoat pocket and laid it on the table. It lay between us like a bubble of blood. 'But now I'm thinking, perhaps you should wear just that one. As a pendant, maybe. There,' he pointed with his knife, 'between your lily-white breasts.'

I suddenly saw what I had not done before. Something that our plans had failed to take into account. The knife in his hand was for throwing. My rejection and flight had slighted him. I had run away with slaves rather than marry him, lived with pirates, given his gifts to whores. I had insulted him and his family beyond any reason and he had no intention of taking me anywhere. He had been merely toying with me. He meant to kill me then and there.

His grip on the knife shifted and he

smiled. I had tried to keep my alarm and fear from my face, my eyes, but he saw it and took clear delight in my knowing that the position was hopeless. I was completely in his power. He could kill me at his leisure, and who would stop him? All the pirates were trussed like fowl on the deck, waiting his order to be tipped overboard. All the pirates but one.

He had neither seen, nor heard her. He had probably forgotten all about her, slaves being beneath his notice. Minerva had come into the room behind him, gliding on silent feet from my rooms into his. I kept my eyes away from her, allowing more fear to flare, my lips to tremble, as if I might start pleading, anything to keep his attention focused on our wordless battle. She took a sword from the wall. The hilt was long enough to take her two hands, the wide blade chased with Moorish designs on razor-sharp Toledo steel. She held it, testing the weight of it, the balance, then she took it in a double grip. She would have only one chance at this. She pulled the sword back past her left shoulder, then brought it forward in a scything motion, a wide blurring arc of grey metal, taking his head off at the neck.

'It was the only way.' Minerva threw the

sword down, and leaned on the back of the chair, taking a deep shuddering breath. Then she reached down, grasping the head by the hair. 'Now we must show this to his people. Without him, they are nothing.'

We held the bloody trophy between us. Men fell away before us as we mounted to the quarterdeck. We held the head aloft for all to see.

'He is dead.' Minerva's voice rang out over the hushed deck. 'I killed him. Now you will be commanded by me.'

They offered no resistance. They knelt before her, as if to some pirate queen.

45

The Brazilian's ship contained fabulous riches. Bales of gossamer silks and shining satins hid still greater wealth. Gems of all kinds: rubies, sapphires, emeralds, diamonds as large as pigeons' eggs. There were pearls of every hue, from black and grey, to pink and cream and purest white. Some were pierced, ready for stringing, others were whole. Some were so small they ran through the fingers like rice, others nestled in the palm snug as a musket ball. Some were perfectly round, others were as oval as gulls' eggs; they warmed to the skin and took on lustre, subtly changing in colour. More and more were collected together. The gems and pearls were poured into sacks ready to be carried from one ship to the other. The men unloaded them like grain, like coal. Each load represented a thousand lifetimes' worth of honest toil.

Then they went back for more: chests of silver bars, gem-encrusted cups and plates, and gold dust, ground so fine that it blew up into the faces of the men who opened the boxes, gilding their sweating skin.

At last the ship was emptied of all its wealth. Not everything was taken. Silks and brocades that would normally have been seized as prize booty lay discarded, blowing across the deck, turning the rigging to gaudy cobwebs. The Brazilian's people watched us, dark eyes in dark faces, awaiting what we would do to them.

The Brazilian's head was stuck on the bowsprit. Now he was his own figurehead. Minerva ordered the guns thrown off the decks, and sent men up the rigging, swarming up the shrouds, knives in mouths, to cut the rigging and slash the sails.

I was about to cast the ruby necklace over the side with the other unwanted cargo, when Minerva held my hand.

'It is over,' she said. 'You are free.' She took the rubies from me and held them up. 'These are just stones now. The magic has gone from them.' She wound the necklace round her wrist. In the sunlight, the rubies had less of the colour of blood. They seemed to take on a milky softness, deepening to a shade of pure rose madder as her skin warmed them. 'They are lovely.

Why destroy such beauty because of him? Besides,' she smiled, 'they are valuable. You must keep them.' She took them off her wrist and gave them back to me. They felt warm from the sun, from her skin. She folded her hands over mine. 'Who knows when you might have need of them?'

We stood, hands clasped. The ships were ungrappling. It was time to depart.

This couple are married
and do agree . . .

46

On the way back to Madagascar, the gems were weighed and assayed on scales taken from the Brazilian's ship. Each one assessed, described, recorded; every man's share entered into a ledger against his name. One large diamond was equal to so many small. What the pirate did then was up to him. If he wished to take a hammer to it, and make forty sparklers, so be it. The booty was divided, fair and square. I went for large stones, selecting by cut and clarity, beauty of colour, the same with the pearls.

'I think this calls for a celebration!' Broom announced when the division was complete. 'By God, it does! You two,' he pointed at Minerva and me. 'Find something fitting to wear. As women. None of your dandy threads. The rest of you scrub down and put on shore-rig. I'm parading the ship.'

We were called to the deck by the ship's

bell. The whole company mustered in the waist of the ship.

'Mr Vincent Crosby. Miss Minerva Sharpe. I would have you join me on the quarterdeck.'

Vincent and Minerva looked at each other, unsure what to expect. Broom had something up his sleeve. I was sure of it, and so were they. His tone was sonorous and over-solemn. His whole face held rigid, as if it would crack with laughter any minute. He waited until they had mounted the steps and stood before him. Then he brought a Bible from inside his coat and opened it, placing upon it two rings.

'I understand that you two intend to marry?' He addressed both of them.

'You know we do,' Vincent spoke up.

'Very well, then. I've been pondering the matter, and I'm not very certain as to a captain's remit to marry on shore. But I certainly know what a captain can do on a ship. And since Mr Crosby has given into my keeping two rings of some magnificence, there seems no time like the present.' He surveyed the couple. 'Do you have any objections?'

They shook their heads.

'Very well, then.' He looked around at the company. 'Anyone stand up for this woman?' Pelling stepped forward with a grin. They had hatched this out between them. 'You'll do. Now, Vincent Crosby, do you take this woman, Minerva Sharpe, to be your lawful wedded wife?'

'I do . . .'

'Do you promise to have and to hold her,' Broom carried on. 'Love, honour, etcetera, till death do you part?'

Vincent looked from Broom to Minerva and murmured, 'I do.'

'Louder,' Broom instructed. 'I want them all to hear.'

'I do!' Vincent boomed.

'That's better. Now, Minerva Sharpe, do you take this man to be your lawful wedded husband, to have and to hold, love, honour and obey, till death do you part?'

Minerva smiled. 'I do.'

'Well then, with the powers invested in me as captain of this ship, I do pronounce you man and wife.' He looked at the company. 'Might not be by the book,' he snapped the Bible shut and held it up, 'but what care we for the book?' He grinned at Vincent. 'You are married good and proper. 'Bout time you made an honest woman of her. Go on, then! Kiss her!'

A great cheer went up from the ship's

company as the couple embraced and the celebrations began. Broom put his arms around the couple, beaming as if they were his own children. He was a wise captain. Death and battle need to be purged by joy and celebration. What better way than a wedding to expunge the memory of the malevolent Brazilian and his bloody demise from all our minds.

The crew crowded round to congratulate the couple. Vincent stood grinning, having his hand rung, and his back slapped and pummelled until he could hardly grip and he was black and blue. The men were almost shy with Minerva. She had changed so suddenly in their eyes, from shipmate, to pirate queen, to bride. They hardly knew how to treat her. They shook her hand, and kissed her cheek and acted most respectfully. There were none of the ripe and ribald comments that might have been expected from such a crew. Or very few. But then it is rare to attend a wedding where the bride might run you through. They brought what they could find in chest or pack to give to the couple. Not gold or jewels, for they already had those in plenty. Simpler gifts that they had about them: a silver rum flask, a nicely worked tobacco pouch, a ship in a bottle, little carvings they had made at sea.

Minerva kissed them all and hugged them, said they were her brothers and that she really loved them. I thought I saw one or two wipe a tear away, but by then the rum had been running freely for quite some time.

I waited until the mêlée around her had finally subsided and I could have my own moment with her. In the waiting, I'd been going over in my mind what I would say and had a little speech prepared, about how much I loved her, how much I liked and respected Vincent, what a good husband he would be to her, how now I had a sister *and* a brother and wished both of them all the joy and happiness that it was possible for two people to have in this world. But when it came to it, all my words fled from me. All I could do was hold her in my arms, and kiss her, and weep upon her shoulder, as she wept on mine.

'What on earth are you two blubbing about?' Broom put his arm around both of us. 'This is a wedding! Come, the fiddlers are striking up! We're waiting for Minerva to lead the dance.'

Vincent and Minerva stepped up as the fiddlers started, and punch and rum were passed round until the decks ran with it.

The party went on long after Vincent and Minerva had slipped away to a cabin especially prepared for them by Abe Reynolds.

'Silk sheets and everything,' he winked at me. 'Courtesy of that Brazilian geezer.'

I was standing at the rail, gazing out at the black night sea, when I felt somebody at my shoulder.

'There's something I forgot to tell you.' Broom leaned on the rail next to me.

'Oh,' I turned to look at him. 'And what was that?'

'Something Andrews told me just before he left.' He stared straight ahead, into the darkness. 'Said he'd met a young chap, a Navy man. New made captain, so I hear. In the Llandoger Trow it was, in your old port of Bristol. Talk came round to women and love, as it often does among sailing men, and someone asks the young captain if he has a sweetheart at all. At that, he declares that he's in love with the finest girl in the world and don't care who knows it. He names no names, but declares that he has her ring about his neck and that she has his, and if he don't marry her, he'll have no other. Andrews wasn't sure of his name,' Broom leaned on the rail and looked at me. 'But he thought it might be William.'

'William?' I looked up at him. 'Every other tar's called William.'

Broom laughed, recognising his words from long ago.

'I ain't staying long when we take 'em back to Madagascar. I'm turning the ship and sailing homeward. Why don't you come with me?'

I was silent, not knowing how to answer him. Part of me wanted to return and find William, but how could I leave Minerva? She was as precious to me as my own heart's blood and I feared that if I left, I might never see her again. I felt a pang at the thought of all the wedding celebrations that would go on and in which I would have no part.

Broom seemed to understand.

'She has Vincent now,' he said. 'And she will have her baby. Her life is here, as it should be. Yours is not. It lies elsewhere. She knows that, even if you don't. Life is short. You've learned that. And not to be wasted. Not a drop of it. Have you still got his ring about you?'

I nodded.

'Well, a tar called William shouldn't be too hard to find. Not with the money we have at our disposal. You will have him, my dear, even if we have to buy the entire fleet!'

481

I did not know what I would say to Minerva. When dawn came, I was still up on deck, having kept my private watch there all night. Decisions must be made. We will be back by morning. It is now, or never. But how to tell her? What should I do? The voice in my head sang like a siren while behind me the rising sun had begun to turn sky and water to pale pink and violet. I was looking away from it, staring towards the dark headland that loomed off our starboard bow like some great crouching beast.

Suddenly, she was there beside me, as if mere thought could conjure her. She looked as though she had risen in haste, her face still half dazed with sleep, wearing a loose linen shirt and breeches too big for her, cinched into her narrow waist with a broad leather belt.

'You must leave,' she said. 'I know.'

I turned to speak, but she put her hand up to quiet me.

'Do not grieve and do not sorrow. We have seen enough of both and we don't have time for all that now. You must go back. I agree with Broom and Surgeon Graham. I know your reasons for staying, but I hate to see you sad and you cannot be happy with your heart divided so. You still love William, don't you?'

I nodded. 'Broom says he's had word that he's waiting for me. But for all I know, Broom's lying to me.'

'Why should he be?'

I shrugged. 'You know what he's like. He tells people the things they most want to hear.'

'And what if he's not? You must stop being afraid, Nancy. That is the trouble, isn't it? You are afraid of leaving me. You are afraid of what will happen if you go back.'

I nodded, staring out at the fast-approaching land. I could not look at her. She knew me better than I knew myself.

'When we first went on the account, you were afraid then.'

I laughed at the memory of it. 'All the time.'

'But you overcame it. You can do the same now.'

'It's fear of a different kind.'

'No, it is not. All fear is the same. You must go back with Broom. Take your chances, just as we do going on the attack.' She paused, staring at the land before us: the red-streaked cliffs, the trees like knots on a tapestry, clearly visible now. 'We will be together, just like then. We are sisters, I will always be with you, wherever you go. And, who knows? Someday, maybe, the sea roads will bring you back to find me with my children playing about me.'

She laughed a little, and I smiled at the picture her words painted. I felt my spirits lifting. She had brought hope to me, as a wind springs from nowhere to take a ship out of a flat calm, to fill her sails and send her singing through the water, speeding on her one true course.

So much had passed between us, we did not need to speak of it. We stood for some time in silence, our fingers interlocked on the rail. Orders rang out around us. Men hauled on ropes to take in sail and the helmsman turned the wheel to bring us safe into harbour. Where I would leave her.

'I will find William,' I said. 'And Phillis, too. And I will come back to you.'

She smiled wide, and her look said that she did not doubt it.

'I meant to give you these last night,' I said, taking the ruby earrings from my purse. 'As a wedding gift.'

She held them up. In the early morning sun, they both flashed like fire, sparking light off each other. She handed one of them back to me.

'You will wear one. I will wear the other. That way, one day, we will come back together. We must have a toast.'

She found rum and two cups.

'To youth,' she proclaimed. 'And freedom.'

We repeated the pirate toast, like a solemn oath.

'And booty,' she added, laughing.

'Aye, and that.'

We drank and threw our cups into the water. She leaned on the rail, her face half in light, half in shadow, as perfect as a statue. The ruby earring flared as the sun struck through it, and her white shirt billowed out in the freshening breeze, her bright black hair streaming like a pirate pennant. That is how I will remember her.

As we stood at the rail, laughing together, I truly believed that there was nothing I could not do.

Afterword

I left Madagascar on the next tide. When the ship reached Cape Town, Broom collected a parcel of mail. In it he found a letter from Graham. The doctor has been busy on my behalf, it seems, and has made good his promise of finding William and speaking to him, which has given me new hope. He has also made the acquaintance of Mr Defoe, who he found to be a man full of curiosity, with a great knowledge of the sea, in deep sympathy for those who make their living there, whoever they might be. A man of discretion, so Graham says, very interested in those who have gone on the account. Mr Defoe plans a further edition of his book, *A General History of the Robberies and Murders of the Most Notorious Pyrates*. The reading public being, so it seems, highly diverted by stories of rogues and reprobates, whether on land or sea. To this end, he has been busy collecting stories from the pirates themselves, both captured and free, and from those involved in hunting them. Graham has started to confide his own history to him. That is what prompted me to begin this writing.

We are nearing the Western Approaches now, and it will not be long before we sight England. I own to feelings of great excitement and anticipation, and even greater nervousness. But I am resolved. When we dock in London, I will deliver these papers to Mr Defoe. Then I intend to find William, and to marry him, if he will still have me. And after that? You may wish me luck, or curse me for a damnable pirate, but do not look for me. I will be gone to parts beyond the sea.